The Rag

Born and raised in Sheffield, Joanne Clague lives in the coastal village of Laxey in the Isle of Man with her husband, children, dogs and other assorted wildlife. She has worked in print, radio and broadcast journalism in the north west for the past three decades and is now a full-time writer of historical fiction set in nineteenth century Sheffield.

The RAGGED VALLEY

Joanne Clague

CANELO

First published in the United Kingdom in 2022 by

Canelo
Unit 9, 5th Floor
Cargo Works, 1-2 Hatfields
London, SE1 9PG
United Kingdom

A CIP catalogue record for this book is available from the British Library.

Print ISBN 978 1 80032 948 5
Ebook ISBN 978 1 80032 947 8

Look for more great books at www.canelo.co

Printed and bound in Great Britain by Clays Ltd, Elcograf S.p.A.

Dedicated to my grandparents

Lily (Hinchliffe) Booth 1920–2016

George William Booth 1919–2017

True Sheffielders

Chapter 1

On a gale-driven afternoon in March, Silas Hinchcliffe breasted the summit of the hill like a swimmer coming up for air.

Except for one detail, the valley beneath his muddy boots was no different to the undulating landscape he'd been stumbling across since before dawn, a runaway's adrenaline coursing through his veins. Here were the same old foggy shades of green and brown, tamed by a jigsaw of drystone walls. Sheep pressed their ropy hides against damp hedges and cows stood in the rain in stoic surrender.

His soaked britches clung to his legs and rain belted his face like gravel, but Silas paid no heed. His narrowed eyes found and followed the movements of a man, ant-sized, who was hurrying across the earth embankment that straddled the gorge below. Silas was a taller than average youth, hard-muscled from farm work, but he reckoned he'd make an equally puny sight, if the man looked up, if he lifted his face to examine the skyline against which Silas stood. But the man didn't. He scurried along, oblivious, his head bent against the wind.

A vast reservoir held at bay by the embankment was the additional detail on the landscape Silas had been told to look out for, the signpost that meant his journey was almost, but not quite, at an end. The bulging mass of water looked barely contained to Silas. It would be a small job for one of those white-capped waves to reach up and devour the man walking so precariously beside them.

A fierce eddy of wind blew fresh rain into his face. He whooped – a nonsense yelp – to relieve the wave of excitement that rose from his innards to his throat, and stamped his feet, pushing his hands through his thick wet tangle of hair. He'd forgotten his cap in his haste to leave. An unwanted sneer echoed in his skull, his father's voice, *Tha not made o' sugar, are tha? Won't melt, will tha?*

A firm nudge into the palm of his hand brought him back to the moment, restoring the bubble of anticipation in his stomach. Silas bent to pat the collie.

'It's stair rods, Shandy!'

He fished an apple from his satchel and chucked it in the air to enjoy the sight of the dog springing and twisting to catch it with a snap of her jaw.

'Good lass.'

He was glad, now, to have her by his side. Shandy had risen from the rug by the cold embers of the farmhouse fireplace, followed Silas out of the house, had waited for him to lift and replace the gate and had stayed at his heel as he had crept down the lane. He'd assumed she would soon turn tail and had ignored her. But she had continued to pad by his side, and then – as dawn broke across the shadowy shapes of roadside foliage, revealing spiked leaves and dew-laden cobwebs – she ran circles around him, threatening to trip him. Silas had imitated as quietly as possible the harsh noises his father made in the field, and gestured back the way he'd come. It had been her turn to ignore him.

The daft dog had only been getting in his path because of her bred-in urge to round him up. It amused him that they had been each trying to turn the other around and he hollered again into the sky. It was a good sound. Freedom. Oh, he'd seen the path set out for him, had understood the role he was expected to play more clearly than ever after yesterday's visit from Reverend James. The vicar had come to speed along preparations for the wedding of Silas's older brother, Peter, to his bride-to-be, Ginny. She was one of several girls that Peter had rolled into the hay, but the first to grow round, and anyway, Peter was twenty now and needed a wife.

Peter would inherit, while he, Silas, wasted his life grafting on a farm he'd never own. That was the way of it. He had no prospects that would convince a girl to roll about with *him*. There was no reward for being the second son. Then the Reverend James, who had conveniently arrived at dinner time to discuss the wedding, had loosened his tongue over the meat and potato pie and told Silas about the town away over the hills and the opportunities that awaited a strapping and hard-working young man.

'Don't turn the boy's head,' his mother had said, too late.

Silas felt the weight of the coins from the housekeeping jar in his coat pocket. *Thou Shalt Not Steal*. He would repay his mother. He would send double the amount he had taken, with a letter to his father, emphasising his good fortune. The good fortune he was bound to encounter.

He pressed his fingertips against the ache on his cheekbone and winced. Peter had beaten him for as long as he could remember and rarely gave an explanation for any of the unexpected blows he landed on Silas's face, torso or back. Brothers fight, his father said over his mother's protests, and just look at the size of the lad. He can take it.

3

Not anymore.

Shandy was at his side, licking the palm of his hand industriously.

Silas bent to tousle her ears and allow her to coat his face with her tongue and her damp doggy breath.

'Father's lost his hardest worker in thee, eh? An' Peter's kicked me across the yard for the last time, ha'nt he?'

Shandy had spotted the man below. She barked, three sharp retorts that were lost in the wide-open sky. The hem of the man's cloak lifted in the wind as he disappeared into a small stone building near the bottom of the embankment.

Silas crouched on his haunches to pat Shandy's sleekly wet head, tracing the thin bones of her skull. 'No goin' back, girl. Never goin' back. Think tha can round me up a hot meal and a warm bed for the night?'

Shandy at his heel, he strode down the valley's steep hillside. He knew, because he had been paying quiet attention to the enthusiastic chatter of the Reverend James, that he was heading for the newest and largest of several reservoirs set like stones in a jewelled necklace on the high ground all around the town. This grey lozenge of water could use a polish from the cloth of a blue sky. Fat chance of that today.

Now, as he descended, the river that led towards the town emerged as a thin grey ribbon from the foot of the dam. He came to a road that ran parallel to the river, about sixty feet above it. A gig that Silas assumed must belong to the man he had seen on the embankment was parked here, the horse hitched to it staring into the rain. Silas fed the horse an apple, his last.

At the bottom of the valley, he came to the deserted pavements of a hamlet of pretty stone cottages and found the river again, walking alongside trees that poked still bare branches into the sky. There was not a soul about, and who could blame them, in this downpour. Silas grinned down at Shandy as he turned east towards the town, the town that was the beating heart of the kingdom's steel industry.

Chapter 2

Harriet Wragg blew a wayward strand of hair from her eyes as she reached the top of the staircase. The bedlinen she was carrying had blocked her view of the floor. If her cousins had left toys on the varnished planks for her to stumble over then her exasperation would be complete.

She could hear the two younger boys playing in the bedroom they shared, the thump of feet on floorboards, a blood-curdling yell. Savages rampaging through a jungle of their own making. She had no wish to investigate. Meanwhile Adam, the oldest at thirteen, should be working on the grammar and spelling she had given him ahead of his matriculation. It was hoped he'd go to boarding school this year, if the money could be found. She passed his door without pausing. Alice was downstairs in Harriet's room, practising needlepoint with all the stubbornness a six-year-old could muster. She'd been stabbing her own pudgy fingers more frequently than the cloth and refused all assistance, even when a drop of blood blotted her stitching.

All the cousins were accounted for, and occupied, thank goodness. Her uncle had called for her to attend her aunt from somewhere in the depths of the house, and now, as she dropped the heavy linen onto the bureau, she heard the front door slam. Walter would be out until mid-evening. On his return, he would host a supper, with Harriet's help.

Harriet quietly entered the master bedroom.

The drapes were drawn and Polly was a hunched shape sitting on the edge of the bed. Harriet suppressed a sigh and went over to crouch before her.

'Aunt. Do you need the…?'

'Yes.' Embarrassment clipped the older woman's voice. 'You're limping today.'

'My foot pains me.'

She bent to help Polly rise to her feet and manoeuvred her across the room, aware the two of them must look like a grim parody of a waltzing couple. She knew that Polly felt as mortified as she, as she lowered her aunt onto the commode.

'Just rise up a little, Aunt.'

Harriet tugged Polly's nightgown out of the way and retreated to the rain-lashed window. The roof of a passing carriage was as blackly velvet as a moonless night.

'I am sorry,' said Polly. 'When I ask your uncle for help, he delays and delays. I sometimes think he enjoys my discomfort.'

Harriet made a sympathetic noise but wasn't really paying attention. She placed a bet on two raindrops meandering down the glass. If the one on the left reached the windowsill first she would be rescued by a handsome prince, a fairy-tale ending to a dark fable that had begun six years ago when her parents died. If the other drop won, she'd be stuck here forever, slowly transforming into a bitter old maid.

'He's gone out with his new acquaintance, Mr Boothby, to solicit business for their venture. House building, if you can credit it. From banking to bricklaying, although of course Walter won't be getting his own hands dirty. And Boothby might be a rich man, but Walter needs to drum up more cash, which is where your brother comes into the equation.'

James. He'd been packed off to boarding school when their parents died and was now doing well for himself in London where he rented a set of chambers in a fine house. Investments, or something like that. Harriet was expected to be grateful for the occasional, if not brief, letter.

The two raindrops converged on each other before reaching the bottom of the windowpane. Harriet sighed.

'There's a high demand in the town, your uncle tells me. I have a demand of my own, I tell him. This was once a relatively quiet spot by the river, but we've been swallowed up. Why, we're in the very stinking centre of the town now! And he wants his own horse and carriage. No man of business can be taken seriously without his own horse and carriage, he says. Mr Boothby keeps several vehicles. A curricle, a chaise… I've finished, Harriet.'

'Hmm.'

'Harriet. I've finished.'

'Oh! Sorry, Aunt.'

Harriet averted her eyes from the contents of the bucket, and helped Polly back into bed, the sharp odour of piss in her nostrils. She washed her hands as quickly as she could in the basin on the bureau. The water was numbingly cold.

'You're forever washing your hands. You're a fastidious child, aren't you?'

Harriet laughed. 'Aunt, I'm twenty-three.'

'I cannot remember the last time I heard you laugh.'

'Well.' She wanted to say she had little to laugh about, but knew she would feel ashamed of herself if she spoke

8

out. Twenty-three. Life was sliding past like a swan on a lake while she was the silly goose on the bank, running in circles around children that were not her own, an invalid aunt, largely absent uncle, and a house that, even after all this time, did not have the comforting scent of home. But no other occupation was open to her and she was not in the acquaintance of any young and eligible men, let alone a handsome prince.

'I would like a cup of tea, if you have time, dear.'

'I have time.' Harriet swept strands of hair away from her face. One of her braids had come undone in the effort it had taken to manoeuvre her aunt onto the commode and back.

'Look at the state of your hair. Come here.'

Harriet knelt by the bed to allow Polly to unravel, tug and twist her hair back into an orderly state.

'You have the same lovely, thick red hair as me and your dear mother,' Polly said. 'I know mine is thinner now but that's what bearing four children and suffering such a loss has done for me. Your mother will be young and beautiful for always. That is a comfort.'

Harriet's eyes smarted. 'I would rather have her here with us.'

She wished to have her mother's gentle fingers comb through her hair, not a woman who gave birth in this bed six years ago and never got out of it, handing the raising of four children to Harriet without a word. Walter talked vaguely of disorders of the mind, while the doctor prescribed tonics.

Polly had finished. She patted Harriet's shoulder. 'Will you take the bucket down?'

Harriet set her jaw as she tugged the wire handle of the tin bucket to free it from the seat of the commode.

Like a snail clinging to a stem, it never came easily, and it sickened her to see the contents sloshing up the sides.

She left the bucket at the foot of the stairs and poked her head into her bedroom, to check on Alice and ensure she hadn't accidentally sewn herself to the armchair. But the little girl was gone, leaving only a discarded piece of cotton on the seat with a needle poking from it. Harriet would have heard her if she had come upstairs to her own room. She frowned, her head cocked for raised voices. She hoped Alice wasn't pestering the boys. They were frequently cruel to her in return. She hurried across to the front parlour where the board games, children's books and some of Alice's toys were stored.

Harriet stopped on the threshold of the room, clapping her hand to her mouth.

Alice was standing in front of a roaring fireplace that dwarfed her, straining on her tiptoes to fan the flames with the edge of her pinafore.

'Alice!'

The little girl jumped in fright and stumbled closer to the grate. Harriet lunged forward, got a tangle of soft hair in her fist and hauled her back. Alice wailed. 'Ow! You pulled my hair! That's mean, Harriet.'

She dropped to her knees and cupped Alice's face. 'My darling. You could have burnt to death. I've told you over and over about this.'

'I was just trying to help!'

Harriet took a deep breath to steady her heart, which was tripping over itself. 'It doesn't help to set yourself on fire, does it? Where's the fireguard?'

Alice pointed to the corner of the room. 'I moved it over there. It's heavy.'

Harriet replaced it on the hearth. 'Yes, you shouldn't touch it. Out you go, go on. Go and visit your mother.'

'Will you tell her on me?'

'Not if you promise to never do this again.'

'I promise. I'm sorry.'

'Then you are forgiven.'

She bent to kiss Alice's damp cheek and went to find Louisa.

Louisa Leigh was paid by Walter to do the heavy cleaning work around the house. She didn't live in, although Walter was her sole employer. The windowless room she had been offered off the kitchen was too small and cold, 'as snug as a bleedin' coffin,' was how Louisa had described it. Walter had employed a carpenter to erect shelves on the back wall and it now served as a pantry. Louisa arrived at six in the morning and worked until four in the afternoon, seven days a week with Sunday afternoons off. Her last task was to help prepare the evening meal and, if time allowed, she would share a pot of tea with Harriet before undertaking the long walk home to Malin Bridge. Harriet cherished this precious time with Louisa. The two young women had bonded over their similarity in age and from this tenuous connection a true friendship had grown, entirely separate from their roles as mistress and maid. At least, that's what Harriet hoped.

She found Louisa sitting at the kitchen table examining her hands, which were covered in red, peeling skin.

'No better, then?'

'Nah,' Louisa sighed. 'That cream tha recommended. No use. Cost a bleedin' fortune, an' all.'

'I'm gasping.'

'Here.' Louisa poured tea into a china cup and passed it to Harriet. 'Does her ladyship want a cup?'

'I'll make a fresh pot for her. Can you take the unguent back? Or I can recompense you for it. It was my idea after all.'

'No, I can give it to Hilda for the baby. Betty's got awful sore bum cheeks from teething.'

Harriet laughed. 'A poorly bottom? Where is she growing her teeth?'

'It's givin' her terrible runs, poor lamb.'

'And how is Hilda?'

'Copin'. War' else can she do?' Louisa sipped her tea and gave Harriet a sly look. 'I've got a bit o' gossip about that situation.'

'Do tell!'

'Her 'usband's been spotted wi' the landlady from the Grindstone Tavern on his arm, no less.' Louisa nodded sagely, then frowned. 'I can't think o' her name now...'

'I don't know it. Doesn't matter. Go on.'

'Seen on the road to Chesterfield! Where they'll be settin' up house together, while poor old Hilda Armitage is left to run a boarding house wi' a babe in arms. Feckless man. I wouldn't 'ave him back if it were me.'

'Oh, my goodness. Will they divorce, do you think, now he's...?'

'Well, Hilda can't get shot o' him, can she? Unless she, y'know, does the same as he's done, and then he can divorce her for adultery. Or if he stays away, she can do 'im for abandonment.'

'Oh my! Poor Hilda.'

'Better off wi'out him, she's sayin'. Led by their... anyway, all men are the same, she reckons.'

'Well, that can't be true. She's upset by this latest development.'

'Puttin' it mildly. She were 'oping he'd been squashed under the wheel of a wagon.' Louisa lifted the teapot and Harriet held out her cup for more. 'Think there'll be any husband material at your uncle's little supper club tonight? Are tha invited to this get-together?'

'I'm helping to host, yes. I only hope they remember they have homes to go to after they've drunk Walter's brandy. And, no.' She grimaced. 'You wouldn't be impressed by any of my uncle's cronies.'

'I dunno. An easy life wi' a maid to empty the grate sounds right up my street.' Louisa paused. 'I'm not sayin' owt against thee, Harriet. I know it's a slog lookin' after this lot.'

'Don't be silly. I might be trapped in these four walls, but I thank my stars I've got you to give me all the gossip of the town.'

'And I shan't let you down, neither.'

The two women smiled at each other.

'Shall I do the honours wi' her ladyship's bucket?'

'Oh! I forgot. I left it at the foot of the stairs.'

Images of the boys upsetting the contents flooded her mind – they were all three of them like giraffes with no idea of the length of their limbs – but Louisa was already on her feet.

'Stay put. Back in two shakes.'

Harriet rested her head in her hands and gazed at the whorls and knots ingrained in the wooden tabletop. When Louisa tramped through with the commode bucket and let herself out through the back door, drops of rain blew in on a gust of wind that fluttered the net curtain covering the kitchen window. Somewhere in the depths of the house a door slammed and Harriet jumped. Perhaps she should ask her aunt's doctor for a draught of elixir.

'Where's your beautiful smile?' Uncle Walter had said the other day. 'Nobody wants to see a mardy face on a pretty girl.' The implication that Harriet would have to try harder than most to present a figure of womanly loveliness, afflicted as she was, was unspoken. And, perhaps, absent. She should not assume every reference to her physical appearance had to do with her deformity.

Louisa blew back in and dropped the bucket in the kitchen sink with a clatter.

'It's silin' it down!' she said. The drops of water in her blonde curls just made her hair look even more lustrous than usual. Harriet always felt ungainly next to Louisa; too tall, too skinny, all elbows and knees. Louisa had rounded edges where Harriet was pointed. At least, she could take comfort from the fact that her road was laid out before her. She'd raise Aunt Polly's children, look after her aunt and uncle in their dotage. Her brother would marry and have children and she would be an aunt who would love her nieces and nephews as much as she loved little Alice. James would furnish a room in his townhouse for her, or perhaps provide a cosy cottage on a tranquil riverbank where she would read and embroider and practise the piano. Hers was a secure existence. She was luckier than most, she knew that. It was only that her foot ached so today, and the pain always worsened in the night so her sleep would be restless again. She had learned as a small child to hide the discomfort. She wanted no more attempts made on a cure, the memory of irons caging her leg from toe to pelvis still there if she chose to dig for them. She did not.

Louisa took down her shawl and wrapped it around her shoulders, lifting the frayed edge to cover her head. 'I should've brought me bonnet. I'll get soaked. Summat to look forward to though. Hilda's layin' on rabbit pie for tea.'

'That sounds lovely,' said Harriet, hoping she didn't sound too wistful. She wasn't talking about the food. She imagined a cosy dwelling with a large fireplace around which the residents would gather, passing red-cheeked Betty between them to rock her to sleep. Harriet recalled the buttery scent of Alice as a baby. No, she shouldn't begrudge the turn her life took when her parents died. She loved Alice as much as she adored her brother, despite his absence.

Louisa opened the door and stuck one arm outside and they both marvelled over the hard drops of rain that pattered off the palm of her hand. 'I'll be a drowned rat by the time I get 'ome. See thi tomorra.'

Harriet watched her hurry down the path and through the gate then closed the door and turned reluctantly into the darkening kitchen. Time to light the lamps. There was a yell and a clatter from upstairs. The deepening voice of Adam ordering the other two about. She ought to check on Alice. If she had been a second later into the parlour...

A cold shudder rippled across Harriet's shoulders as she reached for the matchbox she kept on a high shelf.

Aunt Polly would say it meant someone was walking over her grave.

Chapter 3

John Gunson strode away from the squat cube of the valve house that nestled at the base of the dam, his cloak tugged and yanked by a witch of a wind that shrieked in his ears. The weather forecast had driven him from the relative shelter of the town to the upper reaches of the valley where the elements raged unimpeded. It would appear the Admiralty warning in this morning's newspaper for strong gales had been correct.

Nevertheless, all was well.

As chief engineer of the Sheffield Waterworks Company, Gunson might have sent a subordinate to check on the reservoir, but he acknowledged to himself that it would gnaw at him if he remained snug and dry in his office and something was missed. It was his duty. He had driven his gig over the cobbles of the town, through the industrial districts of Philadelphia and Neepsend towards Owlerton, then headed west through the villages of Malin Bridge and Little Matlock to reach the hamlets of Damflask and Low Bradfield that sat at the foot of the Dale Dyke reservoir.

There were few people abroad. A combination of the foul weather and the fact it was late Friday afternoon and pay day would account for that. The public inns would be busy enough tonight.

He remembered standing in this valley some five years ago – in fact, it had been the very first day of 1859 – when the official ceremony was held to turn over the first sod of earth. The weather had proved challenging on that day too, soaking the fine garments of the great and the good who attended. The gorge they had congregated in was gone now, straddled by the dam, and the commissioning of the reservoir only weeks away. Once the valves were opened and water released to thunder through the pipes, the company would be meeting its commitment to the operators of the corn, paper, snuff and steel mills, grinding works and forges that jostled for space on the banks of the Loxley River. A guaranteed supply of power driven solely by the pressure of seven hundred million gallons of water from the reservoir above.

Gravity, doing its work. Gunson, doing his.

He would inspect the weir before riding back to town. Head lowered against the furious gusts of rain funnelling down the steep-sided valley, Gunson crossed the foot of the embankment to the bottom of the weir that curved down from the reservoir into the river below. It was dry. If the torrential downpours of the past few weeks continued, the overspill would do its job. That point had not yet been reached.

The ride home was uneventful, and Gunson thought he would visit with his wife before returning to the office. He found her in the parlour at the upright piano, a glass of water sitting on a white lace doily on top. Gunson picked up the glass, examined the clear liquid and gulped it down, wiping his heavily bearded chin with the back of his hand. A clean and fresh supply. The townspeople took it for granted.

'Ah, I needed that.'

Charlotte smiled at him and lowered the lid on the keys. 'This is a nice surprise, John. And I must say you're looking very pleased with yourself.'

'Well, I am, I am pleased. I've just been up to take a look at the dam and now I'm going into the office...'

'I thought you were home for the day! Now I'm disappointed.'

'...to check some paperwork, and then I shall return home to you, my dear. What's for supper?'

'Lamb, I think. I'd have to check with—'

'No, no.' He patted his belly, which was continuing its baffling expansion, an accretion of weight that had begun when he entered his fifties. 'The company will be better than anything I could wish to eat.'

'Goodness me. I am flattered. What has put you into such a good mood?'

He bent to kiss her cheek. There was grey in the ringlets that dangled beneath her lace cap. It suited her. There was nothing that could diminish her beauty in his eyes. 'I won't be long.'

'Fortuitous,' she said, 'that you should purchase a house so convenient for work.'

'If you truly hated Division Street, my dear, I would move us into the country. Have cows for company.'

'I know you could not tolerate that, though I am tempted by the thought of the fresh air and net curtains that aren't grey with soot five minutes after they've been washed. Don't get too wet!'

Once outside, Gunson thrust his hands into his jacket pockets. He hadn't bothered with his cloak or gloves for a walk of a few hundred yards and was already regretting this decision. Moving closer to the wall to avoid being splashed by a passing coach, Gunson became aware of a figure approaching from the opposite direction. When he saw who it was, he cursed himself for stepping into the other man's path and doubly so for looking up and making eye contact when he could have kept his head down and forged ahead, the weather being excuse enough against any suggestion of impoliteness.

'Mr Gunson!'

'Mr Webster.'

'And how is life treating you?' John Webster, to Gunson's mind, had the unfortunate capacity to make even the most innocuous of questions sound like an interrogation. He always reminded Gunson of the sparrows that fought in the gutter of the roof, forever jabbing and jabbing.

'Keeping busy. And yourself?' said Gunson, without enthusiasm.

The man was bound to be on some crusade or other, and Gunson was wary of being enlisted into his latest campaign. Lawyering didn't seem to be enough for Webster. He was happy to serve as an Alderman on the town council as well as court magistrate and coroner of inquests. They were of a similar age – they even shared a Christian name, albeit the commonest one – but Gunson irritated himself for always feeling the junior in Webster's company.

'Only fair to middling,' Webster said. 'Fair to middling. Ill tumours breed in weather like this.'

The man was a hypochondriac, but Gunson shivered. He would not be surprised if he was coming down with a head cold himself. What a bother that would be when he had so much work to do. He would ask Charlotte for some honey in his brandy tonight. He looked forward to slipping between clean sheets warmed by the copper hot water bottle he had persuaded Charlotte they should have. She was afraid of it leaking and preferred to add an extra layer of clothing, although at this time of year that might require him to swaddle himself in all the contents of his wardrobe.

'I think I may have caught a chill myself,' he said. 'I've been out to inspect the new dam today and the cold has got in my bones.'

'Ah, yes. Our reservoir to compensate the millowners. Are you content with the progress being made up there?'

Gunson waited for the clatter of another coach to pass. He was impatient to move on, but could not resist any opportunity to talk about his pride and joy.

'We've had heavy rain, as you are aware...'

Webster looked heavenwards and raised an eyebrow.

'...and as a consequence the reservoir is almost full to the brim.' He smiled at Webster, warming to his theme. 'It's a beauty.' Gunson cupped his hands and Webster peered into them. 'The sturdiest cradle we could build. D'you know, the source of it is a little stream, a bare trickle, that rises in the hills twelve miles off yonder,' he gestured ahead. 'We dammed it after four and the results are there to see.'

Webster nodded impatiently. 'So you are satisfied, then, that the Sheffield Waterworks Company is now ready to meet its obligations to the industries in the valley as well as to the inhabitants of the town?'

He talked like the lawyer he was, in precise and seemingly rehearsed sentences, and with a smile playing about his mouth to disguise the sharpness in his eyes. It was no secret that the town council wanted to nationalise the water supply. All Gunson desired was to have this man – to have every man – appreciate the wonders wrought by engineering, a profession that had finally gained the elite status it had long deserved. People were quick to complain when the taps ran dry, but gave no thought as to how their precious supplies were contrived to reach them in the first place.

'Yes, as was promised, of course,' he said. 'In fact, you must excuse me as I'm on my way now to complete the paperwork.'

'Of course, I mustn't keep you, except… well, I note the water rate has gone up again.'

'Has it? That's not my area of expertise, you'll understand. I will say that progress has to be paid for.'

'Yes, indeed.'

'What are we without progress? Back in mud huts. Savages scratching in the mud.'

'Spoken like a true engineer, John.'

This didn't sound like a compliment. 'Thank you,' said Gunson. 'We're really getting very wet standing out in this. It's blowing a gale, too. I must go on.'

'Time waits for no man.'

'Good health.'

'And to you.'

Gunson hurried on. He felt he'd come off better from the exchange. But his genial mood had been snatched from him and carried off like a stick in the overflowing gutter he had just had the misfortune to step in.

Chapter 4

Silas came to a cotton mill, its wheel snug against the outer wall and turning smoothly. He was close enough to hear the discordant notes of water splashing and dripping off the wooden slats. He passed a row of stone cottages and a church with a round turret, like a castle battlement, but with no spire. The church in his village had a tall spire. He could hear the thin wail of a newborn. Somewhere hidden, a dog was barking. Shandy pricked up her ears at this, but continued to pad placidly by his side.

Silas was weary now, focusing all his energy on putting one foot in front of the other. He had hoped to reach the town, but now daylight was fading, and he was prepared to bed down in a barn if it came to that.

The wind resumed its harsh assault when Silas walked out of the hamlet and started up a sloping road fringed with gorse. He looked down, for Shandy. The dog was no longer at his side. Had she decided to abandon him? She could be running back across those hills even now. Silas spun around, his throat already constricted with regret that he'd lost his faithful companion.

A hundred yards back, Shandy sat on her hindquarters in the middle of the road.

'Come on, lass,' he said. She tilted her head, one way then the other, but didn't move. Silas went back to her and tugged at her ruff. 'I'm tired an' all but we can't give up

22

here.' Saying the words was enough to boost his resolve. 'We'll knock on a door, hey? Next place we come to.'

He straightened and clapped his hands.

Shandy turned her back on him and lay down, chin on paws and snout poked forward, facing back the way they'd come.

'Come on, girl.'

The constant moan of the wind in his ears was penetrated by the rattle of wheels over stones and a cab appeared, pulled by two horses and coming from the direction Silas had just left behind. The vehicle filled the narrow lane. Shandy stood up and barked, then came to Silas's side. He grabbed hold of her and shrank against the hedge to allow the carriage to pass.

Instead, the driver pulled on the reins, bringing the animals to a halt.

Silas reached out to stroke the horse nearest. 'Hey, boy.'

It snorted.

'Need a ride, young fella?' The man holding the reins bent towards him, drops of water falling from the brim of his cap. 'You look like a drowneded rat. That your dog feelin' sorry for itsen?'

Shandy was whining again.

'It's been a trek,' said Silas. 'I'm headed to town but I don't know if I can pay you.' The fewer coins he spent on frivolities like carriage rides the better. Still, he put his hand on the handle of the cab door, hopefully.

'Aye, well.' The man looked him up and down. 'I'll take thee as far as I'm goin' for nowt. But sit up 'ere, wi' me. I don't want me carriage messin' up and tha can't get any wetter than thou art.'

'Thanks!'

Silas leapt up beside the driver, reinvigorated, and whistled to Shandy who bounded up after him and planted herself between his legs. She was as soaked through as he, but gave off a damp and comforting warmth. The relief of being off his feet, which were now throbbing dully, coursed through Silas.

'Nice doggo. Not really the weather for walkin', though, eh?'

'I just want to get to the town.' Silas shifted on the wooden bench. 'I've been walkin' all day so I'm right glad you stopped for us.'

'We look out fer each other in this neck of the woods. We're coming into Little Matlock now. I can tek thee all the way into Division Street, if tha wants. That's where I'm headed to pick up me passengers.'

Silas had no idea of the geography of the town. He wondered what Division Street divided.

'I'm after work,' he said. 'I need lodgings first.'

'I can drop thee at Malin Bridge then, at a nice place I know. That'll set thee going.'

'Is Malin Bridge in the town?'

'Near as makes no odds.'

Silas recalled the words of Reverend James, who'd had almost a religious fervour for the new inventions that were revolutionising the production of steel. Silas had no idea what a Bessemer Converter was but he couldn't wait to find out.

'I'm after a job at a steelworks.'

'Ah, reight enough, reight enough. Atlas is the biggest, but there's loads of 'em. Tha'll be tripping over 'em. My boy's in the steelworks, at an armoury.'

'An armoury?' It sounded exotic.

'Tha knows. Armour plate for the warships and steel for guns. Apprentice, he is. About your age. Earnin' a good wage wi' prospects. Tha'll have to work thee way up, mind. And there's harder trades tha should avoid, o' course that's if tha can afford to pick an' choose.'

'Like what?'

'Like what… like what… File grinding. That's one. Day an' night bent over a grinding machine. Pays all right, I'll grant tha that, but tha's breathin' in dust, ruins the lungs an' dead by my age.'

The driver appeared quite old to Silas. 'Your age?'

'Forty.'

The man pulled on the reins to slow the horse as they rounded a bend in the road. They crossed a narrow stone bridge and the man acknowledged the driver of a gig that had stopped on the other side to allow their carriage over. The road steepened and Silas had a view down onto the mills and cottages that crowded the bank of the river. After a while, they levelled and dropped and there were houses and shops and inns on both sides of the road, obstructing the wider view, and people on the muddy pavements, most of them hurrying from one shelter to the next to get out of the rain.

'So I'll drop thee at Mrs Armitage's. She's a lovely lass and is known to take in waifs and strays like thee.'

Silas opened his mouth to protest he was neither waif nor stray and then closed it. He could see the picture he cut, a boy with his pet dog, soaked to the skin, carrying nothing but a satchel with the few clothes he'd hurriedly shoved inside it.

He only realised he'd been nodding off when the carriage jerked to a halt and his eyes flew open.

'Here you go. The one at the far end, closest to the river.' The man pointed out a terrace of two-storey brick cottages that ended at a stone bridge which spanned chop-pily flowing water. 'Tell her Michael sent you.'

Silas jumped down. 'Thank you! C'mon, Shandy.' He watched the driver urge his horses up a steep road then walked to the house at the end of the terrace and rapped on the door. He nervously fingered the coins in the pocket of his smock. He reckoned he had enough for a week's lodgings and food. If it wasn't for the weather, he would have considered bunking down by the river. He briefly regretted his impetuous departure. He could have waited for the balmy summer evenings, but then he might have never acted, and would be subjugated for the rest of his life. He was here now. No going back, that's what he'd told Shandy.

The door swung open and the face of a girl about his own age, maybe slightly older, appeared. Her inquiring smile faded when her glance fell to Shandy. She opened the door wider to reveal an older woman in the room behind her, balancing a baby on her hip. This woman spoke over the girl's head.

'Can I help you?'

'I was recommended your house for a room,' Silas said. He knew he must look a sight and he tugged at his smock that was soaked through where it extended below his brother's waxed coat. 'Michael said to come here. He brought me, from Bradfield way.'

The girl had stepped back so he could duck his head under the doorframe for shelter. From within, there was a rich odour of cooked meat and pastry. Shandy lifted her head, her nostrils flaring.

'You're from Bradfield?' she said.

'No, further off.'

'Stocksbridge way?' She smiled again, warmly, and raised her eyebrows. 'I've a cousin in Stocksbridge.'

'No.' He'd never heard of Stocksbridge and wanted to end this line of questioning. 'The driver – Michael – he were reight kind to stop. I were on me way to town.' He did not want another resident of this town viewing him as waif, stray or vagrant.

'Well, that's all very well,' said the older woman. 'I can make room for thee, but I can't take a dog.'

The baby yawned and reached with a fat little fist for the plait of greyly blonde hair that hung over the woman's shoulder. The girl was blonde too, and pretty. She gave him a sympathetic look.

Silas coughed. 'He's a bonny lad. What's his name?'

The woman absently tugged her hair out of the baby's mouth.

'He's a she. Betty.'

He could tell she was becoming exasperated. The wind was blowing the rain into the room, but he had done the right thing by edging forward over the threshold. It meant she couldn't bring herself to tell the girl to close the door on him. The girl smiled at him and said, 'P'raps we can let him dry off for a bit.'

Silas smiled back gratefully. She was a proper looker with large blue eyes and a plump mouth and pale unblemished skin. Plump and big-breasted. The sort of girl his brother would waste no time in leading into the barn. Her hand, when she lifted it to wave him in without waiting to hear what the older woman had to say, was red raw, the skin rough and peeling.

'And Shandy too?' He appealed to the girl, but she looked away from him, over her shoulder, at the woman whose name Silas had been given and had forgotten.

The woman sighed. 'Aye, alreet. The dog an' all. It's not staying inside, though! You can tie it out the back.'

He followed the two of them, crossing the room in two strides, his eyes flicking over his surroundings. A sampler hung on the wall above the glowing fireplace and a long wooden seat alongside the coal scuttle was covered in embroidered cushions. A rug covered most of the floor. The place looked cosy. He'd struck lucky. In the corner, a white-painted door stood open, a staircase curving out of sight behind it.

The kitchen led off the front room and was just as warmly inviting, the coal fire and hissing gas lamps bathing the walls in a warm yellow glow. Shandy eased past him into the centre of the room and gave herself a vigorous shake, spraying the accumulated filth of their journey against the legs of the small kitchen table and over the flagstones.

'Shandy, gi' over! Sorry, missus.'

'It's Mrs Armitage – Hilda – and this here's Louisa Leigh. Louisa lodges with me.'

'Oh. Pleased to meet you.'

'And d'you have a name, at all?'

'I'm Silas,' he said, '...Hinchcliffe.' There should be no harm in telling these women his name, although he wouldn't put it past his father to set the police on him and have him hauled back to the farm. 'I'm Silas Hinchcliffe.'

'Well, now we've established that, tha can take that towel,' Mrs Armitage pointed to a rag hanging from a hook on the wall, 'and dry theesen off and sit theesen down.'

Mrs Armitage handed the baby to Louisa and opened the bottom drawer of the bureau that stood against the back wall of the kitchen. He watched Mrs Armitage smooth out the knitted shawl that lined the drawer so that Louisa could lay the baby on it. The infant sucked her thumb. She looked very contented to Silas. He wondered whether it would be acceptable to take off his boots and free his feet from his wet stockings. Probably not.

Mrs Armitage beckoned to him. 'Give that 'ere.' Silas handed over his satchel and she hung it from a hook under the mantelpiece to dry. 'Have a seat.'

The delicious smell was coming from a pan on the grate above the fireplace. His mother's kitchen had a larger range and a sturdy oak table that could comfortably accommodate ten people. Louisa pulled out a chair opposite Silas at a table that would not seat more than four and, like the chairs, was constructed of a flimsier wood. He should stop making comparisons and appreciate the good fortune that had brought him here. It was only that his feet were so sore.

'How's hersen?' said Mrs Armitage, to Louisa.

'Aunt or niece?' the girl replied.

Silas eased off his jacket. Shandy was a damp and constant pressure against his leg, keeping very still, as if she appreciated any movement would remind Mrs Armitage that she'd ordered the dog be tied up outside.

'Polly.'

'Bed-bound, still. Gen'rally to be found in the land of nod.'

Mrs Armitage tutted.

'And the niece?'

'Harriet Wragg in her wisdom seems determined to become an old maid,' said Louisa.

'Well, she's comfortably off, at least,' said Mrs Armitage.

'Set for life,' said Louisa. 'I wouldn't call it hard work, neither.'

Silas looked at Louisa's hands.

She caught his eye and curled her hands into fists and put them in her lap. 'I'm sick o' scrubbing lavs and doorsteps in this filthy town. I'm after a bit of fresh air. A gentleman farmer would do nicely. Does tha' know any o' them, Silas Hinchcliffe?'

He coughed. 'Well, I've come off a farm but am set on a different path. I'll be a steelworker. I'll start up me own factory, make armaments for the brave men of war.' It came out more pompously than he'd intended.

'I weren't asking thee to marry me, Silas.'

His cheeks grew hot. 'I din't mean…!'

Louisa laughed. 'I know that, tha daft sod.'

'Johnson wants a labourer, for that new barn he's after building,' said Mrs Armitage. 'They're not far from here. Just in case you can't find owt in town.'

'I'll find summat.' The last thing he wanted to do was end up on another farm. 'I've been told jobs are ten-a-penny here and I'll get an apprenticeship quick as owt.'

'Ah right, good for thee then.'

Mrs Armitage slotted a piece of pie onto a plate, poured thick brown gravy over it and balanced a hunk of bread coated in dripping on the side. Silas was aware of Louisa, who was now sitting with a plate of her own, watching him with friendly interest while he ate. He tried not to gulp his food down. Mrs Armitage sighed when he slipped the bread to Shandy.

'Silas, you can take the attic room, if you've the money to pay for it.' She pointed at his plate. 'Tea is an extra shilling a day. This one's gratis.'

Louisa snorted and leaned over to whisper conspiratorially. 'Hilda must like thee.'

Silas gathered that he wouldn't be paying for his meal. He was tired and it was difficult to keep up.

Mrs Armitage gestured to the dog. 'Outside for that.'

'Shandy's a she.'

'It's a dog. Backyard, or sling yer hook. I've got a rope you can use to tie her. Here you are.'

Silas got to his feet and took the rope. Mrs Armitage gestured to the back door.

It could be worse, he supposed. The back yard was sheltered from the worst of the weather. He went across the yard to use the privy, Shandy on his heels. Back on the kitchen doorstep he turned and told her to sit, which she immediately did, her ears perked.

'Good lass, Shandy. Stay.'

He fed the rope through an iron ring on the wall and around Shandy's neck. She was a well-trained dog, and used to the elements, but Silas felt a pang as he closed the door on her trusting gaze.

Chapter 5

Harriet paced around the dining table, straightening a fork here, a crystal glass there, adjusting the fold of the heavy velvet curtain in the window. Then she counted the place settings, once again, just to be sure, before retreating to the door and leaning against the frame, surveying the room.

'Your aunt's gown certainly looks better on you than it ever did on her,' called Walter from his armchair in the front parlour. 'Not that I can picture the woman in anything but nightclothes.'

The brandy glass she had brought to him only moments ago was empty, which she decided could account for his unkind remark.

'Would you like another, Uncle?'

'No, I'd fall asleep in front of my company, and we can't have that, can we?'

Her uncle was entertaining gentlemen from the upper echelons of society, a rarefied plateau Walter was hacking towards, and the guests tonight would include influential members of the town council and owners of two of the town's biggest manufactories that were not in direct competition with one other, as well as Mr Albert Boothby, the wealthy mason with whom Walter intended to go into partnership, provided the necessary funds could be secured.

Harriet had changed from her day clothes into one of Aunt Polly's evening gowns. The dress was not the finest garment hanging in Polly's wardrobe, but it was Harriet's favourite, an emerald taffeta that her aunt said showed off her green eyes and white skin to best advantage. 'I shan't be wearing it again so you might as well,' Polly had sighed. The fitted bodice was offset by elaborately puffed sleeves that exposed her shoulders and stopped just above the elbow. Her only complaint was the fullness of the skirt. Harriet would, if she ever had reason to, have a dress made in the new style, where the bulk of the material was gathered high in the back, the front flatter and the waist more tightly cinched. Beggars can't be choosers, she told herself. Aunt Polly had watched her lift the dress from the wardrobe and shake it out. 'Don't go near those gentlemen,' Polly had said, 'when they're smoking their foul pipes. Those things have the whiff of the privy and I don't want that smell coming back on my dress.'

Now, her uncle's cruel remark had made her conscious of her bare shoulders and she wished that she had covered them with a lace capelet. She put her hand on the bannister, wondering whether she had time to go and find one, when she was startled by a loud banging on the front door.

'Goodness me!'

'Our guests appear keen to get out of that weather,' said Uncle Walter, standing up and positioning himself beside the fireplace.

More pounding.

'Hurry up, Harriet,' said Uncle Walter.

As she opened the door, her hostess's smile prepared, a young boy stepped back into the road. He was clutching the reins of a horse as sodden as he.

'Uncle?' Harriet called over her shoulder without taking her eyes off the youth. He swiped rain from his face.

'I'm lookin' for John Gunson,' he said, without bothering to introduce himself. 'He's engineer for the waterworks. I know he lives in Division Street somewhere. I were given directions but I've lost me way somewhat.' And then, as if to be certain she understood. 'It's urgent.'

'What's going on?' Uncle Walter came up behind her and Harriet moved aside.

'Sir, I'm reight sorry to bother thee. I'm after Gunson's house.'

'Yes, I heard that. Why d'you want him?'

Harriet knew Gunson was not on her uncle's list of influential townsmen. Probably Walter was just being nosy. Harriet was curious herself.

'Summat's up at the new Bradfield reservoir and he needs to come an' take a look at it.'

Harriet's eyes widened. 'At this time of night? And in this weather?'

'There's a crack in the dam.' The lad looked uncertain. 'A small crack only, but I've been sent.'

'Is that an emergency?' said Walter. He turned to Harriet and raised his eyebrow.

The boy frowned. 'Well, they're sayin' it's safe enough, all them up there that are standin' about in a howling gale starin' at it. But Mr Gunson is needed right away, sir. There's a giant lake back o' that dam.'

'Oh dear,' Harriet said. 'Is there any danger?'

'Nothing we need worry about,' said Walter. 'Dale Dyke's a good eight miles distant. You've ridden all that way tonight?'

The boy frowned. 'Well, aye. I have.'

34

'You'll find your engineer in Division Street. He lives near the waterworks premises.'

'Yes,' the boy said patiently. 'I know that. I got given that. I've just lost me bearings a bit.'

'You've a way to go, yet,' said Harriet. 'Do you know where the town hall is?'

'No, I've never 'ad cause to come into the town before.'

'Oh. Well, turn right at the end of this road, then your first left and that will put you on the main road which you follow to Netherthorpe and then, and then I would stop and ask again.'

'I thank thee, miss…'

'Yes, try those directions,' said Walter, briskly. A gig had come up and stopped a little way off. Presently, there would be a queue. 'Off you go, then.' Uncle Walter retreated into the depths of the house. He could not be seen to greet his own guests on the doorstep.

'Good luck!' said Harriet.

'Cheerio.'

Harriet watched the boy mount his horse and gallop away. The gig moved up until it was opposite the front door and the driver jumped down. Harriet folded her hands and waited for the first of her uncle's guests to disembark. This was the owner of one of the larger steelworks, a portly man. She hoped the boiled mutton would be big enough to go around. Harriet smiled politely as he hurried towards the shelter of the house, the agitated boy already forgotten.

Albert Boothby was the last to arrive and the youngest by far of her uncle's guests. She guessed he was in his early thirties and while his eyes widened in an effusive greeting, the smile on his lips was thin. He had a narrow face and receding blond hair that he compensated for with a pair of bushy sideburns. Polly had told her he was a widower who had inherited his wife's fortune as well as amassing his own and could afford to take a gamble on property development.

During supper, Harriet felt his speculative gaze on her. He did not look away, or even appear abashed to have been caught staring, when she returned his gaze. She lowered her head first. He continued to observe her as she circled the table with the brandy decanter, replenishing the glass of another guest, determined not to glance at him, inwardly cursing the blush that stained the skin of her throat and rose into her cheeks, her body betraying her discomfort.

'Walter,' he said, finally, 'how quaint it must be to have a close member of the family for a housekeeper. That's not to say Harriet is not doing a sterling job. In addition, I hope you do not mind my saying that she is very easy on the eye.'

There was a moment of silence.

'Lining up your next wife, Boothby?' said one of the men.

Harriet's gasp was lost in the guffaws that filled the room. She tightened her lips and put the decanter down on the table. They were talking about her as if she was not present. Well, she would make herself absent. Fingers closed around her wrist. Her uncle.

'Harriet, my dear, they only tease you,' he said. He turned to Mr Boothby, whose eyes were dancing with mirth. 'Harriet is the beloved and only niece of my dear wife,' he said. 'I would rather have her looking after the household and her cousins, particularly dear little Alice, than a stranger brought in from the street. She is house-keeper, but not servant, eh Harriet?'

'Yes, Uncle.' Harriet forced a polite smile.

'I am sure she keeps a good account of herself,' said Mr Boothby. 'Perhaps the young lady would bring that decanter over to me?'

'Please refresh Mr Boothby's glass, Harriet.'

The general chatter resumed as she poured brandy into the glass Mr Boothby held out. He was talking to the gentlemen sitting on his left and now ignored her entirely, which was equally infuriating. He had no manners at all. Harriet fought an overwhelming urge to pour the liquid over his head.

'Now, gentlemen,' said Walter. 'We might discuss our latest business venture. Don't groan! I have more brandy to ease the pain. I shall fetch the cigars myself.'

This was her dismissal. Harriet nodded to the room without meeting anyone's eye and escaped into the hallway. Even in the candlelight, she could see in the hallway looking glass that her cheeks were flaming. She leaned her forehead against the cold surface. There was laughter from inside the room and, from upstairs, the thin sound of water hitting porcelain.

She climbed the stairs and picked up a lamp from the table outside the two younger boys' room, turning up the wick and opening the door gently. They were motionless under their coverlets, only the top of their tousled heads visible when she lifted the lamp over their beds. She closed the door quietly and tiptoed to Adam's room. The lamp jerked in her hand when she opened the door to find a tall figure standing motionless and silent on the rug. Black shapes leapt about the room and Harriet almost cried out before she realised the figure was her cousin, standing over his potty, swaying as he peed. Not all of it was hitting the mark.

'Adam,' she whispered.

The boy looked round blearily. He adjusted his pyjamas and allowed Harriet to guide him back to his bed. He smelled sweet and musty.

'Are they still here?'

'Yes, so straight back to sleep.' She'd had a battle with him earlier. He thought he was of an age where he could join the men and when she had scoffed at that idea he had begged to come down and at least greet his father's guests. This discussion had ended in Adam reminding her she was not his mother. On the other hand, he was happy to allow Harriet to tuck the bedcovers around his chin and kiss his forehead.

Smiling, she said, 'Sleep tight, Adam. Don't let the bed bugs bite,' and leaned against his bedpost so that she could edge the pot back under his bed with her good foot. She let herself out of the room as quietly as she had entered, turned down the lamp, carefully replaced it on the table, and crept back downstairs. Low voices came from the front parlour, serious men's business now under way, her humiliation no doubt forgotten, by them.

She entered her bedroom where Alice was snoring gustily.

In the dark, Harriet felt her way around the bed and undressed quickly, folding her aunt's gown over the back of a chair. She would return it tomorrow, when she took up Aunt Polly's breakfast tray. She would recall some detail from the evening to entertain her aunt while they drank their morning tea. Harriet loosened and removed her undergarments and reached for her floor-length night-gown with a sigh of relief. Through a chink in the curtains that allowed in some moonlight, she could make out her blurred reflection in the dressing-table mirror, her shadow-self making the same preparations for bed.

Harriet pulled the curtains tightly together.

She lifted the counterpane and slipped between sheets that had been warmed by Alice's body. She touched her cousin's back, her fingertips brushing the soft flannel of her nightdress. It would be nice to cuddle up, but she didn't want to wake her. Harriet contemplated rising again to fetch woollen bed socks from the dressing table drawer. They might help ease the ache in her foot. Or perhaps the cold would numb it. But she was reluctant to expose herself to the cold air again. She turned on her side and pulled the sheets higher, glad to be insulated from the gale still raging outside the walls of the house.

Chapter 6

There was heat in Gunson's chest from the brandy his wife had handed to him, which he was savouring, and a prickle on his skin from the leaping flames in the fireplace.

'Where are you going, Charlotte?'

She had got up from her armchair on the other side of the fireplace, skirts rustling. He admired her silhouette in the light from the candles, her hair gathered up to reveal a long and delicate neck. He had the privilege of seeing that hair tumble down her back when she removed her pins at bedtime.

'I'm tired out, John.'

'You're not going to bed at this hour? What is it, nine o'clock only?'

She smiled and bent to kiss his cheek.

'Oh ho!' He took her hand and pulled her towards him. 'You cannot fool me. You have a new book that is more fascinating than keeping your poor husband company.' He tried a pleading look. 'Ask Millicent to bring it down for you. Stay by the fire with me and read.'

But Charlotte was having none of it. 'No, it's too dark in here. The light by the bed is better for reading. My eyes are starting to sting in my old age.'

'Fifty-five isn't old, my love.'

'As I would expect a fifty-six-year-old to say. When do we become old, then?'

'Old age is always a decade hence.'

'So, sixty-six now? And then, in ten years, seventy-six?'

'If we live that long. It would be pleasing to get to the point of saying old age is ninety-six.'

Charlotte shuddered. 'Don't wish your life away. Goodnight, John. And don't stay up late.'

The house groaned in sympathy with the gale raging beyond the shuttered window. Candlelight flickered over the faces in the family portrait that hung on the wall, animating his younger self, bringing to life the hand rendered in oils that rested on his wife's shoulder, warming the serious gazes of their children who were gathered around her. All of them grown now, and scattered like seeds to create their own families. His eyes fell on the celestial globe that sat on a low mahogany table by the fireside, the constellations inscribed in gold on a black sphere that could be rotated within its brass meridian. It was a beautiful piece of nonsense, a wedding anniversary gift from the children. A pleasant wave of tiredness washed over him and his head nodded.

A furious banging startled him awake.

He could hear a female voice – he recognised it as their housekeeper, Millicent – and another unfamiliar voice overriding it. Their conversation grew in volume until a boy was ushered in on an eddy of cold air. Gunson rose to his feet.

'Sir,' said Millicent. 'This here is Stephenson Fountain and he reckons there's a problem at Bradfield, at the new reservoir there.'

The boy ducked his head. 'Well, I'm not sure a'that,' he said, slowly. 'There might be a problem. There might not.'

Gunson looked from the boy to his housekeeper and back. 'Well, is there or isn't there?'

Stephenson Fountain looked at him uncertainly and shrugged. Millicent raised her eyes to the ceiling and exited the room, closing the door behind her.

'Well, boy, I'm sure you're not dripping water on my floor for no reason.'

Stephenson nodded. 'I'm reight sorry, Mr Gunson, but father sent me...'

'Ah, you're Fountain's boy, of course!' He knew Stephen Fountain well. The man was a sub-contractor working on the site and Gunson had found him to be highly competent in all their dealings with one another. 'What's the problem then?'

'It's the dam. There's a crack been found.'

He was instantly alert.

'What sort of a crack?'

'A crack. I don't know. It's been found on the embankment.'

'Where?'

'About twelve feet from the top, in the middle.'

'How bad?'

'Not bad. A sliver only. Father is sayin' settlement, nowt more. Sheffield Harry is sayin' he'll not lose any sleep o'er it.'

Gunson knew of the man. Henry Burkinshaw, known to all as Sheffield Harry. He worked as a labourer for the Sheffield Waterworks Company. He was lodging at Damflask, at the foot of Dale Dyke dam, but had been put to work labouring on the Agden dam, a mile away. Gunson would not give tuppence for Sheffield Harry's opinion.

Stephen Fountain was a different kettle of fish.

'So your father believes it to be settlement, but I needed to hear about this tonight? Why can't it wait until morning? He must have concerns.'

The boy shrugged. 'I don't know, sir.'

'And you were sent out to tell me this?'

'No, sir. Not to tell you. To fetch you.'

Gunson strode out of the room, calling back to Stephenson. 'Go and rouse the stable boy to ready the gig, if you please. Milli— Mrs Leigh?'

He reached the top of the stairs that led down to the housekeeper's domain, her bed and sitting room, the kitchen, scullery and various anterooms that he rarely ventured into. 'Mrs Leigh!'

Millicent tolerated the use of her Christian name when Charlotte uttered it, but affected deafness with Gunson. Some code amongst servants, no doubt. Gunson opened his mouth to shout again but here she came, carrying his Macintosh.

'I am not relishing a second trip out to Bradfield on such a night as this,' he muttered as Millicent helped him into the waterproof overcoat. He fastened the buttons up to his chin. He had walked the length of the embankment and had not seen a crack. He hadn't been looking for one. It would be an easy thing to miss. 'My hat and gloves. Thank you. Would you let Charlotte know that I've been called away to check the dam? Don't wake her if she is already sleeping. I'll be a while. You can leave the door unbolted.'

Gunson drove first to the residence of David Craven. This meant a slight detour from the route to Bradfield and a necessary delay so that he could explain his late-night intrusion. But he wanted the company of the main contractor, the man who oversaw the creation of the embankment from the specifications provided by Gunson. Young Stephenson Fountain's anxious face had set a worm of doubt creeping in his gut. Dams were susceptible to failure. It was in their nature. It was his job to build insurance against nature's vagaries, following sound mathematical principles. He had done that. Yes, he was certain this would be a wasted journey.

The cacophony from hooves striking cobbles, the howling wind and driving rain that made a mockery of the half-canopy above their heads meant that conversing with each other was almost impossible and the two men soon lapsed into silence and their own thoughts. Gunson pulled on the reins at the road bridge at Hillsborough and both men climbed down to peer at the Loxley rushing past. The river was swollen, no doubt about it, and grey crests glimmered in the lamplight as the water rushed beneath them. Craven shrugged. Gunson nodded his acknowledgement. It had been raining for weeks. It would be unusual were the river not in full spate.

They drove onwards.

Light from the Stag Inn at Malin Bridge spilled onto the road. Gunson envied the men, warm and dry, bellies full of ale, whose shadowed profiles were framed in the windows. It would be heartening to stop here, to sit by the fire that would dry his bedraggled whiskers. His wife would fuss over his sodden beard if she was not deep in slumber by the time he returned home. His warm bed was some hours away yet.

Gunson glanced down into the ravine as they ascended the high road, the Loxley now an invisible thread below, its location signposted only by the scattered dots of lights from the tanneries and mills where work went on around the clock. Then the road began to slope down, and grew steeper, as they approached Lower Bradfield. They had passed through the hamlet of Damflask when Craven suddenly lurched forward, staring into the night.

'Halt!' Craven called. 'Stop, please!'

Gunson jerked on the reins. 'What the devil?'

A man was emerging onto the road from a farm track, pushing a barrow in which sat a shawled figure, a grey boulder with an elderly and scowling face painted upon it. She was berating the man who was wearily pushing her along. A younger woman whose long unkempt hair was blowing about her head in the howling wind and three children of varying sizes followed the barrow.

'Ahoy!' said Gunson. 'It's hardly a night to be out!'

'I told him there were no need for this!' The old woman pulled her blanket tighter across her neck. She looked at the younger woman. 'I telt him!' Everybody ignored her. 'It'll be the death o'me, this will,' she muttered.

'There's summat up with the dam,' the man said. 'We got a warning off Ibbotson, who was told by Fountain's lad, and we're off up to higher ground.'

'What were you told?' said Craven.

'I told thee. We got a warning, from up yonder. A crack in the dam.'

The younger of the two women spoke up. 'I said to Billy here that there's no cause for all o' this, but he won't be told. Is that where you're heading? To the dam?'

'Yes,' said Gunson. 'We've been called out to inspect it.'

'At this time o'night?' she said. 'So there is summat up?'

Gunson hesitated. By all logic, he should be telling these people to turn around and go back to their beds.

He should be telling them he himself was not concerned, that there had been heavy weather of late and the new reservoir was filling rather more quickly than had been anticipated, that his dam was sound and any crack in it would be settlement. Go home, he should say, there is nothing to fear. But he could not form the words. Had this afternoon's inspection been thorough enough? It was true he made swift work of it, and had spent most of his time in the valve house admiring the gleam and shine of the pristine machinery that would soon be put to work. He had climbed the embankment and it was solid as a churchman's faith beneath his feet.

He became aware the people on the road were all looking up at him.

'The dam will hold,' he said. 'It's preposterous to think otherwise. But you people must do what you think best. I cannot command you.'

The man grunted. 'Reight then.' He took up the handles of the barrow. 'I've got to get this lot up the hill an' come back for me cows. The pig's being a stubborn git, an' all. I'd rather have him in the barrow than her. He's worth more.'

Craven sat back under the canopy so it would conceal his grin.

The family continued to argue as the gig drove on, their voices quickly fading into the night. Gunson leaned forwards. A hulking shadow gradually materialised, slicing the valley. A hundred-foot-high behemoth.

His embankment.

Chapter 7

Lamps flashed and bobbed like fireflies against the black slope Gunson and Craven were now hurrying towards on foot. A face loomed from the murk directly in front of them, eerily lit by the lamp carried in the man's hand. His stubbled face seemed to float, leering.

'The builder *and* the engineer! They've sent the big guns out then.'

Gunson recognised Sheffield Harry's nasal tones. He stopped. 'I was told of a crack in the dam.'

'It's nowt.'

'Have you seen it, then?'

'Aye. It were Billy Horsfield spotted it on his way 'ome. He reckoned he could just about slide the blade o' his penknife in. Anyhow, the usual suspects 'av come out to have a gander. Self-appointed experts, the lot o' them. A few o' the locals have already taken to the hills.' Sheffield Harry shook his head in sorrow at their foolishness.

'But have you yourself seen the crack?' repeated Gunson.

Sheffield Harry nodded. 'Aye, I 'av. It's the narrowest hairline. Settlement. Nowt to worry about.' He looked from Gunson to Craven and back, and grinned. 'Wasted journey for thee, I'd say.'

'Well, we're here now,' said Gunson.

'And we won't be relying on your say-so, Harry,' said Craven. 'Is Horsfield here?'

'Nah, he went. An' I'm off to. There's a pint wi' my name on it in the Barrel. Who'd be out on a night like this, eh?'

Sheffield Harry stamped past and disappeared into the night as quickly as if he had stepped behind a curtain.

Gunson wrapped his muffler more tightly about his neck. 'We might as well have a look at it.'

They made for the valve house where a group of about a dozen men were huddled together. A figure broke away and trotted towards Gunson and Craven. It was Stephen Fountain, the father of the boy sent for Gunson.

Fountain wiped rain from his face. 'Sorry to drag you out, gentlemen.'

'Fill us in,' said Craven.

'No,' said Gunson. 'Sorry, gentlemen. Let's see that crack first.'

'This way.' Fountain lifted his lantern to guide them. 'Watch your footing. It's treacherous.'

They had staggered up to within twelve feet of the crest of the embankment, by Gunson's reckoning, when Fountain raised his hand to stop them. A gust of wind snuffed the flame in Fountain's lantern as he lifted it towards the earth bank.

'Damnation!' he said. 'This bloody weather.'

He clasped Gunson's arm to guide him closer. Gunson attempted to adopt the same crouch Fountain was in, to get a better look, but his feet slipped from under him, and he went down on his knees, the cold and wet immediately penetrating his trousers. His face was now within inches of the earth bank, his nostrils filled with the smell of wet soil.

'Look.' Fountain took off his glove and Gunson watched as the man's ghostly hand disappeared into the embankment. A magic trick.

Gunson frowned. 'I was informed it was barely wide enough for a penknife.'

'It was, at six o'clock,' said Fountain. 'It's wider now.'

'How long is it?' asked Craven.

'About fifty feet across,' said Fountain.

'Some settlement is to be expected,' said Gunson.

He tested the edges of the crack with gloved fingers. 'There's no seepage. Yes, I'm sure it's a small subsidence only. Have you checked the reservoir?'

'Full to the brim. We opened the pipes, a while since an' all,' said Fountain.

Gunson nodded his approval. Reducing the pressure of water against the embankment would do no harm.

'We had a job on, turning the screw. Took five of us,' said Fountain.

'Thank you. You took the correct measure,' said Gunson. The opening of the sluice gate valves would release water into the river below at a rate of thirty thousand gallons a minute.

'I should be able see the difference in the level of water from the inspection I made this afternoon,' said Gunson. He clapped Fountain on the back. 'You called me away from my warm fireplace on a wild night for this! No, no,' he laughed to see the consternation on Fountain's face. 'I can understand your concern. You did the right thing. All will be well.'

'I hope so,' said Fountain. 'I felt the tremor right through me when the pipes opened. Aye, it's no exaggeration to say the ground quivered. It's like we've woken a sleeping giant and he's about to come at us from out the wrong side of the bed.'

Gunson hid his surprise. Stephen Fountain was not ordinarily given to such flights of fancy.

'I am taking your concerns seriously,' he returned. 'Please do not think otherwise.'

Craven was getting impatient. 'It's a wild night, all right, but this,' he kicked at the embankment, 'will withstand anything the elements can throw at it, and that includes the pipes being fully opened. This dam's five hundred feet thick and there's bound to be some settlement. There'll be more over the coming weeks, mark my words. Are we to come out in the dead of night to record every bit of it?'

Gunson pulled his collar up and set off to climb higher. 'Let's look at the water.'

He was the first to gain the flat path on the top of the embankment and a rising uneasiness made his heart flutter as he did so. Angry waves tossed spray up to his knees. The reservoir the dam held at bay surged restlessly.

Gunson waited for Craven and Fountain to reach him.

'I was here late this afternoon,' he shouted above the wind, 'and it's fuller now. It should have dropped since the pipes were opened. Has anybody checked the weir?'

He didn't wait for an answer, but turned and, braced against the wind, led the way across the top of the embankment towards the overspill. The weir was dry, the river a faint glitter at the foot of it.

'Look at that! Not a trickle! The reservoir's not even at capacity,' said Craven. 'I'm telling you, there's nothing to worry about.'

Fountain shook his head in exasperation and appealed to Gunson. 'You've just seen with your own eyes that opening the pipes has made no difference whatsoever.' He turned to Craven. 'If we don't relieve the dam somehow there'll be a blow up, I'm *telling* you. There's three million tons of water held up here that'll smash this embankment to pieces. And us loitering here like we're debating the price of milk in a coffeehouse!'

'You can't know—'

Fountain cut him off. 'What I do know, David Craven, while we're up here debating the issue, is that a shitload of water once released will go where it bloody well wants!'

'Gentlemen,' said Gunson, glancing at Fountain's clenched fists. He'd had an idea, and hoped he could express it before the two men came to blows. 'Water will go where it *can*. Let us take a further precaution and supply another option.'

He looked into the faces of the other men.

'Blow up the weir?' said Fountain.

Craven shrugged. 'We built in the capacity for it, but I don't think it's necessary. Wait a while, at least.'

'Yes, I understand your reluctance,' said Gunson. 'This may be an unnecessary step, but is it one we can take without damaging the integrity of the reservoir or delaying its commissioning, yes?'

Craven gave a grudging nod.

'Well then. Dynamite the top of the overspill and a goodly chunk of water will be immediately released, and that will relieve the pressure on the embankment. What do you say?'

'Yes,' said Fountain immediately.

The man's sense of urgency was infecting Gunson, or so he told himself. His belly was hollow, although he'd eaten a good dinner – his animal self trying to override his logical brain with that most primal message: *Beware*.

'David?' he said.

Craven wiped rain from his face. 'We've not long finished building the damned thing... All right, I'll get some men on it.' He marched away.

Over the next hour, as the rain eased and stars came out to prick the sky above the reservoir, two attempts were made to demolish the top of the weir. Twice, Gunson held his breath in anticipation of the explosion, and then released it, bewildered.

Craven appeared at his side. 'It must have got wet, the dynamite.'

Fountain hurried over. 'Come and see this.'

Again, Gunson negotiated the steep side of the embankment until the crack was at his feet. He toed it, gingerly. 'It's no wider.'

'Wait,' said Fountain.

Gunson breathed into his hands to warm his face and thought fleetingly about the fireside he had left. Nothing had changed and he opened his mouth to tell Fountain that this must surely now wait until the following day, when he saw the expression on the man's face and followed his gaze to see water was dribbling between their feet and into the crack.

He looked up, dismayed. Water was running down the embankment's face. The reservoir was overflowing. 'But the embankment is solid,' he muttered.

'What did you say?'

'The crack. It's no wider.'

Gunson turned away.

'Where are you going?' said Fountain.

'To check the pipes.'

George Swinden, the site foreman, stood outside the valve house.

'There's no imminent danger,' Gunson said to Swinden, gesturing for him to follow him inside, eager for the shelter of the building. 'I'd like to check the pressures again. Were it not such a wild night…' he stopped when he realised the foreman had not followed him through the door.

'George?'

A cry came from outside, tattered by the wind. It could have been the screech of an owl. Gunson paused, acutely aware of the glass rattling in the windowpane. A wild night, yes. Not a disastrous one.

Swinden darted into the valve house. 'It's going!'

'What?'

'The dam!'

The man was making no sense. Gunson stared at him. 'No, it's not. Get a grip, man.'

'Come on, John!'

Swinden grabbed him by the arm, his grip fierce and desperation in his face. Gunson let Swinden pull him outside.

He looked up, knowing there would be nothing to see, that Swinden was having some sort of hysterical reaction. His stomach caved. The middle of the embankment was collapsing – *crumbling* – and still he could not believe that the entire dam wall could fail.

Swinden pushed him and he almost lost his footing. 'What are you doing, man?'

Distant voices were shouting.

'RUN!'

'GET CLEAR!'

Gunson ran, flailing alongside Swinden for the hillside where Fountain and Craven and the other men were waiting, arms outstretched, to pull them to safety.

It was too late.

He couldn't find purchase in the dirt crumbling down the collapsing bank. He slid and cried out, pushing at the trembling flank of the embankment to regain his balance. Black cracks appeared, abysses to suck him down. He was moving too slowly to escape an unseen monster gaining on him, those childhood nightmares now a reality. He looked up to see Swinden being yanked clear of the embankment. Another shudder and the earth beneath his feet disappeared. He was falling, pedalling his feet into a bottomless void. Then there were hands gripping him, and he was landing heavily on solid ground, face down, choking on dirt. He rolled onto his back, gasping for air.

Craven was bending over him, panting heavily. Gunson reached up and Craven grasped his hand, pulling him to his feet. He cringed as a bellowing roar echoed round the valley. Craven was shouting but he couldn't make out the words. It didn't matter. Nothing mattered. He was witnessing the collapse of his embankment, the entire middle section dissolving in an ear-shattering cascade of rocks and froth.

He tried to speak, but no sound came and this was terrifying in itself. Craven was screaming at him, tugging at his coat. 'Move, man!'

He blindly followed him up the hillside, scrabbling in the dirt.

Fountain was there, swinging a lantern to attract their attention. His eyes were bulging. 'We have to send a warning down!'

'How far?' said Craven. He took hold of Gunson's collar and shook him. 'How far will it go? Damflask? The Stacey Wheel? We have to send men down now!'

Gunson found his voice at last. 'No horse can outrun that,' he whispered.

The monstrous cascade was already past them, the river a snake shedding its skin, discarding the boulders in its bed and the trees on its banks, carving itself a new shape as it raced down the valley.

He cowered as another blast echoed off the hills.

Fountain laughed wildly and Gunson looked at him, aghast.

'The dynamite,' Fountain said. 'It finally went off.'

Craven shook Gunson's arm. 'How far? How far?'

Craven's face was a mask of terror. His men had built that dam, to the specifications Gunson had provided.

He batted Craven away and spoke as calmly as he could, but his voice shook with every beat of his heart. 'The banks might break even as far as Little Matlock but it should subside before it gets to Malin Bridge.' He took a deep breath, afraid suddenly that he would vomit in front of these men. The moment passed. 'If it reaches Hillfoot unabated and joins with the Don... then I don't know. I'm sorry, I don't know. We're in God's hands now.'

Fountain dropped to his knees. 'Then God help us,' he said.

'God help those in the valley,' said Gunson. He ran his hands over his face and head that were gritty with dirt – only now realising he'd lost his hat – and took a shuddering breath. 'God help them.'

There was nothing he could do to halt the avalanche now roaring towards the sleeping town beneath.

Chapter 8

It was nearly midnight and Silas was in a forge, in quiet awe of the vigorous alchemy at work.

He was no longer damp. The heat from the furnace had dried his clothes on to him, stiffly. But he was as exhausted as a stuck cow. Had he been told he was dreaming and would wake up tomorrow in his own bed at the farmhouse he would not be surprised.

Earlier that evening, after he had eaten his fill, Mrs Armitage had led him up to the attic, which was no more than the cramped space where the two sides of the roof met. Under the eaves, the room's meagre contents included a truckle bed, a tin saucer with a candle melted onto it, a bureau made of some flimsy wood only a step above kindle and a metal bucket on the floorboards at the foot of the bed into which drops of water from a leak in the roof were plinking. 'It's cheap enough,' his landlady had said apologetically. 'I've a lodger who's going to fix that leak when he can get round to it.'

Silas had been content enough. A room for the night felt like the first solid proof of his escape. A man's voice called from the landing below. 'Hilda?'

'Ah, speak o' the devil.'

And that was how he met Fred Sharrow, a short, sinewy fellow and foreman of a knife manufactory, on his way to start a night shift. 'Eleven tonight 'til eight in the mornin'.

Come wi' us for a look,' he'd said, after Mrs Armitage explained that Silas was new to the area and looking for work in a forge. 'Strike while the iron's hot!'

Silas had cast a longing glance at the bed before following Fred out of the house and over the stone bridge that spanned the river. They turned right along a lane lit only by the moon. 'If we'd gone't other way,' said Fred, 'we'd arrive at Mousehole forge which tha'll 'av 'eard of.' Silas had been forced to admit he hadn't. 'Anvils,' said Fred. 'World famous, exported round't globe. I served me apprenticeship there.'

'I'm wantin' to be right in the town,' said Silas. 'A big place. An armoury. Atlas. Summat like that.'

'Good to see a kid know what he wants. All in good time. Tha'll need to be apprenticed, get union approved. That can't just walk into a job like this.'

They had walked some distance, the sound of the river never far away, when Fred stopped at a set of iron gates, a brick building behind the thin bars, every window lit with a yellow glow.

Entering the forge had been an assault on the senses. Noise and heat and an alien odour competing with the smell of burning coal, a metallic tang like the taste of a bitten tongue. The far wall was dominated by a floor-to-ceiling metal cylinder being fed coal by two shovel-wielding men in rolled-up shirtsleeves, their forearms muscular and blackened by dirt. Halfway down the long room, a burly man manipulated a series of pulleys to fasten the handle of a bucket to a massive iron hook. Not five feet from where he stood, boiling metal was being poured into crucibles, sweat pouring down the faces of the men handling arm-length ladles.

Fred set him on the job of hauling back the furnace door to allow molten steel to be ladled out to transfer into the casts, where, Fred explained, it would cool until the metal was supple enough to be shaped into knife blades. The molten steel was orange in the furnace, brightening to yellow as it was poured into the crucibles.

At snap time, he'd sat with the men watching them open their tuck boxes, hungrily, his landlady's feast a distant memory. Fred had shared with him a piece of bread and a wedge of cheese and another man had thrown to him a hardened chunk of salted ham that was the best he'd ever tasted.

Now, exhausted, the sound of the scrape of a shovel came to him as the hiss of a snake. He wondered if the bucket catching water at the foot of his bed would be full to the brim by morning, whether he could sneak Shandy into the attic, if tomorrow he would share another evening meal with pretty Louisa Leigh—

'Ey, ey ey!'

He jerked awake. Fred Sharrow, his bald head shining with sweat, had a painful grip of Silas's shoulder.

'Go on, lad, see yonder? That door? Out tha goes, get a bit of fresh air in tha lungs. Tha's dead on thee feet and a splash o' this stuff… well, it'll open tha flesh to the bone.'

'I'm right, sorry.' Silas was chastened.

He stumbled away and through the side door Fred had indicated. It opened onto a narrow strip of ground alongside the river. In the distance, a pair of slim black fingers pointed like sentinels in the sky. Chimney stacks, the smoke they were belching yellowed by the light of the moon. He slid down the wall to rest on his haunches, inhaling the sulphurous air, so foreign to the smells he'd grown up with, the odour of slurry and scent of hedges

heavy with pollen which irritated his nose. He was satisfied he'd made the right decision. Why else would he have
had such a run of good luck if it was not fate that placed
him here, in this spot, bone-tired and elated? It was meant
to be.

Silas tipped his head back against the cold brick. It had
stopped raining.

In the black sky, the moon hung silent and still.

Chapter 9

Harriet woke with a start. There was a body in the bed with her.

She fumbled to release herself from the sheets and was standing on one bare foot and the curled edge of the other on the scratchy wool of the rug before she was fully awake.

A noise like the snuffle and squeak of a hedgerow animal came from the mound under the covers. Of course. It was Alice. She'd forgotten her cousin was sharing her bed. Harriet tiptoed to the bureau at the bottom of the bed and ferreted around in a drawer, pulling out a pair of thick socks. She sat on the edge of the bed, which creaked noisily, and pulled them on, massaging her foot for a few seconds to relieve a cramp, before getting back under the covers.

Alice snuggled against her. 'Where did you go, Lally?'

'Nowhere. Shush. Go back to sleep. It's very late.'

Harriet had no idea what time it was, but the sound of laughter from the front parlour told her it could not be the dead of night.

Harriet's bedroom was at the gable end of the house, downstairs, across the hall from the room where Walter was entertaining his guests. It was a large room that she'd shared with her brother when they had come to live with their uncle and aunt, but now it was hers alone, a refuge, the only part of the house in which she could occasionally close the door and draw the curtains against the world. Not tonight, though. Aunt Polly in her wisdom had suggested Alice might benefit from a night in her favourite cousin's bed. The poor mite was highly strung, and the previous night had woken screaming in fright from a bad dream. She was also frequently to be found swaying at the top of the staircase, fast asleep, and had to be guided back to bed.

'If she's with you,' said Aunt Polly, 'she won't be falling down any stairs.'

Or disturbing her mother's slumber, Harriet thought, but as with so many of her mutinous thoughts, did not say them out loud.

She had some of her mother's possessions in this room, not many. Jewellery and gee-gaws did not figure among her few treasures. She had kept a piece of unfinished embroidery that was propped on an easel in the corner of her room. The outline of a slim girl in a ballgown, holding a closed fan in one delicate hand, a tiara balanced on her head. A princess, her finely drawn features barely discernible. Only the hair piled under the tiara had been coloured in with orange thread. Harriet had no wish to complete it and had resisted Alice's pleas to finish the tapestry. She would leave it as her mother had.

As a very young girl, Harriet had been taught how to peg rugs by her mother and the first rug they made together was now back in her possession. It lay on the floor by the bed, on what was Alice's side tonight.

She found she couldn't rest and rose from her bed again, despite the cold, and ignoring the pain in her foot, padded quietly to the window that looked out on to the side street. Gaslight glistened on the paving stones. It had stopped raining. A watchman was starting his rounds at the top end of the street, his cloak billowing about him as he relit his lantern and turned the corner on to the main road. Harriet wriggled further under the curtain and peered up at the whitely glowing moon. She rested her head against the cold pane and wondered how long she could tolerate the draught that cut through her nightgown and chilled her flesh.

A rustle from behind. Alice was sitting up in bed.

'Lally? What are you doing now?'

Lally had been Alice's first word, even before mama or papa. Harriet had been quietly thrilled by this. Remembering, she smiled.

'Nothing. I'm coming back to bed.'

'What's that sound?'

'It's just that noisy old wind. We'll go out tomorrow once the sun is back out.'

'Will it be sunny tomorrow then?'

'Oh yes. I'm sure it will be.'

Harriet slid back under the blankets and wrapped her arms around the little girl. 'Are you cold?'

'A bit.'

'Shush, then. Let's warm each other up. Back to sleep now.'

Chapter 10

A sudden breeze lifted his fringe as Silas opened the door that led back into the clanging warmth of the factory floor.

He slipped inside, surprised to find he was forced to push against the door to close it behind him, wondering at the strength of the wind that was howling like a banshee once more.

The door rattled against his back and the clamorous roar outside rose in volume. He looked about him, suddenly fearful but with no idea why. Fred was on the other side of the room, his back to Silas, fiddling with the controls of the boiler. The youth Silas had been helping stoke the furnace was standing above Fred on a gantry, manipulating a pulley to send a bucket of molten steel from one end of the room to the other. It swung from side to side. Another worker was hammering steel, close by Silas, but there was something fundamentally wrong with the scene before his eyes. Silas realised he couldn't hear the strike of metal on metal.

He let go of the latch.

The roar intensified and gooseflesh broke out on his arms despite the heat in the room. There was a hammer in his skull, pounding, and he pressed his hands to his ears. Now the tableau before him was of men frozen like statues in the act of whatever they had been doing. Fred had turned to face him with a mildly puzzled look on his face.

The bricks of the wall at the far end of the room exploded inward.

Fred Sharrow hurtled towards Silas, spread-eagled across the boiler, screaming without sound. Silas felt the strength leave his body and the world turned pitch black. The building was coming down on him and he cursed himself for not escaping back into the safety of the back lane. He felt himself lifted, twisted like a knot, and he took a breath but drew water into his lungs and choked. He was underwater, being pummelled by invisible fists. Fingers closed on his head and he thought his scalp would be ripped off. He pressed his lips tight, he must not scream. He had no air left in his lungs. He flailed his arms but there was no up or down, no way to escape and panic filled his mind. He would die.

Something malevolent had taken over his body, jerking him this way and that as if he was a cloth doll. He reached out, blind, and his fingers found slim iron bars. He instinctively curled his fists around the hard metal. Was this the gate, the factory gate? He could pull himself to the top of it, but he was too afraid to loosen his grip even though his lungs were bursting. Repeated blows pummelled his back and then his arms were almost ripped from their sockets. The gate had been torn from its foundations. Silas released his grip and flailed upwards, his head breaking the surface of the water into instant chaos, the roar loaded his ears again, he was in a wild ocean. He had time to gasp for breath, then was pulled down again, into the black and crowded void, then up, popping to the surface like an apple in a barrel.

Searing pain cracked across the back of his skull. It was the branch of a tree. Dizzied, he lunged for the branch and clung on, barely conscious of the rapids that surged around him, adrift on the churning ocean that had once been land.

Harriet gasped into wakefulness.

She'd been dreaming that Walter was berating her for some duty not carried out to his liking and during his tirade all the mirrors in the house had shattered. Polly had sneered from her bed. 'How many years of bad luck have you brought this family, Harriet? How many?' The glass in the mirrors had screamed as the shards fell. High-pitched screams of fear.

Screams. A young girl's screams. A weight on Harriet's face. She realised Alice was crawling over her, suffocating her, reaching for the bedframe above her head. A vinegary stink filled her nostrils and a crashing, rushing sound filled her ears. The chill air sucked the heat from her body.

'Alice, stop! Get off me!' She put her hands around Alice's wriggling torso and used all her strength to push the girl's soft bulk away. She felt rather than saw Alice fall back on to the mattress.

She swung her feet out of bed. Something was dreadfully wrong. Her heart plunged in shock as she fell forward into freezing water. Harriet spluttered and struggled to her feet. She was up to her waist in freezing water. It was not possible. She turned in a stumbling circle about the dark room, searching for a chink of light. A violent shove, a surge, nearly took her off her feet. Harriet screamed and then froze. She was submerged up to her neck, her nightgown billowing up to surround her. She moaned in fear through closed lips. The water was at her chin. They would drown. She *must* still be dreaming. She knew she was not, and that the distraction her mind was trying to conjure could kill them both.

'Alice, Alice!' She spluttered the words. Alice continued to wail so she could not be underwater. Something hard struck her in the chest and she reached for it. Her fingers closed around a slender piece of wood. She reached up to find the end of it, and realised she was holding one of the bed legs. The bed was floating, with her clinging to it.

'Oh no, oh no.'

'What's happening, Lally?' Alice screamed again. 'I'm getting squashed.'

The ceiling. The bed had floated to the ceiling. Again, her mind told her this could not be true. The room could not be filling with water. It was not possible. Harriet fought to keep her voice calm.

'Lay flat, Alice. You mustn't get in the water. Lay flat.'

She squeezed her eyes shut against the horrifying blackness, then dived, Alice's sobs fading behind, for the door. She found the doorknob and tugged at it. It slid from her grasp.

She swam up to touch the ceiling inches above her head. She took a breath of thick, rotten air, dived again, found the doorknob, twisted it and pulled. Nothing.

The window! She would smash the glass, release the deluge into the street. But the blackness was complete. If this room was underwater, so was the world outside.

She swam back up. Only a sliver, a thin crack, of air remained. She gasped, once, and clamped her lips together, clawing at the ceiling as the waters closed over her face.

Chapter 11

Silas was close enough to see the beast's eye roll in its socket as they were carried helplessly along. A horse. It was going to kill him.

Silas's naked body was being scraped against the stone wall, the animal's muscular flank crushing his ribs, its long head too close to his, its lips peeled back in terror to reveal large teeth. Silas's shirt and vest had been torn from his body by the iron rails of the steel works gate. He didn't know when his trousers, stockings and drawers had been yanked away, but it might have been in the whirlpool of debris that had flung him against this wall. Now he would be crushed to death by this hysterical animal. He was going to die in this churning inferno, drowned before his life had even got started. The realisation deadened his panic and Silas was overcome by sadness.

He rose up a little in the water as the horse pushed against him. Stupid creature. Desperate creature. Silas's head was out of the water, but he couldn't breathe. He would suffocate. The stones of the wall were smearing the skin off his chest. It didn't matter about his nakedness, not now the end of the world had come.

Shandy had been right to try to turn him back from this town after all. Was she in this whirlpool? Never try to rescue a dog from the water, his mother always insisted. The dog will eventually find a bank to scramble up, but you won't. You'll be carried off. Stay away from the river. He'd seen a river burst its banks before. Nothing like this. Perhaps the deluge had dropped from the sky. Judgment day. The end of the world. Or perhaps it was some sort of flash flood, a broken pipe, and if he wasn't to be squashed to a pulp against this wall he'd be carried back to dry land. What if everybody he knew was caught up in an endless wave? Noah's Flood. Somewhere, a giant Ark bucked and swayed, but Silas was not one of the chosen ones. His mind churned in endless circles and he sucked in each breath convinced it would be his last.

He gasped in shock as a powerful force shoved him forwards. Whatever it was had freed the horse, for the beast suddenly lurched ahead and away from him. He was freed from the wall that had been an instrument of torture and struck out without thinking – the imperative was to get away from those scraping stones, but this put him back in the heart of the churning mass.

There were houses on either side, the water lapping against upper storey windows, white faces staring from within. The ground could not be too far beneath his feet, but there might as well be an abyss under him. Shouts and cries and moans occasionally broke through the cacophony of rushing water, but he had not seen another soul in the water with him.

Silas was flung against a solid column that knocked the remaining breath from his body. He reached out, through instinct rather than intent, wondering how long he would have to endure before he finally drowned. He realised he'd caught hold of the iron crossbar at the top of a lamppost, just beneath the extinguished gas light chamber. Silas wrapped his body around the iron pole, shivering uncontrollably. He could make out the black silhouette of the horse's head ahead as it continued to ride the rapids. He stared after it until it disappeared.

He thought of the little attic space, of the tin bucket catching single innocent drops of water. The same stuff that had turned fearsome. There was a grim hilarity about his previous worrying whether the bucket would fill to overflowing overnight. How he wished he was in that attic now, in the bed he had paid for, with the water spilling out of the bucket. Let it go where it wanted.

For a terrifying moment, his legs were tugged, hard, then released. He clung on. A wooden container knocked against his body, floating on the waves. The moonlight showed him that it was a crib, a child's empty wooden crib, bucking on the tide of filth. Silas held his chin high as a wave reached up to slap his cheek. He clung more tightly to the pole, a monstrous hissing filled his ears like all the demons of hell were calling to him.

Harriet couldn't help the scream that bubbled from her mouth and nose when her ankles were seized. The door was open and she was being pulled through it, slamming her hip on the frame. She was choking, drowning. What felt like deliberate force tumbled her over and she hit the bannister of the staircase and clung to the bottom spindle.

She was dimly aware of a wavering light above her head, a glimmer in the darkness, and she hauled herself up, spindle by spindle, her head swimming. A shove from behind propelled her forwards and pain exploded in her nose as her face was smashed into the carpet. Her lungs were bursting, her nightgown tangled around her waist.

Harriet reached up and found hands, small hands that grabbed at her fingers and hair. She was breathing air again. She lay, gasping, her head on the dry carpet of the upstairs hallway, staining it with her blood. Three pairs of feet stood close by and the youngest child, only a year older than Alice, was whimpering quietly. Harriet used her last ounce of strength to pull herself out of the water, and stand, gripping the mahogany rail with both hands.

Black water swirled where the staircase should be. It was the most terrifying thing she had ever seen.

She had left Alice down there to drown.

'I'm going back.'

She lurched forwards, but Adam got in her path.

'No!' He shouted into her face. 'Father went down.' He burst into tears. 'He went to get you and Alice. Father got you, so now you have to stay here. You have to stay here while he fetches Alice!'

Harriet allowed herself to be pulled away from the staircase, towards her aunt and uncle's bedroom. The younger two followed. She had to believe that her uncle would rescue Alice. She sniffed hard, swallowing blood, then choking as a fresh bolt of pain ripped through her skull.

She went to touch her nose then dropped her hand. 'What is happening?'

Adam gulped. He had fast hold of her hand, as if she would try to escape and plunge back into the depth. 'We've been watching from the window.' He tugged at her and she got her feet working again. 'Come on, I'll show you. The house, will it fall down, Harriet? Will we get swept away, too? I could hear screaming. Mama said it was pigs squealing, not people. Pigs. I think it was people.'

Polly was in bed, hunched against the headboard. She turned a glassy stare on Harriet.

'Where's my Alice?' she whispered. She held out her arms and the younger boys ran to her, to be enfolded in a fierce embrace.

'Father is fetching her,' said Adam. 'Isn't he, Harriet? Isn't he fetching her right now?'

'The dam must have burst,' Harriet said. She gulped and turned to the basin, hanging her head. 'A boy came, earlier. He knew. He told us.'

'I can't understand you!' said Polly. 'What dam? There's no dam.'

Adam let go of her hand and went to the window. 'There's a proper river outside, Lally. There's all sorts in it. It's right up to here.' His voice was high, on the edge of hysteria. 'There's a horse, look!'

The younger boys pulled away from their mother's embrace to crowd the window, open-mouthed.

'Where's Alice?' cried Polly again. 'Where's Walter? Harriet, I'm talking to you. Fetch the constable!'

Harriet sat on the end of the bed and buried her face in her hands.

'There's a man, I can see his head, he's hanging on to the lamp-post,' Adam wailed. 'Harriet, is that Father? Did he go outside? Come and look!'

Silas clung on as the current flowed around him, tugging at his body, urging him to give up, give in, allow the water to carry him away. It would be so easy. Where there had been a stinging across his chest, he was now numb. There was no feeling in his hands and he stared at his fingers curled around the lamp-post strut, terrified that if he took his eyes off them they would lose their grip and he would be swept along.

Faces stared out from upper-storey windows that were only inches above the fast-flowing deluge, gazing wide-eyed at him amid the wreckage whirling past. Spectators, safe and dry and warm. Silas hated them.

One of the windows was lifted and a woman leaned out, her long hair trailing into the water. She waved to him and shouted words that were lost in the pounding torrent. Silas shook his head. The current was too fierce. He'd be swept past her window before she caught hold. It was certain. He cursed the woman for giving him a grain of hope. It was true he'd had the strength to catch hold of a tree trunk earlier, but he'd been less exhausted then. He should stay where he was, try to believe the flood would subside.

She was still shouting, waving, extending her hand. What was wrong with her? Why didn't she leave him alone? Even if he managed to reach her, if he was able to grab her hand, he'd only pull her out after him, into the maelstrom, and they'd both be drowned. Another silhouette in the window, more shouts. Silas closed his eyes.

A voice whispered in his head. Why not strike out, aim for the windowsill? No. He should stay put, wait and see. He'd only be pulled under, he was convinced of it. But the voice wouldn't let him be. Why not, it wasn't so distant was it? How would it feel to hook his numb and exhausted arms over the ledge, to be pulled into that comforting square of light? Into the dry?

Harriet's heart leapt as the man struck out, his head bobbing in the wrathful eddy and swirl of black water, and she saw he was not Uncle Walter, but he was a life she was determined to save. Walter was rescuing Alice from the bed, and would soon appear with the little girl whom Harriet would hold close to her and whisper *sorry sorry sorry I left you* and never let go, but first she would save this unknown life. Amid the horror, this made sense to her, and the man was here and his mouth was a grim line and his hands were gripping the windowsill.

He stared into Harriet's face as she leaned over him, and their eyes met wide in fright, and Harriet saw that he was young, not much older than Adam, and he lurched an elbow over, then the other, and lunged forward as she grabbed him under the shoulders and yanked, and they were both on the floor of the bedroom and a yell was knocked from her lungs under his naked weight and his wet bare legs entangled with hers. She looked up to see Walter and the boys standing over them and her eyes searched the room while Polly screamed and there was no Alice.

Chapter 12

A tangle of limbs. Gasps for breath, and moans. Were they coming from him? Another body heaving beneath his.

Silas rolled onto the carpet, shivering uncontrollably, his teeth chattering so hard he thought they would break. Instinctively, he curled up, aware of his nakedness amid a roomful of people, one of whom was screaming, a high-pitched curdle that went on and on. The sound of an open-handed slap and the noise abruptly stopped. Near him, a girl struggled to sit up, her bloodstained nightgown rucked up to expose the white skin of her thighs. She had a foot like a misshapen bird's claw and saw him looking and covered it with her hand. That was his blood on her nightgown. Blood from his chest where he had been squeezed and rubbed against the wall like a scrap of cloth. The room swung drunkenly from side to side and Silas closed his eyes.

When he opened them – moments or hours later, he couldn't tell – he was lying under a comforting weight of blankets that covered his head, too. The room was quiet but he could hear shouts in the street, a clatter of bells and a whistle, clear and pure. No deafening roar nor giant's gargling. A faint light penetrated the dense material and he wanted to close his eyes again and escape into the welcoming dark but instead he lifted a hand numbed by cold and pulled the blanket down from his face.

A woman lay propped against the headboard of the bed, a sleeping boy pressed against each side of her substantial bulk, her arms around them. She was staring out of the window at a sky lightening perceptibly from the black of full night. An older boy sat on the foot of the bed, looking directly at Silas.

'What's your name?' the boy said.

He opened his mouth to speak but coughed instead then found he couldn't stop and had to prop himself up to retch. He wrapped the blankets tightly around himself and glanced at the woman on the bed. 'I'm sorry.'

She continued to ignore him completely.

'How old are you?' said the boy.

'How old? Eighteen.'

'That's only five years older than me.'

'All right, then.'

He clung to the blankets as he rose stiffly to his feet, aware of the eyes of all three boys on him, and shuffled to the window. He could hear bells clanging in the distance and two separate whistles were being blown insistently, like the sound of distraught birds. He nodded to the expressionless woman in the bed. Her eyes slid over him and slowly closed. Silas looked outside. There were people moving on the street below, their lamps casting brief light over shattered glass in a ground floor window, a dead dog in a doorway. A woman, wailing.

The bedroom door creaked open and Silas whipped his head round, sending pain shooting across his shoulders. His heart lurched in his chest. A man stood there. A ghost, surely. His face was curdled milk, his britches sodden. His shirt was ripped and his hair stood on end. Silas cringed when he opened his mouth but instead of screaming like the madman he looked, the being spoke in normal tones.

'You'll need some clothes, I think.'

Silas could only nod.

The man opened the door of the wardrobe and began to throw clothes onto the floor behind him. An undershirt, britches, a shirt and waistcoat, stockings. Even a pair of shoes. Silas quickly picked them up, then stood, uncertain. He couldn't relinquish his blankets in this room with the woman on the bed and the boys staring at him. He wondered where the young woman was, the woman who had got him in through the window.

'Adam,' the man said, 'take him to your bedroom so he may dress himself.'

He followed the boy onto the landing, peering over the bannister into the dark void below. The foul stench that rose up made the silence eerie. The boy pointed to a door and Silas let himself into a bedroom darkened by closed curtains. He barked his shin on the end of the bed and sat down on the mattress, resisting a childish urge to burst into tears. He pulled on the trousers jerkily, moving cold limbs that did not seem to belong to him. The britches were big around the waist but too short in the leg. Silas wiped his hand across his chest. It stung. He pulled on the vest quickly and then the shirt, his biceps straining against the soft material. A wave of nausea overcame him and he sat down again on the bed.

When it had passed, he wondered whether he should wait for the man to come to him, or venture out. He could hear water trickling and was seized by thirst. A jug on the bureau had a couple of inches of water in it and Silas drank it down. Water had never tasted so fine. He was alive. He fought the urge to laugh, knowing he was not in his right mind. He wondered again where his saviour was, the woman who had beseeched him to strike out for

76

her, who had pulled him to safety, and he stepped outside the room to find her.

A smell like wet sheep and sewage emanated from the stair carpet. He moved downwards, crablike, clinging to the bannister, although the staircase was clear of obstacles. At the bottom, he stepped through a glutinous layer of sediment, afraid the ill-fitting shoes would be sucked from his feet. A shaft of sunlight blinded him to the detail of the ruins he was surrounded by, and he was glad of it, afraid of what he might see. Would there be human limbs in this mess? How close had *he* come to being a water-swollen corpse?

The front door swung like a drunkard from its hinges. An internal door lay flat. In the room beyond, a ribbon of dusky pink wallpaper licked hungrily around a gaping hole under the window, like a cow's curious tongue. On the doorstep, Silas stopped to stare at the object that blocked his path. After a few seconds he recognised it as an anvil, tipped on its side.

He edged around the contraption's black bulk as though it was a hellhound there to prevent his exit, only pretending sleep, ready to leap up and clobber him. He thought suddenly of Shandy, his gentle lass, and what had become of her, then was immediately seized by fresh horror when the glint of white bone in the middle of the street caught his eye. His heart continued to hammer even as he realised he was looking at a stripped-bare tree trunk resting on the mud-covered road, like the spine of some great monster picked clean by scavengers.

A bird trilled, filling the curiously peaceful street with liquid notes, and a horse stepped delicately over the trunk, the rider giving Silas a nod of acknowledgement as he passed by. The man did not stop or speak. The horse, a handsome black beast though its shanks were encrusted with mud, did not seem to be even of the same species as the panicked and helpless animal that had rolled a wild eye at Silas in the maelstrom.

The faint warmth of the sun, still low in the sky, caressed his face, and this reminded him again that, miraculously, he was alive. Silas took a deep breath and watched the progress of horse and rider down the street to the corner, where a dozen people stood in a loose grouping near a seven-foot-high pile of metal junk. Now he had seen them, his ears were penetrated by their chatter.

There was some commotion as a ladder was brought and laid against the mound and men's voices quarrelled over whether it was safe to climb or better to wait for the arrival of the properly equipped fire brigade. He saw the reason for their urgency. A pair of naked legs dangled from the debris, shockingly tender against the tangle of iron. A barefoot child darted forward and began to clamber up the rungs of the ladder, and was ordered down and pulled into the road by a man who clipped him round the ear. A woman took the child's arm and hurried him away.

Silas felt a presence behind him and knew instinctively she was there before he turned to confirm it. His rescuer, last seen in a bloody nightgown, now dressed in a high-necked black blouse and long black skirt. Her red hair was pinned in a loose bun and she held a handkerchief to her nose. Her eyes were swollen.

'How did you hurt your face?' he said.

'My uncle, he was trying to help me. He did help me.' Her voice was muffled but she kept the handkerchief in place. 'He came down to get me and Alice and he pushed me up the stairs.' She looked down the street. Silas followed her gaze to the pile of debris. 'I thought Alice would be safer if she stayed on the bed. I couldn't get the door open.'

'Who is Alice?'

'My cousin. She was with me in my bed when the house filled up with water and now we can't find her.'

He followed her gaze down the street. There was no sign of the fire brigade, but a horse-drawn flatbed cart had arrived. Men jumped down from it and set about retrieving the body.

'It's a man,' said Silas. 'The body.'

He'd meant to reassure her, but the woman said, 'Then what chance does a small girl stand?'

'The little lass might have been rescued,' said Silas. 'Like I was.'

She removed the bloodstained handkerchief from her face and looked disinterestedly at the blood smeared in it. She cleared her throat. 'What will you do?'

'Find my lodgings an' my dog. I were in a forge last night.' He looked past her, down the road. Fred Sharrow flew through the air towards him, screaming but making no sound. Silas blinked. 'I'm not from round 'ere. I come yesterday, looking for work.'

'Then you are very unlucky.'

'No,' he said. 'That's daft. I am lucky. I am standin' 'ere, alive.'

'True,' she said flatly.

There was a whistle from the street. 'Oy! Gi' us a hand, lad?' Two men were trying to shift the tree trunk that lay in the path of the cart. Silas walked over, showing them the raw palms of his hands.

'I can try,' he said.

The trunk of the tree was astonishingly smooth and heavy, more like a rock than wood. Silas put all his effort into helping release it from the sticky mud and shift it to the side of the road, the mistreated muscles in his arms and legs quivering in protest. He straightened, breathing heavily, and went to lean against the cart, but the heaped bed was covered by a sheet and Silas could guess what was under that. He approached one of the men instead, wiping his nose with the back of his hand, wondering whether his nostrils would ever be clear of the horrible stench.

'Where thou goin'?'

The man took off his cap and swiped beads of sweat from his forehead. 'Workhouse. They're layin' out the bodies there, for folk to come and identify.'

'Is that near to Malin Bridge?'

'Nah, lad. It's in town.'

'Then which way is it to Malin Bridge?'

'Opposite to the way we're goin'. Thanks for tha help,' the man called back as the cart trundled away.

Silas looked back at the house, at the gaping wound in the gable end through which the wave had poured. The houses beyond on the rising slope of the street appeared unscathed. The woman with the red hair had disappeared. He had never asked her name, nor given his. He was a stranger here. If he had drowned last night would his parents, the people in his village, ever know about it? He was untethered. Anything might happen.

He stood in the early sunlight and clenched his fists, focusing on the pain in his hands to fight the wave of panic that threatened to engulf him. There were more people on the street now. A man was stuffing the dead dog into a sack. Silas took stock. He was hungry and had no money to buy food. He needed directions to his lodgings.

The sooner he returned to Mrs Armitage's cottage the better. He'd left his satchel hanging in the kitchen, he remembered now. There were clean clothes in it, and money.

He walked a few paces along the filthy pavement. The crowd had dispersed now, except for an elderly man dressed in dusty black trousers, waistcoat and jacket who was scoring lines in the mud with the end of his walking stick. He might know the way to Malin Bridge.

The man peered up at Silas, wonderment on his face.

'It came and it went,' he said. His eyes were crinkled to slits in his crumpled face. 'Just like that, son. It came and it went.'

Chapter 13

Harriet stood on the threshold of the kitchen and put her hand to her mouth, but the taste of the foul muck was already in it. A layer of mud she reckoned to be a foot deep covered the floor like a grotesque carpet. The dresser lay flat, shards of broken crockery sprouting around it. The table was upturned by the back door, as if it had tried to escape, legs poking into the air like a half-buried insect. The fireplace was a ruin of soaked kindling and coals.

The stench came from the grave.

Harriet shrieked when, from behind, Walter put his hand on the doorframe above her head and leaned into the room to take a look. He smelled of sourness, of rotten eggs.

He ignored her, bending to pick up the large iron skillet. The mud released it with a wet, smacking sound.

'Uncle, where have you been?'

He turned bright, empty eyes on her. 'Where have I been? I've been searching for Alice. I haven't found her yet. You know,' he said, his tone conversational, 'it's quite bizarre that just a few yards up the hill you wouldn't know anything had occurred. And then you step in the other direction, and there's carnage. I walked to the town hall where some of the survivors went. They're sitting round the fire telling their stories and people are already turning up with clothes and food for them. That's heartening, eh, Harriet?'

He threw the skillet down, making her jump, and suddenly his eyes flashed with anger. 'It was that dam after all! That blasted dam!'

Harriet was afraid of him. This was the Walter who had screamed in her face during the long night prior. He had plunged into the black depths repeatedly, searching for his daughter, and when the waters slowly receded, had turned over every stick of furniture hoping to find Alice still alive. He had not found her yet. In the night, Harriet had dared to suggest Alice might have been swept along the road and rescued like the exhausted youth who lay in a stupor on the bedroom floor. Walter had roared at her. 'She's six years old! She can't hang onto lamp-posts!'

He was staring at his hands now. They were filthy, streaked with dirt and blood.

'You have hurt yourself,' she whispered.

'It's nothing. I scratched my hands in the dark,' he said.

Feeling for Alice's soft body in the tangle of broken furniture. Harriet shuddered. Walter had saved his crippled niece, but did not rescue his daughter. He must wish it were the other way around.

He tapped the doorframe briskly. 'We will have to do what we can with temporary repairs to the house. I shall call on my good friend Albert Boothby to send some men.'

She was aghast. 'Uncle, we cannot stay here.'

'My dear.' He gave her a patient look. 'We have to stay for when Alice comes home. What will she think if there's nobody here? She'll think we have all abandoned her—'

His eyes suddenly bulged and Harriet gasped as he grabbed her arm for support and vomited grey water onto the kitchen floor.

He straightened, gasping. 'I'm sorry. I swallowed rather a lot of that filthy water.'

'Uncle, please let's go back upstairs,' Harriet pleaded. 'Just for a moment, to sit with Aunt.'

'She's in her bed, so no change there. The boys will look after her.' He gestured around the kitchen. 'The structural damage can be repaired, I believe. We have a lot of clearing up to do. Will Louisa be here today? Yes, we have a lot of work to do. Lots to do.'

Harriet shrank back as Walter stamped past. He had lost his senses. She followed him reluctantly towards the front of the house. He pointed to the plume of white smoke rising from the chimney of a neighbour's house. 'Come along, Harriet. Perhaps you'll let our neighbours know our downstairs rooms were flooded and we have no wood or coal. Perhaps they will provide Polly with a cup of tea. Perhaps Alice is sitting by their fire eating crumpets for breakfast.'

Walter paused and grabbed his scalp with his fists. A low moan came from him that terrified Harriet. Then he stepped into the street and marched on without another word.

There was a creak from behind and Harriet jerked around. Alice! But it was Adam, standing on the stairs in his dressing gown, his hair stuck up on one side. Poor child.

'Can I go out and look?' he asked.

'No. Of course you can't.' She shuddered. 'It's not safe. Back upstairs, Adam.'

'I want to see!'

'No, you don't! There's nothing to see, just… a lot of rubbish and mud.'

'What's that smell?'

He was right, there was another smell now permeating the house. It was sharper than the rotting mouldy stink that was everywhere, coming in on a light breeze to sting her nostrils. A tannery was on the flat plain on the other side of the river. What cocktail of poisons had been swirled into the deluge?

'I'm sorry, Adey. Come with me.' She took his hand and he clung to her in a way he hadn't since he was a small boy. She hauled him and herself up the stairs. Harriet's throat was dry, her tongue thick in her mouth, but there was no clean water to drink. Polly lay on the bed.

'Has Walter gone to bring Alice home?' she said.

'Yes, Aunt.' Her voice trembled. 'He's going to find her. Where are the boys?'

'I don't know.'

'In their bedroom,' said Adam. 'They want breakfast. I'm hungry, too.'

Harriet focused on the burgundy flock that covered the wall behind the bed, a repeating pattern of frond-like swirls, and, yes, just there, was the section in which she had always seen an animalistic face, her eyes obeying the human instinct to find a face in random patterns. This one had always been a benign and comforting bear, with large dark holes for the eyes and a friendly snout. But the familiar pattern twisted to show her something different now. She was gazing at the empty eye sockets of a small skull.

Harriet looked away, her desperate eyes falling on Adam.

'Adam, you must go and fetch us something to eat and drink from Stacey's grocers at the top of the hill. Mr Stacey will supply us on credit. Off you go. And please be careful.

Don't go down to the river.' She turned to Polly. 'Aunt, I'm going to find you a warm shawl. You're shivering.'

'Alice will be very cold in her nightgown,' Polly said. 'I hope she does not end up with a chill. Do you remember that high fever she had in January?'

Harriet wrenched open the wardrobe door. The inside smelled of cigars and lavender with a slightly acrid undertone of sweat. Comforting enough to wrench a sob from deep within her, which brought fresh pain to her injured nose. She wanted to climb inside the dark recesses and close the heavy mahogany doors behind her. She would crouch in the corner on the dusty wardrobe floor, make room for herself among the shoes and boots, wrap her arms around her knees and rest her head on them.

Anything other than gaze on the scene arranged behind her, the child that wasn't there, filling the house with her absence.

Chapter 14

It was a ruin.

Patchy early morning mist clung to the sides of the valley like sheep skein, but the air was sharp and the sky blue over what remained of his reservoir, as if nature was mocking him by showing him the clearest possible view of his failure.

'A sight for sore eyes.' David Craven had followed him down the steeply sloping field behind the High Bradfield farmhouse owned by Joseph Mason in which the two townsmen had spent a sleepless night. 'And yet I still cannot believe it.'

Gunson nodded. He could not trust himself to speak.

A shallow pool of water lay in the bowl of the lake. Beneath it, at the foot of a jumble of rocks and mud, the river flowed innocently along its newly carved out route. Gunson looked back at the gouge in the earth, thinking about a seaside holiday his family had taken, long ago, when his oldest was a stout-legged little boy. The two of them had built a watercourse in the damp sand and a dam to divert the buckets of water they fetched from the sea. They erected a castle and a moat. The boy had wanted to stand on the dam to survey the kingdom he had created, but the soft sand crumbled quickly under the weight of his bare feet.

Here too, it seemed a careless foot had stamped on the embankment and destroyed his life's work.

He clasped his hands together to hide the tremor in them.

'Subsidence,' said Craven, decisively. 'An underground spring, perhaps. That eventuality cannot be foreseen. We were unfortunate. There were no faults in construction. We had some flooding in the puddle wall but not over-much and certainly nothing out of the ordinary. I think…'

'David.'

'Yes?'

'Would you wait at the site? I'm sure a delegation will soon be on its way. You can take my gig back to town.'

'Where are you going?'

Gunson had already begun to stamp back up the field. He called back over his shoulder. 'To borrow a horse from Mason. I need to see the extent of the damage.'

As he rode down, the contours of the valley solidified in the strengthening light and ghost-like figures emerged from the evaporating mist, men, women and children descending from the hillsides to pick their way through the tangle of uprooted trunks and branches and gather in knots along the riverbank. The ripped-off limbs of trees were everywhere he looked, glutinous mud thick under the horse's hooves. The animal snickered and Gunson brought it to a halt and patted its muscular neck, as much to reassure himself. He had fully expected the riverbanks to be devastated here, so close to the dam, but witnessing it was a different matter, and his hand shook as he soothed the horse.

There was sudden movement at the side of the road and a figure leapt into his path. A boy of ten or twelve, who threw him a startled look then made to run off down the road ahead.

'Here! Wait!'

The boy stopped and looked back.

'Will you wait for one moment?'

Gunson dismounted and fumbled in his pockets. He had raised three sons and knew how difficult it was to keep boys in one spot, even for a moment, especially if they thought they were about to be berated for some mischief.

'Look at this.' He held up a coin. 'A shilling now to look after my horse and another when I return.'

The lad jogged back. 'All right, then.' He examined the coin. 'Got nowt else to do except gawp wi' the rest of 'em.'

He took the reins from Gunson and led the horse over to a felled tree trunk and sat down on it. Gunson felt the lad's eyes on his back as he struggled through the mess of stones and branches and mud. The edge of a piece of sandstone, pale as bone in the black mud, caught his eye and he bent and used both hands to pull it free. The stone was rounded, the size of a loaf of bread, and could have come from any building or bridge in the path of the flood. He could not say why he was certain this was a relic from the valve house.

Bile rose in his throat and he dropped the stone back into the mud and walked on, moving closer to bank of the river that ran through the middle of the hamlet of Lower Bradfield.

Two men stood in the flooded garden of a half-demolished cottage, their arms hanging by their sides. Gunson felt their eyes on him as he passed. A tangled stew of detritus, wood, rocks, roof tiles and bricks were piled high on the flank of the river, like a hastily constructed defence of a child's play. A ragged gap revealed the Loxley itself, a shallow brook once more, innocently burbling, tickling the sides of a grey boulder that almost spanned its width.

'That thing weren't there yesterday. Must weigh sixty ton.'

Gunson turned to see who had spoken. There was a man by his side, as square and solid as a brick. He pointed to the jagged remnants of a low stone wall nearby.

'And that's what's left o' my mill.' The man laughed mirthlessly. 'It were a waste of effort lugging the wheat up two floors. Blasted thing took the whole buildin', the wheel, all the stock, the pig in its sty, slaughter bench, bacon.' He paused for breath. 'Got the cows up the hillside though, an' saved the wife an' kids. The mother-in-law, an' all, for all her bleatin'.'

The miller peered at Gunson. 'I know thee... but I can't place thee.' He shook his head. 'Me mind's addled.'

Gunson was deep in thought. How many people, like this man, had known enough to flee in time and save themselves from destruction?

'You had a warning?'

'Of sorts. It were young Stephenson Fountain stopped off and said there were a crack in the dam. Jon Ibbotson, the landlord at the Barrel, sent a couple of men up and they reported back that they thought it would burst for sure.'

'They said it would?' Who were these men, and how had they known so much more about it than Gunson himself? 'How could they be sure?'

The miller shrugged. 'Don't know. I thought I should take precautions, though. I were right to, an' all. I've lost everythin' except my family.'

'I'm sorry to hear it.'

'Don't thee worry.' The miller banged his broad chest as though he was trying to dislodge a cough. 'A claim's goin' in to the bastards that did this. See across yon? The schoolhouse?'

Gunson raised reluctant eyes to examine the bleakly scoured landscape and shook his head.

'Exactly. It's gone. Not even the foundations left, nor the rock beneath. Just a hole. That'll want rebuilding, and the church, and Chapel bridge. Smashed to smithereens.'

'Did you see it?'

'The flood? Not hardly. It were pitch black. Heard it though. Like a thousand engines lettin' off steam all together, tha knows? Me missus thought it were the end of the world.'

Gunson could only nod.

It had been a mistake to come here. He should have ridden straight back to Division Street where he could re-examine over five years' worth of meticulously prepared specifications and drawings that had guided the construction of the reservoir. He should be searching for the flaw. If there was one. He could not allow himself to believe there was.

'We will do everything we can,' he said.

'Who's "we"?' The man didn't wait for an answer. 'I can tell thee right now there's a bairn drowned.'

'What?'

'Tha might well look shocked. Joe Dawson's wee bairn. Joe, the tailor, tha knows? He got his older two boys out the house then went back to get his missus and the bairn. They were in bed on account of her 'aving had the baby only two days since.'

The miller bent to prise a piece of wood from the mud – it looked like half a stable door – and Gunson wanted to put his hand out, to stop him. He was convinced the small white limbs of an infant were about to be revealed. The miller flipped the wood over, grunting with the effort, and Gunson closed his eyes. He stumbled, dizzy, and opened them to see a stone rolling into the mercifully empty indent in the mud. When he looked up, the miller was moving away, picking up branches and tossing them aside.

Gunson followed him.

The miller pointed to the filthy façade of a row of cottages, the windowpanes replaced with jagged black holes that glared balefully, accusingly, at him, at Gunson.

'Y'see, they were tryin' to get across the field, but it were no good, the water were closing in on 'em and they ran back for the house.' The man swung his head slowly from side to side. 'She dropped the bairn and he were whisked away. Joe managed to get her upstairs, right back where she'd started from. Even then, they were up to their necks until it passed. She's gone up Bradfield in a sorry state. Joe's out lookin'. Not found the bairn yet, far as I know. Tiny creature could be miles downriver, prob'ly never be found.'

Another man was approaching, as tall as Gunson, but willowy and wild-haired. A dandelion clock of a man, swaying this way and that through a dazzle of sunlight.

'This here's the schoolmaster. He nearly copped it an' all.'

'Thank you, Billy. I already have my wife reminding me I'm a fool.' The man turned to Gunson. 'I went back into the house, to fetch this.' He tugged the sleeves of his overcoat. 'It's a sorry sight, isn't it?'

For a confused moment, Gunson thought the school-master meant the coat he was wearing and opened his mouth to politely protest it was in fact a fine garment then he realised that the man was talking about the devastation all around them. He clamped his mouth shut. Fool, fool.

'What did tha mean,' said the miller, 'when tha said "we" before?' He stepped back from Gunson, the better to glare at him. 'Who's this "we"?'

'Dear me,' said the schoolmaster. 'I'm sorry for my friend, sir. We're all...'

'Who is he, though? A gentlemen ghoul from that cesspit of a town, come to ogle at us in the valley?'

Gunson spoke quietly. 'No, I am not. I was here last night, when the dam burst. I work for the waterworks company.' He almost told them he'd been nearly swept away himself, but it would sound too much like an appeal for their sympathy, which he neither wanted nor deserved.

A crow cawed in the weighted silence that followed.

'Then p'raps,' said the miller slowly, 'if it belongs to thee, tha can tell us what happened up there? Were tha the fella that stopped to tell us it were nowt to worry about?'

'We did stop, briefly, but in the dark—'

'Aye, well, it were me.'

The schoolmaster put a warning hand on the miller's arm and Gunson wondered whether he might end up sprawled in the mud from a punch with the weight of that compact body behind it.

'We will try to establish the cause,' he said. 'We, we...'

'There's that "we" again.' The miller hawked and spat on the ground.

Gunson took a deep breath. 'I am the resident engineer. There was a crack. I was shown it last night.

It was certainly not there during my inspection yesterday afternoon.'

Was it not? Had he missed it? Doubt gnawed like a rat in his gut.

'We don't know the cause of the burst, but it had nothing to do with the design or construction. They were sound.'

The schoolmaster spoke gently, 'Clearly, they were not.'

The miller shook his head in disgust and walked away, towards a group of men and women who were shifting rocks and branches from the front of a collapsed building. 'Oy! Got a man 'ere from the waterworks, them that built the dam!'

A couple of the villagers straightened and looked in Gunson's direction.

He turned to the schoolmaster. 'I am not here in an official capacity.'

'Well, then,' said the schoolmaster, 'I would suggest removing yourself from this place sharpish. Nobody's in their right mind this morning, and I should think that includes you, sir. Good day to you.'

'Please, let me…' Gunson reached for the man's sleeve but skidded in the mud and lost his footing, falling forwards into the filth. He lay there, his humiliation complete. His gaze was level with the schoolmaster's retreating feet. He got to his hands and knees, yellow mud oozing through his fingers, and finally onto his feet. He walked carefully away, a dull pain in his knees and back, cringing against anticipated jeers from behind but there was only silence.

He didn't look back.

Chapter 15

The boy was sitting where he had left him. When he spotted Gunson, he jumped up and held out his hand for the promised coin, his eyes widening as Gunson got closer.

'Tha's clarted in mud.'

'I fell.' Gunson gave the boy his shilling and swung into the saddle.

He left behind the wrecked riverbank and the people wandering it and took the higher road that would bring him above the wooded riverside hamlet of Little Matlock. Here, the waist of the river was pinched between the steeply wooded valley sides, the banks of the Loxley lined on both sides with mills and forges, workers' cottages and stone bridges, an industrious area that had sprung up to take advantage of the faster flowing waters. He'd driven Charlotte to Little Matlock in the gig on numerous occasions and talked about how they would one day purchase one of the pretty cottages with the river flowing by at the foot of the garden, a lovely spot in which to enjoy retirement, away from the jumble of grimy streets and factory smells of the town.

Dale Dyke was to have been his last project, the sign off on a long and satisfying career.

Gunson steered the horse down the lane towards the river. It gave onto a wasteland.

He yanked on the reins. This area was known to him like the back of his hand and, much as he might wish it, there had been no wrong turn. Little Matlock had been wiped from the face of the earth.

A mess of broken machinery poked from of a sea of thick mud on the wide slope that fanned up from the river. People stood in groups of three and four on the fringes of it. Two men in stovepipe hats were posing for a daguerreotype, standing grimly to attention on either side of a toothed iron wheel that was partly submerged in the rubble but still dwarfed them. On the other bank, a woman was dragging a sack out of the mud and Gunson saw it was not a sack but a limp body, a mop of lolling black hair, a small child's narrow chest, and his heart scuttered with the horror of it. The woman sat in the mud and covered the lifeless child with her arms. She stared ahead and made no sound, but the man stumbling towards her was yelling his grief to the sky.

The horse whinnied and he turned her, picking their way back onto the main road. A fire cart with six uniformed men hanging from it rumbled past. Gunson rode on towards the town. He would come to Malin Bridge next.

There was something he was missing, and the rat was busy in his gut.

He stopped on a narrow stretch of road to allow a cart to pass. From here, he had a clear view down to the riverbed.

The realisation swung into his skull like a tilt hammer. The view below was wrong, so fundamentally alien that he had not been able to see the evidence before his eyes. There should be thick shrubs, treelines, dense woodland stretching all the way to the bottom of the valley, to the very edge of the industrial district of town.

The woods were gone. Swept off like crumbs from a table. To fall where? The enormity of the disaster was far greater than he had comprehended, so great that he could not reckon it out, could not find the edges of it and pull it into a recognisable shape that he might deal with it. He could not breathe.

Gunson dismounted outside the Methodist church in Malin Bridge and walked carefully over the layer of dirt that petered out a short distance beyond the graveyard gate. The door to the church stood open. He peered inside. If he had hoped for a few moments of quiet respite he would not find it here. The place was packed with people, huddled in pews or standing in the aisles, a chorus of voices swooping and diving. A man carrying the handles of a large metal cauldron in his meaty fists gently nudged him with an elbow. "Scuse me, sir.'

'Forgive me.' Gunson flattened himself against the door to allow the man to pass. 'Forgive me.'

A tiny, white-haired woman followed, the bulging sack over her shoulder nearly as big as she. With a grunt, she dropped her burden in the nave. Breadcakes, bowls and spoons rolled out that were quickly collected by the congregation who then queued up for the soup being doled out. A bowl was pushed into his hands, a spoon offered, and Gunson obediently joined the queue and collected his ladle of soup. The pews were full so he lowered himself down to sit on the flagstones. He would be one of these people, for a while. Their chatter washed over him like pebbles in the tide. A respite after all.

He continued his journey, witnessing horror piled on horror. Where the Loxley met the mighty Don, his worst fears were realised. The deluge had blown apart brick and stone buildings and bridges as if they had been made of straw. People swarmed over the ravaged ground. He recognised the Chief Constable, on horseback, directing a gang of men who were trying to lift a tilt hammer, a giant piece of machinery weighing God knew what that had been flung from an exploding factory and carried on the wave. There was a shout and a lifeless body was pulled from under it, and then another. Gunson rode on, averting his eyes from the sight of two men carrying the limp body of a woman between them, her long blonde hair trailing.

He made one more stop on his way towards the centre of town, dismounting at the iron footbridge that straddled the Don as it passed under Ball Street. He would have to ride on, to cross the river at Lady's Bridge or perhaps even beyond, if that ancient structure had also been destroyed by the wall of water. What was left of the Ball Street bridge dangled into the debris-choked river, twisted like a corkscrew. Cold iron should not be able to adopt such a shape.

Gunson turned south towards Division Street a shade after midday, according to the clock tower on the roof of the Green Lane foundry. There was no sign of the catastrophe here. He was relieved to be back on the familiar cobbles and to be invisible to the townspeople scurrying hither and thither, the calamity on all their lips. He went to the stable block first and took his time settling the borrowed horse, afraid to face his wife, to admit his failure.

He entered the house via the back steps into the scullery. The kitchen was deserted, no fire in the grate. The house was silent. Then he saw the front door stood ajar. 'Charlotte?' His wife was out on the street, wringing her hands as she paced up and down. Her eyes widened at the sight of him and she ran into his arms, all propriety forgotten. He hugged her fiercely in return, burying his head in her lavender-scented hair. The stream of passers-by parted around them like water around a rock. He closed his eyes and wished he could close his ears to the sounds of the street.

Finally, Charlotte pushed him away to search his face. 'I thought you dead!' She patted his arms and his chest as if to confirm he really was standing before her. 'Look at you, you're absolutely filthy.'

He rubbed his face and flakes of dried dirt fell from his beard to the ground. She lifted his hands to examine them, tutting at the black muck under his fingernails.

'Tell me what happened up there. I've been listening to gossip and speculation all morning. No. It will wait. Come, come inside.' She kept talking as she led him through the house and into the kitchen. 'Millicent has gone to the town hall. She's worried about her daughter.'

He pulled out a chair and sat. 'Where does her daughter live?'

'She's in lodgings at Malin Bridge.' Charlotte was twisting a towel around in her hands and he wanted to console her, but could not lift his arms he was so suddenly wearied.

'That bridge is gone. All the bridges.'

'It hit Lady's Bridge and that still stands.'

'Yes, I crossed it. It is deep in muck.'

'I hear they're finding wreckage downriver as far Doncaster but that's twenty miles away!'

'Doncaster?' He was bewildered. 'It got so far? Well, perhaps. Such a tremendous force…'

Charlotte dropped the towel and took his face in her hands. 'Oh, John, I can't tell you how terrifying it was to wake in the night to hear all the alarms sounding and then to discover you were gone.'

'I'm sorry.'

'Is it very bad outside the town?'

He didn't know how to answer. His reservoir had turned into a ravenous monster gobbling up and spewing out the mills and forges that lined both sides of the riverbank, swallowing who knew how many of the poor souls who lived at the water's edge, who could ever have believed their river would betray them so fatally? He had not been able to do anything except watch from the hillside. If he had known then that the wave would go on to devastate the heavy industries in the east end of town, drown the inhabitants of Hillsborough, Owlerton and Neepsend… Well, he might never have come home.

Gunson pulled away from her gentle touch.

'I would have to say that it is very bad, my dear. Very bad indeed.'

Chapter 16

Silas needn't have worried about which direction to take to get back to his lodgings. As the dawn brightened into full morning, he found himself among the growing number of people streaming upriver on a macabre pilgrimage.

He stepped aside for a cart that rattled ahead to disgorge a dozen men into the knots of villagers clamouring for help; grim-faced and purposeful men wielding shovels and picks and jumping ankle and knee deep into the mud to be surrounded by angry men and women and urged to dig, and dig deeper still. A stretcher was placed on the ground, ready to receive a small body that a constable had pulled from the mud. He ignored the stretcher and carried the limp child in his arms to the bed of a wagon piled with bodies, his face a grizzled ruin of grief above his black cape.

A human limb, an arm – as pale as a fish belly in the sunlight – was jammed in the spokes of a mill wheel that lay flat on the riverbank. Next to this, the corpse of a small black dog was draped over a branch, as if the animal had been put there to dry. It hung, paws limp. Silas shuddered. He'd tied Shandy up in the backyard. He'd looked into her trusting amber eyes as he closed the door on her. Three men were dragging a dead horse towards a pit of animal carcases. Another man waited for them, leaning on a long-handled spade, a tub of lime at his side. Silas wondered if this was his horse. He would never forget the animal's fearful eye rolling in its socket. He hoped it had survived the wild ride they had shared and was not the creature now having lime shovelled onto it. Two men and a woman were waist-deep in a hole in the ground, pulling at something unseen. An old man sat on a stone beside them, quietly weeping.

Silas passed a stable yard where a row of corpses had been arranged neatly on the flagstones, his gaze snagging on a boy in a tattered nightgown streaked with orange clay. He wondered why a slab of stone had been placed on the stomach of one of the bodies, then realised he was looking at the ground through a hole in the man's torso.

The landscape was reminded him of the scorched earth left by a grassfire, but on a massive scale. The foliage and buildings that had, for long stretches on his journey by foot and carriage yesterday, hidden the river from view were either gone entirely or crumbled into ruins. The river itself was little more than a glutinous mud flat punctuated by stagnant ponds. Pieces of metal and stone and wood poked out, like a monstrous half-digested meal. The cries of survivors were like the cries of gulls, plaintive and hopeless. He was choked by the need to find his dog, to be reunited with Shandy and bury his nose in the thick ruff of her neck, breathe in her familiar scent and be reassured that the world had not ended.

He walked on.

All he knew was that Mrs Armitage's cottage was near a stone bridge and he should stay close to the riverbank. He crossed the foot of a steep road, pausing to allow a carriage pulled by two horses to turn to make the ascent, the white discs of faces staring out at him.

When he reached his lodgings he would discard these ill-fitting and foreign-smelling garments. As fine as they were compared to his rough farm clothes, they were not his. And then what? He could continue to walk on, put the ruined town behind him. Over the hills and home, with his tail between his legs. He'd have a tale to tell, all right, but he'd be the whipping boy again in no time at all.

'Goin' for a look at it?' A man appeared alongside Silas. He was heavily whiskered, wearing a farmer's smock, and reminded Silas of his father. 'Or are you searchin' for your people?'

'I don't have any people,' said Silas. 'Not round 'ere.'

'Well, that's p'robly a good thing.'

'Well, I mean to say, I'm not from 'ere but I know people. My landlady who gave me a roof, and Betty, her baby. A girl called Louisa.' He thought of Louisa's dimpled smile. 'A man who were in the flood wi' me – he were goin' to gi' me a job, I think – and a young lass who saved me. I might not be 'ere were it not for her.' His unnamed saviour with the pale skin and shocked, swollen eyes.

'So tha does know folk, then. I'm sorry if tha's lost them.'

'I don't know. I don't know if I've lost them.'

The man raised his arm to gesture to the hillside, his shovel-like hand streaked with dirt. 'I farm up topside and woke up to this. They say the dam's gone, that it's an earthquake brought it down and all those millions o' gallons o' water after it. Like when Moses parted the Red Sea then it crashed back down on the pursuing horde.'

Silas was astonished. 'You din't hear it?'

'No, lad. Nowt at all. Stone deaf in one ear an' this don't help in me good lug'ole.' He dug around in his ear and came out with a crumb of brown and crusty wax that he flicked onto the ground. 'Nowt wrong wi' me eyes though and they were on stalks when I went out to feed the pigs this mornin'. I come straight down, helpin' where I can. Dug some bits o' a body out from under a wagon. That were grim. There's bodies scattered all o'er the place. Some bein' laid out at Webster's inn. He won't like that, havin' his pub used for a mortuary. Place'll be haunted for evermore.'

'Aye.' Silas shivered.

'What's tha story, then?'

'I were in a forge in town when it hit. Got swept out.' Fred plastered to the monstrous boiler, mouth agape. Silas, lungs bursting, trapped in the torrent, his bare chest flayed by a brick wall. Panic clenched his throat and he coughed to disguise it and spat on the ground.

'At least you're 'ere to tell of it,' said the man, and clapped Silas on the shoulder. 'See that hostelry up the hill there? There's a fire and hot grub on offer for them that's in need. I'll take thee, if tha likes. Tha looks done in.'

'I thank thee for offerin', but I need to get to Malin Bridge.'

'Son.' The man peered at Silas as if he was simple in the head. 'This is Malin Bridge.'

Inside the public inn, Silas joined a group gathered around the roaring fireplace and accepted a tot of rum. Lamps glowed in the gloom. It was comforting after the harsh reality outside where the early spring sun cast too bright a light on the devastation. Somebody here would know where Mrs Armitage lived and point him in the right direction. He hadn't even a proper address, had no idea what street his lodgings were on. He'd gone straight out with Fred, thinking he'd have time to get the address and pay his rent later, time to relish his new life, all the time in the world.

The landlady was handing out bowls of steaming soup, thick with chunks of potato and carrot, and Silas took one gratefully and wolfed it down, earning another brimming ladle and weary smiles from those seated around him. The warmth of the room and the hushed talk had a soothing effect. He listened, lulled, his eyelids drooping.

'It were a deafenin' sound.'

'Like thunder when it's right o'erhead. Right in the 'ouse, in fact.'

'It were like that, reight enough. So loud I din't even see the water at first, cun't take that in at all...'

'Me and the mester got the kids on the roof an' prayed the 'ouse wouldn't go. We saw the neighbours sail off like they were on a raft.'

'People screamin' in the water.'

'I'm glad in a way that it were dark.'

'They're laying out some o' the bodies in't stables next door.'

'We lost all the stock in the shop.'

'Sheffield Harry come off worse.'

''ow so?'

'He's among them bodies at stables.'

'Him that reckoned it were nowt to be worried about? Allus were a cocky sod.'

'Tha shun't speak ill o' the dead.'

'D'you know, I saw Armitage's place fall reight before me eyes.'

Silas jerked upright.

'... the whole front o' it just sank like lead and 'twas gone, and all inside swept away.'

'Same wi' Megsons' place on't other side. No warnin'.'

'Terrible, terrible.'

'I 'eard a man screamin' his head off. Couldn't see him, though.' A pause. 'He soon stopped.'

Silas leaned forward. 'What were that about the Armitage house? Is that Mrs Armitage? Hilda who has the baby?' He searched the faces around him, but nobody was paying him any attention.

'We got out on our roof an' all, never been so bleedin' scared.'

'He had to punch a hole through wi' a broom, din't you, love? That saved us.'

'Me mother's in Wadsley so we're goin' to her. I had a roof o' me own yesterday.'

Silas sprang up to stand in front of the fire and face the people sitting around it. 'What about Mrs Armitage?'

'Out the way, lad. All yer doin' is warmin' yer own arse.'

The landlady came over and put her hand on his arm. 'D'you know her?'

'I'm lodging there.' He looked at the upturned faces. 'If it's the same place. It might not be. Hilda Armitage. She's got a baby.'

'Betty, her baby's name,' said the landlady. 'I'm sorry, son, but the place is a ruin.'

'Are tha sure?' said Silas.

'Yes, love. We've seen nowt of Hilda or Betty. Louisa Leigh lived there, an' all. An' Hilda had a lodger…'

'Fred Sharrow? I know Fred. I were wi' him. I think, I think he might be dead.' Silas put his fist in his hair and pulled at his scalp. He didn't want to break down in tears in front of these people, but the landlady's face blurred and the image he struggled to blink away was not of Fred but of the baby, of Betty being laid in a nest of blankets in an open drawer while Mrs Armitage dished up his meal.

'What's that about Fred?' An older man, small and wiry, clutched Silas's arm. He shook him off.

'An' me dog was tied up outside, in the backyard. Shandy, her name is.' He looked at the faces around him. 'A collie.'

The man spat on the sawdust. 'The dead animals are bein' put in pits and I weren't askin' about tha dog. What about Fred, then?'

'George, we'll find out soon enough,' said the landlady. She turned back to Silas. 'I bet she's a good dog, yes? Sheepdogs are survivors. I wouldn't go looking in the stables. Most of the people laid there have come from further up the river. I don't know what's happened to Hilda or to Louisa. They might have escaped, love.'

'I did. I escaped,' said Silas. 'I got swept under and I escaped.'

'Well, then, lad, there you go.'

He asked for directions to the Armitage house and was sent back the way he'd come. He stopped to watch a commotion outside a partially ruined house. The front of the house was missing, its contents scooped out, leaving only the floorboards of the upper rooms spilling down like unravelling entrails.

A knot of people stood before it, all peering up, a woman at the front wringing her hands. 'Come on, love, jump down. He'll catch tha!'

A constable stood in the shadow of the building, legs braced, arms outstretched. Silas followed the man's gaze to the upper storey of the house. A child, a girl of no more than eight or nine, was crouched against the back wall, balancing on the last remaining plank of wood on what had been the floor of the room.

'Can't tha fetch a ladder?' The woman who had been shouting to the girl was now tugging on the constable's sleeve. 'Look at her, she's petrified!'

'You can't put a ladder against that,' a man said. 'It's not stable.'

Silas approached a man standing a little way off the others.

'I'm lookin' for Mrs Armitage's house. Can tha help me?'

The man jerked his thumb over his shoulder – 'End o' this row' – and turned away. Silas crunched towards the end of the terrace, where a gable-end chimney stack pointed accusingly into the blank blue sky. In the gaping maw where the house had stood, roof beams hung or were scattered across the ground like tossed matches. At the foot of the bank, the river flowed by. There was no sign at all of the bridge the coachman had dropped him off at the day before. Was that only the day before? Silas felt he'd been wandering this wasteland for an eternity.

A ragged cheer rose and Silas turned to see the woman lift the child from the constable's arms, who now strode towards him. The girl, crying for her mother, was borne away.

'Oi, you boy. Wait up.'

He reached Silas, breathless from the rescue. 'It's not safe here. This whole row's coming down, one way or t'other.'

'This is Mrs Armitage's house?'

The constable's nod removed the last shred of hope in Silas's head.

'I lodge 'ere.' Silas looked up at still intact roof slates. 'The attic.'

'Not anymore you don't. Have you anywhere else to go?'

Silas shook his head. 'No, I've...' He gasped for breath. 'My dog! I left my dog tied up in the yard. She'll be frantic. My bag's in the kitchen, my money, clothes.'

He picked his way over a pile of bricks towards the rear of the terrace.

'There's no dog nor nowt else back there! No kitchen nor attic neither!'

Silas ignored him and the man made no move to follow. Perhaps he already knew what Silas would find.

'Shandy!' She would come, to his call. 'Shandy, Shandy, here girl! Come on, girl!'

Rubble rose like a frozen wave against the walls of the surviving houses. There were no privies, no back-yard walls or gates. The door he had closed on Shandy yesterday evening had gone, swallowed by the wave.

'Shandy!'

She could be trapped under the rubble, injured, waiting patiently for Silas to rescue her. He kicked at the pile but the toe of his flimsy borrowed shoe struck metal, sending a bolt of pain through his foot. The mass was solid. She could not survive under there, so she must be somewhere else.

'Shandy!'

He had tied her up. It was all he could think about. He had tied her up.

There were shouts in the distance and a heavy, drawn-out rumble. Silas froze. Another flood come to sweep him off his feet and he knew in his bones that this time he would not survive it. His luck had run out. Another rumble, louder than the last but nowhere near the deaf-ening roar of the flood. Silas crouched in the rubble, put his hands over his ears and squeezed his eyes shut.

More shouts, closer.

'It's comin' down!'

'Gerrout the way, the lot o' you!'

The constable, the same one as before, pulling on Silas's sleeve. 'Come on, scarper, before this one goes an' all!'

Silas staggered to his feet as the exposed guts of his lodgings released a ceiling beam, spear-like, into the broken bricks beneath.

'I already told thee, there's nowt to find here.' The man sounded more exasperated than angered. 'Get along, now. Go on.'

'I'm goin', he mumbled.

Silas wandered away from the river and up a steep lane. At the top, he looked out over a cluster of factory chimneys. Smudges of grey floated serenely across the pale blue sky.

'Shandy!'

She could be teasing him, stalking him, belly on the ground, nose twitching. Playing a game. If he turned at the right moment – 'Gotcha!' – she'd bark in delight and bolt towards him. Or follow him, at a distance, and he would have to win back her trust. Every glance back filled him with fresh despair. But better that, better that than accept she was lying crushed under the rubble.

'Here, girl! Come on, Shandy.'

Silas waited.

On the riverbank below, a house released a tide of roof slates – a glassy cascade of sound – and a raven glided implacably away. He watched the bird flap upriver then turned to gaze again at the factory chimneys belching out smoke. No money, no lodgings, no job. He was nobody here, with nothing at all. But hadn't that been the case when he first arrived? And he had something many now did not. A life to live.

Silas set off, back towards the town.

Chapter 17

Gunson placed his hat on the wide shelf under the window inside the double doors of the workhouse, adding the topper to what looked like a landscape in miniature of squat black chimneys. He turned to Millicent Leigh, who had stopped on the threshold, her face ashen.

The Kelham Street workhouse was a place of last resort, and now, he reflected, of last repose. The first bodies had been brought here within hours of the disaster and the macabre deliveries of the unclaimed dead would continue for several days yet. He'd been told the wave had thrust itself into the workhouse, throwing the heavy doors open like an unwanted guest, but although the beds in the women's hospital and lunatic ward were said to have been afloat, the waters quickly subsided. He could barely comprehend it had been a mere fourteen hours since he was scrabbling for his life on the collapsing embankment.

'Mrs Leigh.' He went back to her. 'Would you like me to go on alone? There is a bench outside and it's a tolerably mild afternoon. You can wait there.'

She looked at him as if he was an imbecile. 'She's my daughter. You don't know her.'

He was an imbecile. 'Yes, of course. I'm sorry. I wasn't thinking. The past night has affected...' He trailed off, ashamed to be complaining of a lack of sleep.

In the first ward they came to, the bodies were laid out in rows. He thought there must be fifty or sixty of them. All but the deathly pale faces were covered in sheets. Someone had combed out the long dark hair of a young woman and draped it over the sheet that covered her torso. She could be sleeping, were it not for the deep gash that ran down the side of her face from forehead to neck. Gunson squeezed his housekeeper's cold hand.

'How old is your daughter?'

'Louisa. She is twenty years old.' Millicent moved to the next row. 'She has lovely blonde hair, curly. She's not in here. I'd know her sleeping face in an instant.'

A wail rose from another part of the building, an animal sound of despair that lifted the hairs on Gunson's neck. A woman in a nurse's uniform gave him an apologetic nod and went to investigate.

'No, she's not in here,' said Millicent faintly.

'Right.' He guided her back into the corridor. Two men carrying a stretcher were heading towards them. Mrs Leigh put her hand to her throat but the body on it was that of a bloated white-haired woman. Gunson glanced into a side room to see a man and woman on their knees as if in prayer, pressed together shoulder to shoulder. They were leaning over a small marbled body, as still as statues. A nurse stood over them, writing in a book she had balanced on her arm.

In the next room Gunson saw a doll had been incongruously placed across the upper body of a bearded man's corpse so that its round, hairless head rested on his shoulder. Like the doll, the man was clothed in a long nightshirt and looked for all the world as if he was peacefully sleeping off a night on the ale. Gunson's gaze was drawn back to the doll's cherubic and unblemished face and he could finally accept the truth he gazed on. Nothing so exquisite could be manufactured by anything other than nature. Lustrous lashes resting on a plump cheek waiting for a mother's kiss, wispily arched eyebrows that had barely had chance to come into being before they were set in time. A tiny placid mouth that should have been rosy with life.

'Terrible, terrible,' said a familiar voice at his shoulder, 'but at least they are together now, for all eternity.'

It was John Webster and, behind him, a group of men. Gunson recognised the town clerk among them and nodded to him, but the man just stared back at him. Was he in shock or did he blame Gunson for the calamity? The man must understand that this had been a freak accident, that no accusing finger could or should be pointed at the chief engineer. Gunson felt Millicent pull away from him, walking towards the next room, and realised how much he had been depending on that small physical contact. He went to follow her, but Webster laid a hand on his arm.

'Have you lost someone, John?'

'No, no. I have brought my housekeeper to see if her daughter is here. The girl lives in Malin Bridge. She hasn't turned up and she's not in the infirmary.'

'Then I fervently hope she will make her way to you and not be discovered here.' Webster patted his arm.

Two of the men had come forward to peer into the room and were conversing in low tones.

'It was known the dam was dangerous on Friday morning, I heard.'

'Aye, I heard the same, and that the alarm was raised in the valley before the thing burst. At least, at Damflask. Why didn't we get a warning at Matlock?'

'I was told there was water leaking from a crack two days before and the contractors said that was usual.'

'They would say that, wouldn't they?'

Webster caught the men's eyes and put his finger to his lips. 'I'm sorry, John. This is not the day for apportioning blame or speculating on the cause of the disaster. These are the jurymen just empanelled for the inquest. We've opened it at the Sheffield Union House. Do you know, there are a hundred bodies laid out in that building alone? There are temporary morgues all over the town.'

Gunson grimaced.

Webster said, 'I must say I've never seen so much lime scattered about. They've already started flushing out the sewers. It's a filthy business. Mark my words, there'll be more deaths from this.' He sighed. 'In any event, the sanitary committee certainly has its hands full.'

'It might now live up to its name,' said Gunson.

Webster laughed. ''Twill be the first time.' He turned to the men in the corridor behind him. 'Gentlemen. We have seen enough, I believe, and I'd like to suggest we return to the court where we have bereaved witnesses waiting to give their evidence. Then we may allow the town to bury its dead.'

A couple of the men with whom Gunson had a loose acquaintanceship nodded to him as they walked away. Webster lagged behind. He clearly had more to say.

'The cause of death is a foregone conclusion. The cause of the catastrophe less so. I'm organising a visit, John, to Dale Dyke to take place as soon as practicable. So I shall probably see you next at the scene of the crime.'

Gunson stuttered, 'There was... there was no...'

'It's merely a turn of phrase, John.'

'It seems as though you are trying to rile me.'

'Not at all. But I should inform you I have been told – and very confidently told – the reservoir was in a dangerous state. I wonder also whether this dreadful loss of life could have been prevented by a timely warning. In any event, I'll be setting an adjournment so the matter can be thoroughly investigated and we shall see whether there is any criminal liability. Good afternoon, John.'

He watched Webster walk away.

'Mr Gunson.' It was Millicent. 'Louisa's not in there either. Where else can we try?'

Gunson peered up at the longcase clock in his study. The plain white face decorated with black Roman numerals rested a few inches above head height on a slim and unornamented case of varnished oakwood that concealed the pendulum and weights from view. Charlotte thought the thing rather plain and ugly – it was why it stood behind the door of this room – but Gunson was not concerned with its beauty or otherwise. The casing might not be fancy, but the mechanism inside was renowned for its accuracy, if correctly wound, a weekly task he preferred to carry out himself.

So, he had to admit that the time was correct. A few minutes before nine o'clock in the evening. Less than one full rotation of the Earth about its axis had passed since the torrent exploded onto the valley below. In that time, he had been plucked from the flood's path, seen with his own eyes the extent of the devastation in the valley and on the industrial east end of town, met with his employer and the company's lawyer, accompanied Millicent Leigh on a fruitless quest to find her daughter, and eaten a light supper with David Craven that was interrupted by the town clerk calling by to arrange a visit to the scene – 'of the crime', as Webster would have it – with the inquest jury. This would take place first thing Monday morning, two days hence. Tomorrow he would collate all the relevant paperwork and specifications, for he had been assured that although this was no criminal trial, the waterworks company was very firmly in the dock.

Through the adjoining wall he heard the back parlour clock chime the hour, inaccurately. It was two minutes to nine. He could hear Charlotte and Millicent talking in low voices, a soft music like water over stones. He ought to join them in their vigil.

He put his hand on the oak casing, waiting for the clock to come to life. The town clerk had told them that a mantel clock discovered intact in the ruins of a house at Hillsborough was stopped at twenty-seven minutes past midnight, and the claim was this indicated the exact time the wave hit that district. This seemed far-fetched but it had not seemed a point worth arguing.

The longcase clock chimed four times before it was drowned out by a volley of bangs on the back door of the house.

Chapter 18

Silas lay wrapped in blankets on the stone flags of the lounge room at the Red Lion. He'd fallen in with a rag-tag of homeless survivors who had been offered shelter for the night by the landlady of the inn. Lulled by the whispered tales of escape being told around the fireplace, his eyes closed, but sleep refused to come. He felt a nudge, his cheek gently dabbed by a cold wet nose and, without opening his eyes, he put his arm around the inn's little dog that he'd made a fuss of earlier. The animal snuggled down in the crook of his arm and Silas folded his lips tightly and soundlessly allowed the tears to run unchecked down his cheeks.

Prone under a starched coverlet, Harriet watched guttering candlelight play across the ceiling of the unfamiliar bedroom. Mr Boothby had insisted the family spend the night at his property and Polly had been persuaded to make the journey when Walter told he she was free to remain in her own bed if she chose to take the risk of the house falling down around her ears. Walter had left Harriet and the Boothby's maidservant to help settle her aunt and had ridden home to sit in the armchair he'd dragged from the master bedroom into the upstairs hallway that afternoon. He was waiting for Alice to return and could not be persuaded otherwise by Mr Boothby. Harriet had not spoken for fear of further riling him. She watched the haunting shadows thrown by the dying candle, praying tomorrow would bring news, while fearing it, too.

A dog was barking. Gunson marched to the end of the unlit corridor, aware of Charlotte and Millicent on his heels. He dismissed a fleeting thought that this was a mob come to drag him out of his house and set about him. But he could not deny he was rattled.

He hesitated. 'Who's there?'

But already Millicent was reaching past to twist the key, lift the latch and pull open the door. There was no mob. Only a young woman reaching out to embrace Millicent, a black and white collie dog leaping up and down at her side.

Chapter 19

The road above the high stone arches of Lady's Bridge was busy with traffic rattling in and out of the town centre, pedestrians streaming up and down the pavement on one side, the other blocked by a scaffold about halfway along. Harriet's destination lay across this bridge and she was eager to cross, but her escort had stopped to observe the scene and therefore so must she.

'Mr Boothby?'

'Indulge me. Your uncle and I gained the contract for these repairs and it pleases me to see the work progressing.'

The top three rungs of a ladder were visible beyond the scaffold. Harriet laid her gloved hands on the rough granite of the parapet and peered over the side. The end of the ladder rested on a platform suspended by ropes a few feet above the sluggish brown waters of the Don. Here, the river was hemmed by tall brick buildings that channelled it east as far as the eye could see. The ancient structure Harriet had stepped onto had survived the tumult that had flattened the previous fifteen bridges in its path like dominos. Tons upon tons of wood and iron, and worse, much worse, had slammed up against Lady's Bridge, clogging the arches and ripping chunks from the stonework. Bodies had been found lodged in the structure. Harriet leaned harder on the wall, fighting a sudden wave of nausea.

'Are you quite all right, Miss Wragg?'

She gulped. 'My foot is somewhat sore. I need a moment only to rest it.'

'I should not have suggested we walk. I am thoughtless.' He laughed in a way that seemed to suggest she ought to contradict him. 'Well,' he continued after a few moments had passed, 'you must take your time, of course. This evening, I shall drive you home.'

Harriet took a deep breath of the familiar smell of the town, of smoke and coal and horse dung, a cold metallic whiff from the river. She focused on the scene below.

Two men balanced on the platform, the younger of the two clutching the rope and looking decidedly ill at ease to be on such a makeshift contraption. The older man stood with a board in one hand and a trowel in the other, placidly chopping and mixing mortar. The youth was taller and broader than the older man at his side, with a mop of dark hair. His shirtsleeves were rolled up to his elbows, exposing strong brown forearms. There was something familiar about the way he pushed his fingers through his hair, the way he flexed his shoulders.

At her side, Mr Boothby took out his pocket watch, glanced at the time, replaced it and adjusted the necktie around the high collar that corralled his abundant side-burns. The necktie was silk, polka-dotted, and matched Mr Boothby's waistcoat. In fact, Harriet considered, he was kitted out as handsomely as if he was promenading about the park rather than delivering her to the town hall. She was dressed more sombrely in black taffeta, and felt like his shadow.

Nine days had passed since the catastrophe.

Polly was back in her own bed, complaining about the musty smell the house gave off. 'It's drying out,' Harriet had explained. 'The structural damage is repaired, but the walls cannot be repapered just yet.'

'You seem to know a lot about it,' said Polly.

Harriet had shrugged, her head bent over her bone-handled crochet hook. 'I listen when Uncle and Mr Boothby talk.' She laid the hook down. 'Aunt, would you not consider rising again? I can make you comfortable downstairs. A change of...'

Polly had looked away. 'Do not badger me.'

Alice had not been found, although she appeared nightly in Harriet's fevered dreams, slipping into the room to announce she had fooled them all with her game of hide-and-seek, or pounding up the stairs to wake her parents, water streaming from her hair and nightclothes. Or unseen, calling Harriet's name entreatingly, the voice she adopted when she wanted to play a game or have Harriet help her with her embroidery. That was the dream where Harriet woke sobbing. She knew Mr Boothby had observed that Walter could not stand the sight of her – that her uncle's eyes slid away when he was forced to address her, to focus on her shoulder or the ceiling or the lace cap on her head, anywhere but directly at the face of the girl he had saved, the wrong girl, the one whose very presence only reinforced his failure, and her own. That was why Mr Boothby was doing her this kindness. What other reason could there be?

'It's voluntary work, of course,' he had told Walter. 'Nothing so demeaning as a waged job. I shall be happy to take her under my wing. Now, Miss Wragg, you are to help record claims from the survivors of the disaster.' He had turned back to Walter. 'You too must apply for compensation from the waterworks company. For the damage to the house, and for the new furniture and right down to the silver teaspoons. Other property owners are doing the same, the mill owners, the landlords from their country piles, and the poor who only rent their cottages and even before the flood had barely a pot to piss in. Excuse my language, young lady.'

'But where are the poor living now, if their homes were swept away?' asked Harriet.

Mr Boothby had dismissed her with a wave of his hand. 'They can apply to the guardians and go to Kelham Street, if it comes to that. We need not concern ourselves with fellows who find themselves become paupers and vagrants. They could not have been so far above that status before. Now, it shall be my pleasure to escort you to the town hall and return you home afterwards. You start tomorrow. We should walk. It is predicted to be a fine day.'

His prediction had proved correct. Harriet glanced up at a pale blue sky striated with plumes of smoke from the surrounding factories. She looked back down at the two men on the platform over the river. The younger one had begun to scale the ladder. He squinted as a shaft of sunlight crossed his face. Something about this – the light, or his expression, she did not know – penetrated the numbness that enveloped her and she drew her own brows together in puzzlement.

'Shall we continue?' said Mr Boothby.

She blinked. 'Yes. Yes, I am quite recovered.'

When they drew level with the works, she glanced across to find that same youth standing there, on the bridge, and staring. At her. She drew in a breath. She knew those eyes, had seen them before, desperate and fearful, and also full of sympathy in the dawn light and, now, round with surprise and pleasure. And she found an answering smile of recognition was spreading on her face, and warmth kindled in the pit of her stomach. She had grasped those muscular arms, had felt the hard weight of his body fall on hers, the shock of his pelted nakedness under her fingertips. She lifted a gloved hand in greeting.

'Mr Boothby, I think I see...'

But Mr Boothby wasn't listening. He had hold of her elbow and was steering her along the busy pavement. She lost sight of the youth as a carriage passed, then there he was again, standing in the same spot, continuing to stare after her. For the first time since that terrible night she felt something other than numb sorrow. She desired something, even if it was simply to cross the road.

'Can we...'

'Come, come, Miss Wragg.' His grip was firm.

She was being pulled along like a child and a cold fury swept over her.

'You are squeezing my arm.'

'I only want to get us out of this crowd, Miss Wragg. We shall end up under the wheels of a cart if we are not careful.'

'I would like to...' but then she stumbled, turning over on her bad foot and gasping in pain.

Mr Boothby only increased his grip on her. Harriet cast a last glance over her shoulder, but her view was obscured now by the blank faces all around her.

The road inclined steeply once they were over the bridge and into the district of Castlegate, once the entrance to a medieval castle in which, Harriet had learned as a child, Mary, Queen of Scots had been imprisoned for twelve years. It now led, rather more prosaically, to the town hall that sat at the crossroads at the top of Waingate. They hurried past the taverns and shops that had sprung up to serve the growing population of the town – Parkin's tea dealers, Dalton's cabinet makers, Riley's grocers, the Bull and Mouth tavern, which Harriet noted already had drinkers inside it despite the early hour, and the Anvil, Rose and Crown and White Hart. Harriet was breathless by the time they arrived, from a combination of avoiding bumping into other pedestrians, the throbbing ache in her foot and the encounter on the bridge. The entrance was busy with people. Inside, a queue was forming along the wall opposite a large fireplace that dominated the foyer.

'The lucky survivors,' said Mr Boothby. 'Come to claim some compensation.'

'These people cannot all be waiting for me,' said Harriet.

'No, no. There are others recording claims besides you.'

'I'm sure I'm not qualified.' Panic fluttered in her chest. 'This was a mistake.'

But again, Mr Boothby wasn't paying her any attention. He hailed a group of gentlemen who were approaching the staircase and bent to whisper in Harriet's ear.

'There ascends the legal team and witnesses for the waterworks company.'

Harriet tilted her head as if in acknowledgement, intending to break the contact between her cheek and the thin blade of Mr Boothby's cold nose, but he had more to say and leaned closer. 'They are attending the inquest into the catastrophe.' It was all she could do not to shudder at his touch.

'Mr Boothby, what am I supposed to do now?'

'Wait here.'

He left her standing, striding away to confer with a gentleman whose arms were full of papers. Harriet smiled timidly at the man in a shabby overcoat and battered topper who was taking her in from head to toe and back again. The smile was not returned. Was this one of the petitioners for compensation? Harriet's throat tightened. How could she help this aggressive person? She was unequal to the task and should not have agreed to under-take it.

'This way.'

Mr Boothby was back. He guided her through a door at the far end of the foyer. It opened on a narrow corridor and he led her into the first room on the right, which was small and gloomy with a window that offered a view of the adjoining room rather than the outside world. A man in a police uniform glanced up from his desk and nodded. Harriet tentatively returned his nod and looked around the room. It was sparsely furnished with two chairs on either side of an oak desk, a worn carpet on the floor. A thick leather-bound ledger sat under a lamp on the desk, pen and ink and blotter laid out. Harriet sat behind the desk and tentatively rested her hand on the ledger.

'Ah, a constable. You are in good company,' said Mr Boothby. 'Here, let us light the lamp. It's rather gloomy in here. A clerk is coming who will explain precisely what you are to do. I imagine your task will be quite straightforward or they wouldn't have a woman doing it, eh?'

Harriet laughed lightly through clenched teeth. 'Indeed not.' She would not give him the satisfaction of knowing he had infuriated her with his comment. 'Thank you, Mr Boothby.'

'I'll return at five o'clock to escort you home.'

Harriet sat behind the desk and put her hand on the ledger. But it was not the task at hand that occupied her mind, however daunted she might be. Instead, she saw the youth on the bridge again, his delight when their eyes met, the thrill she had felt, that she felt still, and she dipped her head to hide the smile that she could not suppress.

Chapter 20

Silas supped his ale and smiled ruefully. Jim was explaining to the pub at large why his workmate was the soft arse of the week for buying useless trinkets from a girl in the street. They were sitting at a table in the King's Arms where Silas had found lodgings. Handy for a pint. The hostelry was near the river but set at a good height, being perched halfway up a hill with a scribble of trees and bushes hiding the water from view, and therefore, as far as he could ascertain, safe and sound. He knew there was no longer a body of water hanging over the valley, but could not explain why the sight of the river set his pulse racing.

'What use has tha,' said Jim, 'for a dainty cup and saucer and a statue of a… wha' is it?'

'A cat,' said Silas. 'A miniature of a cat, painted purple an' all.'

'A purple fucken' cat.' Jim shook his head.

Silas spread his hands. 'P'raps I just can't say no to a bit of dainty porcelain.'

'Daft fucken' apeth.'

The truth was that he'd been touched by the red-eyed girl who had spread a woollen shawl on the mud of the riverbank to display undamaged items she'd recovered from the wreckage of the house behind her. She'd looked up when Silas approached then carried on cleaning a teapot with her skirt. Both teapot and skirt were encrusted with dirt. 'Did tha' live here?' Silas had asked. She had raised her chin. 'Me father lodged 'ere. I've not stole owt. These are all mine now, but I have no use for 'em.'

Silas had picked up a teacup. 'I'll gi' thee a shilling for this.'

She had taken his coin and Silas stuffed the teacup into his trouser pocket. She'd held up the saucer to go with it and the small figurine of the cat to boot. 'Have these, an' all. Have 'em as mementoes of the calamity.' She had begun to cry again. Silas had gently taken the saucer and the cat and given her another shilling. He could afford it.

He put another drink down in front of Jim.

'Anyhow, tha's the one,' said Silas, 'that paid to get a picture of theesen balanced on a bit o' twig up Penistone Road.'

He grinned at the mock-affronted look on Jim's face. Left behind when the waters receded, a two-ton log was still sitting like a prehistoric beast in the middle of the road, waiting for somebody to come and cut it up, and attracting plenty of attention in the meantime. Silas had seen an artist set up his easel the other day to paint it.

'A twig? That's gettin' recorded in history, I'll have you know. It's a sight for sore eyes. More impressive than a fucken' teacup.'

Silas laughed. 'All right, all right. Drink up thee beer an' tell me what's next on the agenda.'

The repairs to Lady's Bridge were finished and Silas had no wish to re-enter a forge. He had not told anyone about the recurring nightmare that had him struggling up from sleep, thinking he was awake, fighting for air, to find Fred Sharrow standing at the foot of his bed, unmoving, staring at Silas, a horrible grin burnt into his charred face.

Silas told himself hundreds of men put out of work by the flood would be flocking to the bigger manufactories and there'd be no room for him, a foreigner, but it was hard to hide from the truth. Some had predicted the flood would destroy the town, but the wheels were already back on the cart, so to speak. The town would feed the greed for steel, and grow fat itself on it, and he was glad to be here. Silas told himself that labouring on building sites was his education to the ways of the town and he would be back in a forge one day. Just not yet.

'Regiment's barracks at Hillsborough, I reckon. Wave broke through't boundary wall and filled up the Sergeant's house. Drowneded two of his bairns.' Jim shook his head. 'That outer wall were three foot thick, tha knows, solid stone. That din't do it a speck o' good, though. I were lucky I never saw the great wave but it rolled across an open field to demolish that wall. Some fucken' wave that must 'av been, eh? Well, tha knew about it, I suppose. Silas?'

'Eh?'

'Are tha listening to a word I'm sayin'?'

'Yeah, I mean no. Sorry, Jim. Gi' us a minute.'

His attention was on the two men who had entered and were being served whisky at the bar. They disappeared into the snug.

'What's up?' said Jim.

'When I were rescued...'

'Oh aye, tangled up in the arms of a young lady in the lass's bedchamber, no less. Some 'ave all the luck.'

'T'weren't her bedroom.'

'Details, lad. Anyway, what's it got to do wi' that pair?'

'One of 'em's the man o' the house. I borrowed his clothes. I never did manage to find where they live. I had

130

a wander round, but this town is a bleedin' maze. I wanted to thank the young lady.'

'I bet.' Jim leered. Silas ignored him. 'D'you not have the address then?'

'Nah. I had somewhat o' a merry ride to their place and weren't really paying attention to street names. I saw her, tha knows. She were wi' a man, walkin' o'er the bridge. I should 'av gone after her, but the boss would've 'ad me guts for garters.'

'Aye, tha's told me this tale, such as it is. More'n once.'

Silas stayed on after Jim bade him farewell. He would help clear up when the place closed. The landlady waved a cloth at him from behind the bar and Silas gave her a thumbs up. She had a soft spot for him. He'd won her over by asking her to write a letter home to reassure his family he was alive and well. He had given his address, enclosed money to replace the coins he had stolen and wished them well. He'd hesitated over mentioning Shandy and, in the end, did not.

The moment he was waiting for finally came. Silas followed the two men outside, his heart thumping. One of them, not Silas's target, staggered off the kerb and into the road.

'Whoops,' he said, returning to the pavement.

'Sir, can I have word?'

The man whose arm he had touched turned around, his eyes widening in instant recognition.

'Ah!' He turned to his friend. 'This is the ruffian who landed like a fish on my bedroom carpet.'

The other man laughed lightly. 'I heard of it.'

Silas held out his hand, and the two men, in turn, reluctantly shook it.

'I want to thank thee for… to express my gratitude to the young lady who… well, she saved my life from that flood, gettin' me to swim for the window. Elsewise, I'd've been swept away for sure and drowned. I saw her, in the town, but there wasn't the opportunity to speak to her. I'm reight sorry for babbling on. My name is Silas Hinchcliffe and I'm very pleased to 'ave bumped into you.'

'Walter Simpson.' He looked Silas up and down in a way that made him feel ashamed of his working clothes.

'Aren't you going to introduce me, Walter? I'm Albert Boothby, Mr Simpson's business partner and a friend to Miss Wragg.'

Silas nodded quickly then turned back to Walter Simpson. 'I'm back on me feet, workin' to help repair the town, an' I lodge here, at the King's Arms.'

'Then, well done.'

'I just wanted to thank thee for saving my life. I still have the clothes tha loaned me.'

'Oh, I did not save your life. That was my niece. You may keep the shirt and britches. I have no need of them.'

Mr Boothby laughed, then hiccupped. 'It's a night for losing your britches, eh, Walter?' He turned to Silas. 'We've been to Mrs Exton's in Eyre Lane. Are you aware of the establishment?' Silas shook his head. 'Some fine rides. Your saviour here likes to partake of a ride, even though he still has no horse!' The gentleman seemed to find this uproariously funny.

'I didn't save him,' Water muttered. 'Just a moment.' He patted his pockets. 'I have no coin on me.'

Silas clenched his fists. 'I don't want tha money!'

'Well, I shall say goodnight then.'

'Goodnight,' said Mr Boothby.

Walter strode a few steps down the street. He looked back and waited for the other man to fall into step beside him. Silas followed. He wasn't finished.

'Mr Simpson, can you slow down for a minute before I go arse over elbow on these cobbles?' Silas raised his voice. 'Wait up!'

Walter stopped and turned to face him.

'I'm not sure how my family can be of further assistance to you,' he said, coldly.

'I'd just like to give my thanks to the young lady in person.' He reminded himself of his mother, *putting on the posh for the vicar*, his father would say. 'Mr Simpson, your niece saved my life and you very kindly allowed me to remain in your house until the flood subsided and I would like to call on you.'

Walter waved his hand in the air. 'Well, Harriet is...'

Silas beamed. 'Ah, her name's Harriet? I never did get 'er name. Harriet.'

The other man snickered.

'Yes.' Walter glanced at his companion and lowered his voice. 'Well, Harriet is shortly to be moving down to London. She's going to live with her brother. The flood, you see, it has had a terrible effect on her. She wants to put it behind her, to make a fresh start. We shall miss her, of course.'

'Aye.' Silas scratched his head. 'Still, if I could just come an' say—'

'She'll be leaving in a few days, I'm afraid, and is very busy in the meantime.' He raised his voice. 'Mr Boothby, shall we away?' Walter Simpson gave Silas a thin smile. 'I am glad you are well. I am sorry to seem abrupt, but we lost our darling Alice in the flood and I am not well myself. My chest.' He put his hand to it. 'So the weight of the world is bearing down.'

'I'm sorry,' said Silas. 'I'm reight sorry about your little lass.'

Walter looked at Mr Boothby then back at Silas. 'I want to help you. Silas, was it? Shall we return to the hostelry and find pen and paper and you may write Harriet a note of thanks? Will that do?'

Silas frowned. 'Write her a note?'

'Yes, yes, a short letter conveying your gratitude and your good will, et cetera. I will be sure to pass it on to Harriet.'

'Ah, no. No need. I shouldn't've bothered you.'

'We'll be on our way, then. I shall be sure to tell Harriet I bumped into you and she will be pleased you have made a strong recovery.'

Silas watched the pair of them stride away. Walter laughed at some comment from the other man as they rounded the corner and Silas had no doubt he had been the object of a snide remark. He wondered whether they had a carriage waiting. It was a tolerably warm evening for early spring. Perhaps they were on foot.

There was only one way to find out.

Chapter 21

Sheffield Harry was holding court at the Barrel Inn on the banks of the Loxley. A gale raged beyond windows that were black as death.

'I've no dependents and I'm glad o' it. No missus to hand the pennies o'er to. Accountable to nob'dy, that's me.'

Gunson watched the odious man swallow the dregs of his pint and smack his lips. A growing sense of dread was blooming in his chest. He couldn't bring himself to look directly at this braggard beside him or the leering regulars that crowded his back. He knew he would see two hundred and forty souls behind him, should he care to turn and look. He had not realised the Barrel had the capacity for so many bodies. Instead, he bowed his head and continued trying as unobtrusively as possible to keep his feet clear of the tide of swampy filth that was creeping across the flagstones. Charlotte would be furious if his new shoes were ruined.

'I told 'em all. Frost crack. I know dams.' Sheffield Harry's voice rose along with the wind that rattled the walls. 'I know dams right well and there's nowt wrong wi' this one. Bunch o' old women, the lot o' 'em.'

Gunson swallowed. There was a hard lump in his throat. He tasted earth and gagged, spitting clods of soil and gravel onto the bar. A pale worm wriggled in the muck. He recoiled and looked, finally, into Sheffield Harry's pitiless face. 'Help me, Harry.'

'It's Mr Burkinshaw to thee,' the man said, and as he spoke a stream of fat bubbles rose from his mouth towards the ceiling. Sheffield Harry's hair stood on end, swaying like fronds of seaweed, and his eyes were merciless silver marbles.

Gunson woke, gasping like a beached fish. His wife slept on, a hunched shape under the covers in the early morning light, snoring lightly. He told himself it had been only a dream, a nightmare, and couldn't understand why a wave of plunging doom was continuing to tighten in his chest. Then he remembered.

He was due to take the stand today.

'We have made eight reservoirs.'

'Then you have made eight mistakes!'

Gunson gripped the polished walnut of the witness box, stung into speechlessness.

John Webster, now sitting as the coroner of inquests, one of the many hats the man wore, was implying – nay, stating – that the principles upon which all the reservoirs surrounding Sheffield had been built were unsound. That any one of Gunson's creations might fail as Dale Dyke had.

Perronet Thompson, the barrister brought in to act for the Sheffield Waterworks Company, raised one finger and spoke mildly into the echoing silence that followed.

'Sir, might I suggest that these are observations which ought not to be made in the presence of the jury?'

Gunson looked across at the impassive faces of the jurymen. He had been engaging so intensely with John Webster that he had entirely forgotten he was in a courtroom packed to the rafters with townspeople. The largest courtroom in the town hall had been allocated to the inquest. It was a room designed to endanger fear in the accused, not that, he reassured himself, he was being held on trial. The dock beside the box he stood in was empty. However, the seating allocated to the jury and the bench at which the coroner and his clerks sat were elevated so Gunson was required to look up to address Webster, like a supplicant. And members of the public crowded the upper galleries that ran along both sides of the room, as well as standing in every available space not taken up by bulky benches and chairs and tables. The overall effect was to make him feel claustrophobic, as if he stood at the bottom of a well with everybody peering down at him.

To make matters worse, and despite the room's high ceiling, the air was stuffy with bodily odours. He would give anything for a breath of town air, a whiff of chimney soot and sulphur coming in on a light breeze or the heavy scent of hops from the brewery to tickle his nostrils.

'Why should I not speak freely?' said Webster. He poked his head forward like a man sniffing blood. 'I am merely asking this engineer to speak like a rational man. If there was a fracture in a pipe…'

'We do not know what caused the catastrophe,' said Gunson quietly.

'…how could you be alerted to it? There is no access to the pipes once they are laid and buried and all the evidence is certainly destroyed now. Your work at Dale Dyke not being perfect…'

'I thought the embankment perfect up to the time of its giving way.'

'…have you not reason to think that your Agden reservoir that is now under construction…' Webster broke off. 'I'm sorry, what did you say? About the perfection of the dam?'

Gunson cursed himself.

The company's barrister finally met his pleading eyes, but merely raised his eyebrows under his shock of thick white hair. Gunson wondered why Perronet let his hair grow so long at his age and why he was not defending him more robustly. But when he opened his mouth to reply to Webster, intending to explain himself more fully, Perronet gave an almost imperceptible shake of his head. Webster would not wait long for a reply, and he didn't.

'Everybody else can see that the method of construction was full of danger!' Webster waited for the grunts of assent and bursts of chatter to subside. 'This is a most serious matter for we have lost hundreds of our fellow townsmen from an accident that ought not to have happened.' The man's voice was tight with emotion. 'Was this an accident that might have been avoided?' He looked directly at Gunson, who met the man's glare with what he hoped was a calm gaze.

But when he spoke, his voice was high-pitched, strangled by the injustice of Webster's attack. 'I have acted as engineer for this company for nearly thirty-three years.' He took a deep breath and made a deliberate effort to lower his voice. Webster had reduced him to a shrieking fishwife. 'From my experience there was nothing left undone that could have been done as to safety of construction.'

The coroner cast his eyes like a net over the jurymen. 'No man who has looked at the place could say this accident might not have been avoided.'

Gunson glanced again at Perronet, who had bent his neck and was absorbed in the papers on his desk. He wanted to protest, to appeal to the jury, to explain that he followed the instructions of the consulting engineer to the letter and that there had been nothing wrong with the dam, nothing at all. *Then why did it fail?* Gunson studied the faces filling the room, strangers all. Did these people who did not know him blame him, personally, for the deaths of so many of their fellow townsmen and women?

He recalled the silhouettes of the patrons of the Stag Inn at Malin Bridge, framed in the window on the night he rode out to the dam. How could he have known he was glimpsing future ghosts? Sheffield Harry, for all his bluster, had perished when the wave hit his lodgings. He had been on his way to the Barrel Inn when Gunson saw him. Had he stayed out drinking he would have fared no better, for that establishment was engulfed and swept away too. And so many children, and infants now in eternal innocent slumber. And forty orphans made. Forty. Sorrow clogged his throat and he coughed, covering his mouth with a shaking hand.

People were turning to each other, exchanging whispered words. Perronet lifted a hand to gain the room's attention.

'In re-examination, Mr Gunson, we have heard from the consulting engineer, Mr Towlerton Leather – and I would like to quote from his testimony here.' Perronet lifted a page and read from it. '"Mr Gunson was not my servant. He had the superintendence of the works, occasionally consulting with me. He would not deviate from my plan." Perhaps you can tell us how closely you oversaw the works.'

Gunson looked at the closed faces of the jurymen sitting across from him. He glanced at Webster, a man who painted his face with his emotions. At least he knew where he stood with him, even if that was on the lip of his own downfall. He reminded himself this was an inquest, not a criminal trial. It had been convened to determine the cause of death of all those poor souls, and no more. Yet it had become an inquisition. He ran a shaky finger around the inside of his collar and clasped his hands together.

'Mr Gunson?'

'I beg your pardon. Can you repeat the question?'

'How close was your supervision?'

'I visited the dam three or four times a week, and sometimes oftener than that. In addition, I generally went on a stormy day, to see the effect of the wind on the water.'

'And did you go on the day of the flood?'

'Yes. I'd seen Admiral Fitzroy's prediction of a gale and that the wind would be blowing down the valley. There had been torrential rain on and off during the course of that week. I recall some remarkable downpours.'

Several heads nodded in acknowledgement and a woman exclaimed that she'd got nothing dry that week, the inside of the house had been festooned with sheets and knickers. There was laughter and Webster banged his gavel to restore order.

'Mr Gunson,' said Perronet, 'would the wind and rain – torrential rain, as you say – have an effect on the embankment?'

'Not an effect such as this. I have seen the wind and the waves ten times worse at Redmires reservoir.'

'Then what might have caused the crack that was reported to you?'

Gunson paused. 'When I first saw the crack, late in the evening, I thought the action of the wind and waves, which had been playing against it all the afternoon, might have loosened the material of which the inner slope at the top of the embankment was made, and this might cause a crack to form. I do not know. It wouldn't cause the embankment to collapse so...' He stopped himself from saying 'spectacularly'.

Perronet nodded. 'There is a rumour that you had said, during the day, something about the embankment giving way.'

Gunson inhaled sharply. 'Is there such a rumour?' It was the first he'd heard. Why had he not been prepared for this question? 'I would never say such a thing! I never expected the dam to burst.'

Perronet nodded again, satisfied. 'Thank you, Mr Gunson. You may step down.'

Webster nodded his assent.

Gunson remained in the chamber, standing at the back of the room to listen to the government inspector give some statistical evidence. This man recited in a droning tone the Chief Constable's latest report detailing the number of persons who lost their lives to the flood. A rustling sigh of dismay swept around the room when the inspector named the official dead as two hundred and thirty-eight in number, although more bodies had been found in the days since the return was made. The ages of those accounted for ranged from two days – Gunson's stomach dropped, that would be the tailor's son – to eighty-seven years. In addition to the human loss, fifty horses, thirty-eight cows, eight donkeys and two hundred and fifty-eight pigs.

Gunson was holding his breath as if underwater. Beads of sweat ran down his face and he jerked involuntarily and gestured for the man beside him to move aside so he could open the door that led into the corridor.

'I wish to say more.'

Gunson paused. The government inspector had raised his voice and seemed to be aiming his words at Gunson's back.

He waited, gripping the door handle, staring beyond the room at the floorboards he would tread on. Spectral bodies, young and old, stretched before him as dead and still as the lacquered planks of wood. He rubbed his hand over his mouth and looked over his shoulder at the witness box, but the inspector was not regarding him. Instead, the man was staring intently at the editor from the *Sheffield Independent*, who was hunched over his notebook in the corner of the room. This was the man he addressed.

'The velocity of the flood between the dam head and Owlerton, a fall of four hundred and fifty feet in total, shows the water travelled at a rate of twenty-six and a half feet per second, or eighteen miles per hour.' The inspector surveyed the room, his gaze sweeping over Gunson and on. 'This is a velocity I can form no conception of. The public ought to have this information given them, that after the dam broke a Derby horse could not have carried the warning down the valley fast enough.'

Gunson did not wait to hear more.

Outside at last, he stopped and rested his hand on the solid stone arch of the new drinking water fountain latterly built into the wall of the building. He twisted the spigot to splash a few drops into the marble basin and watched the water drain away. He could acknowledge there was a small consolation to be had from hearing the information relayed for the benefit of the townspeople, that once the dam was breached there had been nothing anybody could have done to save the victims in the valley.

Back in his office, Gunson could not settle, although there was plenty of work on his desk. A door slammed somewhere in the building and he heard the chairman's raised voice.

'That damned coroner! He's acquired experts from France and Germany purporting to tell us how to build reservoirs. That man, what's his name, he lives here in Sheffield, who worked on the dams of Australia *of all places*. Yes, with sugar please. No, wait. What time is it? Get me a brandy instead. Well, Mr Leather—' Ah, he was talking to Gunson's immediate superior '—I am greatly interested in the revelation that you as consulting engineer visited the Bradfield workings on only two occasions during the past five years.'

John Towlerton Leather sounded unperturbed. 'The day to day was always the responsibility of Mr Gunson, in whom I have the utmost confidence. I have made no more than his acquaintance in work, but I do know that his chief pleasure is in that work, which he discharges with extreme conscientiousness. Within our profession, and far beyond the bounds of Sheffield, John Gunson is regarded as a mathematician of great natural abilities. He came from Leeds, I believe.'

His voice faded and Gunson stepped out of his office. They had gone into the boardroom. The corridor was empty. Gunson put his ear to the door.

'So he's from your neck of the woods, Mr Leather,' said the chairman. 'And Mr Gunson is a clever gentleman with a modest disposition, there is no doubt. But did he make a mistake, as the coroner claims? Is he still making them? You are aware that the town wants this company and will look for any excuse. The damned council think they can run all this better than we do. We have to protect our shareholders. Have you seen the share price? It's plummeted.' There was a beat of silence. 'And the people. We are for the people too, of course. I must show you our plans for the public baths. We'll be subsidising that, offering exceptionally generous terms…'

Gunson rapped gently on the door.

'Yes, who's there? Come in.'

He entered and carefully closed the door behind him. Both men were standing by the window, silhouettes against the light behind and he couldn't make out the expressions on their shadowed faces.

He remained by the door. 'Gentlemen. No mistakes were made in the creation of Dale Dyke. The design was not defective nor were the engineering principles unsound.' He waited for Mr Leather's nod of assent. 'The collapse was not due to bad workmanship and I would—'

The chairman interrupted. 'The future of our company depends upon convincing the jury that we are not culpable in this terrible disaster.'

'Yes,' said Gunson patiently. 'And to that end I wish to be recalled. I have some new evidence. I believe it will exonerate us from blame.'

Chapter 22

Harriet hopped down from Mr Boothby's curricle and hurried inside, happily unaccompanied. It had been pouring with rain when they crossed Lady's Bridge, the deserted workings barely visible. There were few pedestrians and none of them showed the unnamed youth's face.

'Are the works to repair the bridge almost complete?' she had asked lightly.

'I believe so,' said Mr Boothby absently. 'It is a small job only.' He chuckled. 'I can tell you that business is booming for Boothby, Simpson and Sons. We did a grand job flattening all those ruined cottages in Malin Bridge and I have men all over the town now, building new dwellings. There's a great demand, and not just from the flood. The town is growing quickly, and so are we. Here we are. I'll return at five, Miss Wragg.' He paused. 'I wonder whether you and your uncle will agree to dine with me tonight?'

Harriet forced the corners of her mouth down in a show of disappointment. 'I should not leave my aunt alone so soon. I'm sure Uncle Walter will be agreeable.'

Her uncle, she thought, would be glad to escape the house. We must not wallow in our grief, he had told her the day before when he came across her sobbing over a piece of Alice's sewing and the heartbreakingly messy stitches. We must forge on, he'd scolded. Her uncle's mood was the mood of the town. Foreigners from the surrounding counties and even as far away as London continued to trickle in to visit the site of the disaster and marvel over the charm of the rugged hills that encircled the town. They also complained about the stink of the smoke-filled basin and the rabbit warren of streets. The locals shrugged. Industry equalled money and money put food on the table and clothes on their backs. 'We must put it behind us.' Walter coughed.

His cough was getting worse, although he denied it. Harriet was often woken in the night by the sound of his harsh barks in the room above. He was thinner, too, but that could be attributed to the grief he also tried to deny.

Harriet passed the usual queue, catching the words of a woman holding forth. '—and I opened the back gate to a load o' dead pigs piled up in the lane. Nearly gave me heart failure, that did.'

'There's been worse sights than that, Ethel.'

'Oh right, tell me that when you've clapped eyes on a load of mangled flesh same colour as yer own in yer own backyard.'

Setting out her writing tools, Harriet congratulated herself on having made the perfect excuse to avoid dinner with a man who seemed to have invaded every part of her life. Not even Mr Boothby could argue with her wish to remain with her aunt. The first petitioner of the day poked his head into the room and she put Mr Boothby out of her mind.

Harriet smiled warmly at him. 'Please, sit.'

The man did, his eyes narrowed on Harriet's hand as she turned to the top of a fresh page and asked for and recorded his name, Thomas Cowley Fawley, and occupation, owner of the Philadelphia Leather Works in Neepsend. He threw a sheet of paper on the desk.

'Here, I have listed it all.'

Mr Fawley sat back and folded his arms across his substantial chest. 'Do you understand it? Please read it aloud so I can be sure that you do. I'd have preferred a man.'

'I'm afraid you have me.'

Harriet picked up the sheet, ran her eyes down the list and read a line at random. 'Across the tannery, fourteen thousand, nine hundred and seventy-two pelts lost.'

'Each valued between eight pennies and one pound eleven shillings.'

'Yes, I can see the values are noted here.'

'It's not just the skins. There's a lot more expense to tanning than that.' He poked a finger at her. 'I wouldn't expect somebody like you to know.'

'Then please enlighten me.'

'The materials, for one. Vitriol, shumac, lime and alkali. Two tons of tallow at thirty-six pound per ton. See it? And the wages to workers I've had to lay off. And the dog shi— I mean… you know what I mean. Ten casks of that stuff, forty-five shillings per ton.' He paused for breath. 'You can see what I have lost from my final claim.'

Harriet found the figure. 'You're putting a claim in for four thousand four hundred and forty-six pounds, ten shillings and nine pennies, Mr Fawley.'

'It is a fair claim. To speak plain, I shouldn't be having to deal with a woman on matters of such importance.'

Harriet returned his challenging look. He was glaring at her, that was true, but she could see the fright in his eyes.

'It was my business.' His voice shook. 'I've lost it all.'

The rainstorm had swept through by late afternoon. Harriet returned the ledger to the clerk's office and walked to the end of the corridor where, as she had been promised in the letter she had received, there was a door that led onto a quiet side-street. She checked the time on the wall clock before opening the door and stepping outside, bonnet-less, glad to feel the weak warmth of the spring-time sun on her face. She did not have long to wait.

Louisa Leigh came strolling towards her, her long striped skirts partially hiding the black and white collie at her heel.

'Hello, love,' she croaked.

Harriet kissed her friend. 'I am so happy to see you.'

The collie jumped at her and Harriet took its paws in her hands, and laughed. 'Alice would love you!'

'Shandy!' Louisa smacked the dog's snout. 'Get down.'

'She begged for a pet,' said Harriet. 'A dog, a rabbit. We should have got her one.'

'Well, this one's not by choice, but she looks after me, tha' knows. Guards me 'gainst unsavoury characters.' Louisa coughed. 'Sorry. I've had a poorly chest ever since.' She hugged Harriet. 'Bet my letter were a surprise.'

'A lovely one.'

In it, Louisa had explained that the doctor she visited had told her she had poisoned water on her lungs – many survivors had swallowed an evil brew of engine oil, lime, all sorts of muck, and would in his opinion have been better drowned in the first place – but she was young and strong and should recover, in time. She and Millicent had moved into a cottage together, and she said she was enjoying her mother fussing over her. For the time being. Mother and daughter were living off Millicent's wages, so Louisa would have to find work she could carry out with a pair of exhausted lungs. And she had suggested a meeting, having been informed by a gentleman of her acquaintance of Harriet's work at the town hall.

'Why didn't you come to visit me?' said Harriet. 'I've missed you so.'

'I din't think Walter would appreciate me turnin' up on his doorstep.' Louisa looked away and a shadow passed over her face. 'He'd think I were after 'is money.'

'How do you end up with a dog?'

'Shandy. She belonged to a boy who were lodgin' wi' us. He'd only arrived that day… the day of… If he's still alive I don't know where.'

'I'm sorry to hear of Hilda and Betty,' Harriet said.

'And I'm sorry about your little cousin.'

They looked at each, sombrely, then Louisa laughed and hugged Harriet again.

'I can't leave thee alone, can I?'

'I'm glad of it.'

'Here.' Louisa fished in the pocket of her jacket and pulled out a newspaper cutting. 'I'm told Alice has not been found. I thought tha might be able to do summat wi' this.'

Harriet took the cutting from her. It was a public notice from the town's coroner.

> *A MAN, unknown, lying at Joseph Taylor's, Don Close, Greasbro' — about 25 years of age.*
>
> *A MAN and GIRL, unknown, lying at the Holmes Tavern, Kimberworth — Man about 40, Girl about 10 years of age.*
>
> *One MAN, a BOY and Three WOMEN, unknown, lying at the Ship Inn, Kilnhurst — Man about 45, Boy about 16, Women about 4, 28, and 47 years of age.*

'I only thought,' said Louisa, 't'would be a shame if Alice was put in the earth unknown. Polly would never rest. They're burying the poor souls if nob'dy comes for'ard. She might be one o' these, layin' at Kimberworth or Kilnhurst.'

Harriet's eyes filled with tears. 'Thank you. I'll take it to Walter.' She folded the cutting into her purse. 'Louisa, can I come and visit you one day?'

'A'course tha can! I'm in most daytimes, out most evenin's but tha won't be coming at night, will tha? I gave thee the address in the letter.'

'I shall come on Saturday afternoon, if that suits you, when Uncle takes the boys on the green to watch the football game.'

'It suits me.' Louisa squeezed her hand. 'Come on then, Shandy. See me 'ome.'

Chapter 23

Gunson was both rattled and exhilarated from his exchange with the chairman and eager to get home to Charlotte and the easy pleasures of home life. As he stepped onto the pavement of Division Street, a woman blocked his way. She was heavily shawled despite the clement spring day. He nodded warily to her and made to pass but she put a grubby hand on his sleeve and opened the dirty cloak she wore to reveal a woollen smock stretched into holes by a heavily pregnant belly.

'Excuse me, sir. Let me speak to you, begging your patience to indulge a wife and mother,' she said all in a breath.

'Are we acquainted?'

'Aye, I should say as much, through disaster.' Her voice shook with indignation and he saw her make a conscious effort to calm herself. He braced himself, knowing what was about to come. He was frequently accosted by townspeople in his acquaintance, the lower classes wanting financial aid; the others being gentlemen suggesting in most ungentlemanly tones that the water-works company should not be allowed to further wreck the town in order to satisfy its shareholders.

'How can I help you?'

'You're Mester Gunson.'

It wasn't a question. Gunson nodded.

'D'you know how many people are destitute from that flood? We are. Destitute. An' now we're told we'll be unlikely to get owt in compensation from this miserable lot.' She gestured to the building. 'Nowt for losin' our home, employment, all of it. I've got five mouths to feed. Soon to be six!'

'Yes, I can see. Did you apply…?'

'Turned down. Rented cottage, rented tools. Nowt were ours. Landlord found us summat, a couple o' rooms above a shop in town you can't swing a cat in, but he wants payin' and we've not got two pennies to rub together.' Her voice rose on a wail. 'We'll all end up in Kelham Street at this rate.'

Gunson took out his purse. 'I can give you…'

'That don't help! What about next time the rent's due? I want to see some proper justice gettin' done.'

'I'm very sorry. I'm not the correct person to ask.' Gunson began to walk away, his gut squirming in shame. 'You might get some restitution if you enquire at the town hall. I do wish that I could help you.'

'Wishes are all well an' good.' Her voice rose shrilly. 'You've made paupers o' us! It'll be my bairn that'll bear the shame of a birth certificate with the workhouse address printed on it.'

He knew the family would be split apart as soon as they passed through the workhouse doors and become inmates. Segregated according to age and sex. She was following him down the street.

'As I said, I am sorry for your plight.'

She shook her head, in disgust. 'Gi' me the money, then.'

Gunson handed over all the coins he had on him. 'I'm sorry it's not in my power to help further.'

She looked away from him, flinching away from a passing carriage, her hand rubbing her belly.

'May I help you cross?' he said.

'Aye, I suppose.'

On the other side of the street she walked away without a word.

Gunson opened the front door of his house to the sound of his wife at the piano. He didn't pretend to have any musical knowledge. He considered himself a man of science and there was art enough in that. But he was forced to admit there was a particular comfort in the fluttering ribbons of velvet echoing through the house from Charlotte's tender fingertips to his tired ears.

She stopped playing abruptly when he entered the parlour.

'John. You look worn out.'

'The inquiry,' he said. 'John Webster has appointed himself judge, jury and executioner.'

'Come.' She led him to the card table and took out a deck. Gunson smiled at her, bemused. 'A game of Patience,' she said. 'You can assist.'

He watched her lay the first seven cards face down then turn the first over and work through the remaining rows. He had to admit the elegance of her gestures had a soothing effect.

'Will there be criminal charges, then?'

'I don't know. Five of clubs under six of hearts. I have an opportunity to give more evidence when the hearing resumes tomorrow.'

'Oh? Aces along the top, silly.'

'Yes, I knew that.' He edged one of the rows of cards back into perfect alignment. 'I have a theory, well, more than a theory. I should admit I have Craven to thank for it. He spoke with a man who lived close by Dale Dyke who told him that cracks had appeared in the walls of his house *before* the dam burst.'

'But why must you give the evidence? Why not Craven, or this other man whose house was cracked?'

Gunson flapped his hand impatiently. 'Do you see what this means? Would you like to hear it?'

She carefully lay down another card. 'Of course. Go on.'

'Imagine, an ancient underground spring, undetected despite our best efforts, that has caused a landslip that undermines the embankment. Cracks appear in a building close by, hours before the burst. Now, how could that occur without some subsidence of the land?' He leaned back triumphantly. 'You've missed that one there.'

'I see it.' She placed the jack of spades card under the queen of hearts. 'I recall your survey of the land had been a thorough one. I remember you talking about it. I remember you debating whether you should move the site of the reservoir slightly.'

'And?'

'So why was an underground spring capable of bringing down an embankment of that size not detected, and if it was, why was it not acted upon? Where does the blame lay for that?'

'My dear, the point is that it was not poor workmanship on the embankment itself, as is being claimed. My dam was sound.'

'I don't want to offend, John, my love, but you are not being logical and that's most unlike you.'

He was stung. 'What do you mean?'

'Wait.' Charlotte swept the cards together to reshuffle them. 'I could see that game coming to nought. My dear, listen to me.'

He frowned. 'I am.'

'John, are you labouring under a delusion that this inquiry is being held to find the cause of the catastrophe?'

'That is the whole purpose of it!'

She put the cards to one side and reached out, wordlessly asking him to put his hands in hers. He did, a little reluctantly.

'You are being paraded before a town that wants justice.'

'Yes,' he said slowly, 'they want the truth…'

'No, the truth is unimportant.'

Gunson shook his head. 'This is gibberish.' He stood up to pace the room. 'When will dinner be ready?'

'I'm simply trying to tell you that the town isn't interested in the truth. The people are looking for somebody to blame for all the anger and grief they feel. John, be still.'

He stopped and stood before her. 'What are you saying?'

Charlotte sighed. 'Forgive me for voicing it, but I'm afraid you have been put forward as an easy target.'

Later, in bed, as Charlotte lay gently snoring beside him, Gunson reflected on her words. He could see the truth in them, but history would prove him right, even if the townspeople failed to appreciate that no fault lay at his door.

His dam had been sound.

Chapter 24

Harriet was in the porch, collecting the boys' outdoor gear which they had unceremoniously dumped on the newly laid chequered tile, when Walter returned. White-faced, he marched past her and straight upstairs and she knew that he had not found Alice among the unclaimed dead in Kimberworth or Kilnhurst. She followed him, her arms full, waited for him disappear into the room he shared with Polly and leaned against the wall so she could tap her foot against the boys' bedroom doors.

'Adam! Help the other two get ready. It's almost time to go.'

She dropped their boots and coats at the top of the stairs and hesitated outside the closed door of the master bedroom, listening to Walter coughing wretchedly and the indistinct murmur of Polly's voice. She was about to knock, but jerked her hand back when her uncle raised his hoarse voice into a shout.

'We can't both take to our beds, woman!'

Adam came out of his room. 'Harriet?'

'Your mother and father are resting. Are you looking forward to our outing?'

'Can we go and see where the dam burst?'

'No, no, there is absolutely nothing whatsoever to see there. We're off to the botanical gardens near Ecclesall. I've made a picnic. Won't that be lovely?'

She ignored his groan of dismay. 'Come on, Adam, get your brothers down.'

A smart rap on the front door startled her. 'He's here! Come on, boys.'

Harriet descended the staircase slowly. When he made his invitation, Mr Boothby told her he had little interest in garden landscaping or the bounty of flora contained within the high walls of the botanical gardens, but he had a substantial shareholding that granted him, and any guests he might wish to invite, access into the town's Eden, and it was something she might enjoy. Harriet had accepted fulsomely and added that her cousins would be delighted, too. 'I had not thought the youngsters would have much interest in the gardens?' Mr Boothby had said. 'Oh, yes, they do,' said Harriet, 'and they will be so excited when I tell them they'll be going on a carriage ride.'

She thought it a job well done. Mr Boothby would escort his business partner's family about town, and Harriet could answer Louisa's half-jesting 'Is he courtin' thee?' with a firm no.

She painted on a gracious smile and opened the door.

For a second, her eyes refused to recognise the tall figure who stood on the doorstep, she had been so certain she would be forced to meet Mr Boothby's self-satisfied smile. Harriet inhaled sharply and put both hands to her throat. The same face she had seen at Lady's Bridge, the same shock of dark hair, that sturdy frame suggesting pent-up energy and easy strength. The work clothes she had last seen him wearing had been exchanged for smart trousers, a collared white shirt and dark blue waistcoat. She was not mistaken.

She breathed out. 'It's you.'

'Ta da!' he said weakly.

Now she had a name for him.

'Uncle,' she said, as Walter came into the parlour to see what all the noise was about. The younger boys were dancing about excitedly, Adam standing to one side, shyly observing Silas who had drawn himself upright and braced his shoulders when Walter entered. 'Uncle, this is Silas Hinchcliffe. It is the boy who...'

'I know who it is,' said Walter.

'Sir,' said Silas. 'I came here because I wanted to thank Harriet for saving me...'

'You saved yourself,' said Harriet, beaming.

'...before she leaves for London.'

'What?' Harriet frowned. 'Before I what?'

Walter was coughing into a handkerchief, so Harriet turned to Silas for an explanation.

'Your uncle said you're leavin', goin' to live with your brother...'

'Going to James? Why would...?'

Now Walter spoke. 'How did you find us?'

'Uncle!' She couldn't understand why he was not being at least civil. 'Silas has come to say thank you...'

'I followed thee out of the King's Arms, a little while since. This is the first chance I've 'ad to come back this way.' He turned to Harriet and took her hands, which seemed to bring on a fresh bout of coughing from Walter. 'I owe you me life.'

'No, not at all.' She blushed.

Walter started to speak, but then bent double as another coughing fit took him.

'Oh, dear, excuse me a moment.' Harriet ran down the corridor and into the kitchen where she poured a glass of water and brought it back. What had Walter meant about London? She wondered whether he had some plan for her he was yet to reveal. But why tell Silas? He was clearly displeased to find Silas in his house. She did not want to believe her uncle had lied to discourage him. She would put it out of her mind.

On re-entering the parlour, Harriet had half-expected, and was dreading, to find Silas gone, but he was still there, standing in the middle of the room, like a miracle, but looking somewhat helpless. She smiled at him warmly. Walter stood at the window, wiping his mouth with his handkerchief. 'My uncle has been unwell ever since... well, ever since.'

She handed Walter the glass and he took it with a nod of thanks and pointed to the street. 'I see Mr Boothby's carriage arriving.'

'Oh! Oh yes.' Harriet was dismayed. She had temporarily forgotten about the jaunt she was to take with Mr Boothby. Then the idea came to her and the words were out of her mouth before she had time to think about them. 'Come with us, Silas, today.' Impulsively, she reached for his hand. The trip was now an altogether more pleasant prospect; Mr Boothby would just have to make the best of it.

Silas's fingers entwined with hers and a thrill coursed through her. She pulled away, feeling a moment's resistance from him, and met his eyes, which were merry. She wondered if he could hear the deafening thump of her heart or see the fluttering pulse in her neck.

'Where are you going?' he said.

Harriet collected herself. 'To the botanical gardens, with a picnic. There's plenty of food to go around.' She paused. 'Unless you are busy.'

'That sounds grand, miss, I'd be glad to.'

'I already said I should be pleased if you would call me Harriet.'

Walter collapsed abruptly on a chair. She could see he was trying to control his breathing, a handkerchief balled in his fist. He coughed into it, a horrible choking cough. When he took the handkerchief away from his mouth, the white linen was flecked with blood.

Chapter 25

Silas peered into the bear pit. It was empty.

'We had a black bear. Bruin was his name.'

Silas, Harriet and the three boys all turned to see who had spoken. A skinny, middle-aged man in a flat cap was trundling a wooden cart filled with pots of seedlings towards them. Silas smiled at him.

'What 'appened to Bruin?' he said.

'Well, he were a layabout by all accounts. Got replaced by two brown bears, but they weren't no fun either, just sat in the bottom there, when they could be bothered to come out. I am told we had a bear that did leap about, even managed to climb out.' He patted the top of the wall and winked at the boys. 'The story is the man who had this job before me gave it a biscuit and scarpered. There were some lady visitor thought she had a way wi' animals and went after it, but she weren't taking account of the size of the claws on the bloody thing and it ripped 'er to shre—'

Harriet interrupted. 'What happened to the bears?'

'Dunno. Sold for meat, I expect. Ended up in a tasty stew, eh?' He laughed, exposing brown molars. Silas clocked the anxious frown on Harriet's face as she glanced at the boys.

'Nah,' he said. 'They went to a retirement 'ome for bears. There's one where I've come from, full o' lazy old bears it is.' Harriet smiled gratefully at him. 'Harriet,' he whispered, 'I 'av to ask thee why Mr Boothby, whenever he looks my way, has his lips as pursed as a pig's bum.'

He was gratified to see Harriet splutter with laughter and at that moment Mr Boothby appeared.

'Ah, here you all are. I'm sorry I was waylaid. I had a little business to conduct at the curator's residence. Silas, I hear you mention where you come from, where is that exactly?'

'Over the hills and far away.' He winked at Harriet and was thrilled to see the blush rise in her cheeks.

They nodded to a couple passing by, a young couple who were arm in arm. The weather was cold but dry and there were plenty of fine people perambulating about. Probably the only exercise they ever got. He wished he could take Harriet's arm. His brother Peter would have done by now. In fact, he'd have already found an excuse to get her alone, behind a tree or bush or one of the giant green fronds in the conservatory where he would plant a kiss on her mouth.

She was talking now, but he'd been too busy thinking about kissing her. She looked pale under that black bonnet that hid her lovely red hair. Black was too severe a colour on her. He'd find an excuse to buy her a new bonnet, a blue one to match his new waistcoat, with a red ribbon.

'… and away from the town smog. We could be in another world.' She took a deep breath. 'All this fresh air.'

'I got enough o' that at 'ome,' said Silas.

'So you say you came to town the day of the disaster,' said Mr Boothby.

'Aye.'

'Alone?'

'I came wi' a companion. A dog. I lost her in the flood.'

'Oh, no!' said Harriet. 'I am sorry, Silas.'

'A mere dog?'

'Others 'ave suffered worse, I know,' said Silas. 'I'm only tellin' thee my tale.'

They had reached a wide expanse of grass near a mound planted with saplings.

'Let's have our picnic here,' said Harriet. 'Adam, give me the blanket. Thank you for carrying the basket, Silas.'

'Can we go and look at the pond?' said Adam.

'Yes. Be careful.'

'You ought to go along with them, young man,' said Mr Boothby to Silas.

'I'm sure Silas would like to have some food first,' said Harriet, 'before the boys return. They are like locusts.'

He could feel the hostility coming off Mr Boothby in waves. It was worth it, though, to be in Harriet's company. She seemed a serious sort, but they had exchanged a glance or two where her eyes were full of warmth. He watched her busy herself setting out the picnic.

'We must return here, Harriet, when the gardens are in full bloom,' said Mr Boothby.

Silas watched her nod her agreement, glance quickly at Silas and away.

'So, are tha the Boothby of Boothby and Simpson?' Silas asked.

'I am. I'm a director, along with Harriet's uncle, Walter Simpson.'

'Ah,' said Silas. 'I've done some labourin' for tha firm. Small world, innit?'

'Indeed.' Mr Boothby pursed his lips.

Silas caught Harriet's eye and was gratified when she turned her back to Mr Boothby so he would not see the wide smile on her face.

The next day, Silas was sent to Brick Row to finish the job on a house that had been partially destroyed in the flood, a day's work for a team of four men.

'The fall is always quicker than the rise, eh?' the foreman said, handing Silas a slim-handled masonry hammer. 'Can't go too quick, though, or it'll be on tha head. Lit'rally!'

The three-storey building stood at the foot of a hill beneath a terrace of cottages that looked untouched by the flood. The wave had taken the side of it off. He'd heard of this house; it was famous in its way. A newspaper report dismissed by the regulars at the King's Arms as overly sensational told the story of the brother of the tenant of the house. The tenant was called Joe Dyson and his brother had been asleep on the top floor when the wave hit. This brother smashed his way through the roof to sit there, naked as the day he was born, waiting for the waters to recede. No one seemed to know this man directly, or his name. He was always the friend of a friend or a cousin to the man who rented a grinder's wheel at Neepsend. Unfortunately, Joe Dyson couldn't confirm the tale because he was dead, along with his wife, five children and two lodgers.

Silas stood on rubble-strewn open ground that had once been the interior of the front parlour, looking up at the sky through a jagged hole in the roof tiles still hanging overhead, imagining Joe Dyson's brother reaching his arms through it to the black night. On the walls, about twice Silas's height, a tide line marked the level the waters had risen to. An engine from the fire office had already pumped out the flooded cellar, leaving a thick layer of rot and a scent that played around Silas's nostrils, as far removed from the earthy, organic odour of the farm as it was possible to be. It was the smell of death.

He looked up, squinting against the white sky, to a small window at the apex of the gable end. The glass in its six tiny panes was intact. Not for much longer.

The foreman stamped over. 'That were the brother's bedroom. Bedrooms below all flooded to the ceiling, so the rest o' 'em never stood a chance. It weren't just the water, though. These houses were chucked up on contract. Flimsy as a sheet o' paper. Come on, stop moonin' about. Time to get the scaffold up, get this stinkin' thing down.'

Silas weighed the hammer in his fist. Bodies were still being found in the nooks and crannies of ruins like these. His eye caught a glint on the ground a few feet away, a wink of light, there and gone again. He walked over and scuffed the dirt away with his boot then stooped and brought out a plain gold band. It barely fit on the tip of his little finger. A slender woman's wedding ring.

'Keen eyes, that's down to tha youth.' The foreman took the ring from Silas and tucked it into the top pocket of his waistcoat. 'Old Pearce has given over his warehouse for a lost and found. I'll give it him.'

A wedding band. He wondered whether it had belonged to the wife of Joe Dyson or had been long buried and now excavated by the wave.

He thought of his brother. Peter would be a married man by now, and soon he would be a father and Silas an uncle. Silas would return to visit his niece or nephew. He would be a man of the town now, safe from Peter's fists, with a beautiful wife on his arm. Harriet's face swam before him, that anxiously guarded face that was transformed when she smiled and made him feel glad in his heart. He wanted to make her smile always.

Imagine if he turned up at the farm in a carriage with Harriet sitting beside him. His mother would immediately fall in love with her, his father would be speechless in the face of Silas's good fortune. Peter would try and fail to hide his envy.

Silas kicked a fragment of brick. He had little to offer Harriet, but she did not send the warm glances Silas received in the direction of that pinch-faced Boothby fella. The man was staking his claim though, whether Harriet knew it or not.

Walking home that evening, he came to a clearance site with men still swarming over it, making the most of the dying light. Smoke was pouring from the stacks of a nearby steel works, only slightly further up the incline of the road but enough to have escaped the flood. He recalled the ferocity of Reverend James talking about the Steel Age and all its wondrous new inventions. 'I've seen a Bessemer convertor stoked up,' he'd told Silas. 'A furnace quicker than a crucible and hotter than the sun.'

'It sounds dangerous,' his mother had said, mildly.

'No, madam. We're in the modern age where we can easily transform the raw power of iron into steel. God, Empire, Industry, Prosperity! And God bless Queen Victoria.'

But the vicar had not seen Fred Sharrow lifted and carried, stuck against one of these furnaces like a swatted fly. If he had, he might have understood Silas's reluctance to re-enter a forge. His nightmares were still filled with the roar of the wave, the ease with which it had destroyed those machines of which he'd stood in awe. He couldn't see himself back inside a forge, trapped like an animal if disaster befell him again. Better to be labouring in the open air, using his muscles, building his strength. He'd escaped a gruesome death by the skin of his teeth. Only luck had saved him. Luck – and Harriet.

Chapter 26

Gunson crossed the foyer buoyed with renewed hope, although his wife's words echoed in his skull. He was content — he had built a sound embankment and would prove it today. He smiled and tipped his hat to a young woman reclining against the ledge of the tall window next to the staircase, her red hair a fiery halo from the sunlight fractured through the small square panes. She returned his greeting with a nod and smile that animated her pensive features and Gunson vowed he would not allow himself to become riled by Alderman John Webster today. He would seize the opportunity to put forward a theory that would absolve the waterworks company, with the evidence to support it.

A man in a peacock-blue waistcoat sat with his legs stretched before him on a bench outside the courtroom. Gunson recognised him as Matthew Jackson, a fellow engineer about his own age, who was to give evidence based on his experience of supervising the building of reservoirs in Adelaide and Melbourne and Bendigo. Gunson had been introduced to him during an inspection of the remains of the embankment two days after the disaster and they had travelled on together to look at Agden, the newest dam under construction, both marvelling that their paths had never before crossed. He admired Jackson's methodical and calm demeanour and ability to listen to the person he was conversing with, rather than simply waiting his turn to speak. The opposite of the coroner, in fact.

John Webster heard only the details that suited his agenda.

'Matthew, I'm pleased to see you again.'

'Hello, John. I thought you'd already been put through the grinder.' He gestured with his thumb to the closed door. Gunson could hear the hum of chatter from within.

'I must be a glutton for punishment. Have they begun?'

'Not yet, but it's already standing room only.' He yawned. 'I thought I'd give my legs a rest.'

Gunson resisted the overwhelming temptation to ask what Jackson would have to say about the Dale Dyke embankment once he was on the stand.

'Good morning, gentlemen. I'm a little late.' It was Perronet and his wild shock of hair. Webster followed behind, his clerk on his heels, arms stuffed with folders.

'Hello, John,' Webster said to Gunson, as warmly as if he was greeting a long-lost friend. 'I hope you are well.'

Gunson rubbed his hand through his beard. Webster's geniality was unsettling, coming as it did before the man would no doubt once again tear into him in the public forum.

'And here is Mr Jackson, our engineering expert,' said Webster. 'I'm looking forward to hearing your evidence.'

'Good day to you, sir.' Jackson got to his feet. He was as tall as Gunson and towered over Webster and Perronet. 'I have had the opportunity of visiting the site and Mr Gunson has been most helpful indeed. A terrible tragedy. I can sympathise with the heavy burden the waterworks company is shouldering.'

'It's quite ironic, isn't it,' said Webster, poking his beak forward, 'that the very reservoir built to supply the mills on the banks of the Loxley should instead prove to be the instrument of their destruction.'

This sounded rehearsed, but Gunson couldn't let it pass. 'This town's population has quadrupled in the past fifty years and every resident expects a ready water supply, from the housemaid to the mill owner.'

Perronet nodded in agreement. 'Indeed, indeed. Sheffield is certainly a sizeable town now, for the north.'

'And the people continue to flow in,' said Gunson.

Matthew Jackson laid his hand on Gunson's arm. 'An apt analogy, John, if somewhat insensitive in the present circumstances. Well, shall we go in, gentlemen?'

Smarting from his gaffe, Gunson braced himself for more from Webster who always ensured he had the final word. Sure enough, the man spoke up. 'Would that this town had the control of the flow of its water supplies.'

Gunson stamped into the room, his earlier equilibrium destroyed.

The rustle of papers and murmur of voices subsided as Gunson stepped into the witness box. He glanced at the newspaper editor, who was watching him with weary eyes, his chin resting on an ink-stained hand. Gunson straightened his shoulders. He would not show how wounded he was by the evidence Matthew Jackson had just given, how it pierced his heart to hear his fellow engineer blame poor construction for the disaster. It was one man's opinion only.

John Webster immediately went on the attack.

'It would not be so bad if the water company could admit they had made a single mistake in the construction of this dam. You assume that everything was perfect!'

'Not perfect,' said Gunson. His hand was shaking and he tapped the rail of the witness box to cover it. 'Not perfect, no, but we did everything for the best so far as our knowledge goes.'

'Very well then,' said Webster, nodding sagely. 'I am sorry you have so very little knowledge.'

He would bear this so that he could deliver his point. 'It is a great misfortune.'

'When destruction is visited upon us, you say the work was perfect.' Webster banged both fists upon the table. 'This will not do at all!'

There was a stir in the jury box and the foreman raised his hand. 'Coroner, you might wish to take this more deliberately.'

'It is difficult to do so when the work has destroyed nearly three hundred of our fellow citizens!' But Webster subsided and had the grace to look somewhat abashed.

'Mr Gunson,' said Perronet.

'Thank you.' From the corner of his eye, he caught a flash of peacock blue leaving the chamber. He hid his dismay. Matthew Jackson would not hear the assertion Gunson was about to make. He spoke slowly and deliberately. 'It is my contention that the catastrophe was caused by a landslip and not by any fault in the design or construction. The downstream toe of the dam was built on an old landslide area. I believe this is the true cause of the disaster and that no fault can be laid at the door of my employer.'

'Is there any evidence of that?' said Webster.

'It may have taken place and then been covered by the ruins of the embankment,' said Gunson. He saw that Webster was about to interject and raised his voice. 'But it has recently come to my knowledge that on the night of the disaster, cracks appeared on the wall of a house near the reservoir.' He appealed directly to the jurymen. 'The cracks in that house were caused by a landslip, the same landslip that caused the crack in the embankment and resulted in its collapse.'

'Why, we must visit that property and view these cracks,' said Webster.

Gunson hesitated. He looked at Perronet who closed his eyes briefly and nodded. 'Unfortunately, I'm told the house in question was swept away. What we do have is the word of the occupants who escaped the deluge.'

'Do you? Well, words are cheap. Or perhaps not, eh, Mr Gunson?'

Webster was implying that a bribe had been given. He left Gunson floundering. Gunson gasped, then found his voice. 'I'm sure the farmer concerned would be willing to give evidence to say cracks appeared in his walls.'

'But are we then expected to leap to the conclusion the cracks he says he saw were caused by a landslip? No, I think we have gone as far as we can with this,' said Webster, folding his arms.

Whispers spread in a creeping tide across the room. Gunson rubbed his beard and found the eye of Perronet, who nodded, telling him without words that he had successfully introduced an element of doubt. He'd done all he could to save the reputation of the Sheffield Water-works Company, and his own.

When Gunson arrived home, the front door stood open. Just inside the threshold, Charlotte was tying the ribbon of her bonnet.

'I have had a most draining day,' he said.

'A cold supper is already laid out for you,' she answered briskly. 'I must hurry or I shall be late. I'm being collected shortly.'

'But where are you going?'

She handed him a piece of newsprint. 'Did you know that more than four thousand homes were flooded?'

'Yes, of course. I hear of nothing else on a daily basis.'

'And the poor people who didn't lose their homes entirely couldn't make a fire to warm them because the coal cellars were swamped. There are people who still have only the clothes they stand up in, or slept in. Working men who didn't lose their lives lost their tools so how are they to making a living?'

'It is terrible...' said Gunson.

'Yes. It is. I am meeting the ladies of my music club tonight at Union House. We intend to organise some urgent relief, to assist the general fundraising being done. You really have no idea how terrible this situation is for the poor and dispossessed.'

Gunson peered at the newsprint. The owner of a furniture shop on the Wicker was offering to sell his damaged stock of beds, bedsteads and mattresses '*at a great sacrifice in price*' at the auction rooms in Fargate. He looked up at Charlotte, bewildered. 'Do you want a bed?' She shook her head in an exasperated way and pointed at a notice in the corner of the page.

'There. It is our meeting.'

'You didn't mention it.'

'You have been busy.'

He sighed heavily. The intimation behind her brusque responses was as clear and unassailable as a wide open sky. He was a self-absorbed man; overanxious about his reputation, when he should be thankful that he had not perished in the flood. She was also telling him that he should be working alongside her to help those less fortunate; he should witness their suffering and see that his own was not so great. But he was not ready, yet, to acknowledge it.

'I'm not sure the wife of the company's resident engineer should be involved in such a high-profile rescue mission. You should not be in the public forum.' He rubbed his beard. 'Charlotte, I ought to forbid it.'

'Yes, dear.' She lifted her chin. 'But I have not given you the space to do so. Ah, here is my transport.'

She swept past, leaving Gunson to stare after her help-lessly. There were people on the street, observing him, and he retreated into the house, slamming the door behind him.

Chapter 27

'May I note down your name?'

Harriet spoke gently to the man sitting opposite, who was twisting his cap in his hands. He had a long thin face, not unlike Mr Boothby's, but without the bushy sideburns. This man's cheeks were covered in dark stubble and there were grey smudges under his eyes.

'Bert Crookes. We were at the foot o' Watersmeet Road but now we're in a room at...' he rubbed his temples and then shook his head impatiently, 'where the... I can't think o' the address...'

Harriet put down her pen. 'Mr Crookes. Please take your time. I'm in no hurry. Would you like me to fetch you a glass of water?'

'No, but I thank thee. Am I in't right place? I've come to lay a claim for loss o' life.'

'Yes, you're in the right place.' She wrote his name at the top of a fresh page. She was halfway through the ledger now and her confidence had grown as the pages filled. She looked up at the man.

'A loss of life?'

'Aye. Me son, me eldest. Thirteen he were, 'ad a job at a skinner's.'

'I'm very sorry.'

'Aint tha fault.' He glared at Harriet in a way that would have distressed her only a short time ago. Now, she calmly poured water into a glass from the jug she was supplied with each morning and pushed it towards him. He drank it down.

'I've got a bad chest from nearly drownin' in the filth, but I won't make the mistake o' callin' the doctor out again. Thievin' git only put me in more debt. If it gets so as I can't breathe, I'll get mysen to the infirmary.'

'Would you like another drink?'

'Aye.' He laughed. It was a bitter sound. 'Whisky, pref'rably. Anyhow, this claim. I've been advised already to not bother claiming for me lad's little sisters. They brought no money in, nor the wife.' He squeezed his cap, over and over. 'I might be able to claim for their clothes, though, I am told?'

His honest, inquiring look was heart-breaking.

Harriet cleared her throat. 'I'll make a note of it. Can I clarify, you lost all your children and your wife?'

'Aye. I were out, doin' a night shift. House got swept away.' He gazed into the adjoining room where the constables filed their reports. It was empty today.

His hands stopped their restless movement. 'Elise, that were me wife's name. Lovely, in't it? Elise.'

'Yes, it is. It is a very lovely name.' Harriet dropped her eyes to the page so he would not see the tears in them and busied herself with her pen. 'Now, Mr Crookes, I think we could include more in your claim, if you are agreeable. We can but ask.'

At noon, the clerk came to tell her that she was not required for the rest of the day.

'Am I to return tomorrow?' said Harriet.

'I'm not sure. I'll check and let Mr Boothby know.' He smiled at her over the top of his spectacles. 'You have been of great service.'

'Oh.' She could not hide her disappointment. 'Well, I have greatly enjoyed the work. It is gratifying, to feel useful. If there's anything else I can do...'

'You are very kind. Thank you. Excuse me.' He hurried off.

Harriet was thankful she had informed Mr Boothby that she would not require his escort home today, supplying the pretext that an unaccompanied stroll would clear her head, and promising not to linger on the street. She had her stick to lean on to save her foot.

So there was no reason to wait, following her early dismissal. Still, she found herself wandering across the foyer, between the tall columns she had found so imposing on first sight, away from the door that led into the street. Perhaps she could find an official and offer herself up for a new voluntary role. She stopped at the tall window near the staircase and leaned on the ledge, observing the uniformed officials, gentlemen and working folk, chatting in groups of two or three, or striding purposefully about. She had been one of them.

A man was walking towards her. He was fiercely bearded and had a determined set to his brow. Was he going to ask her to leave, accuse her of loitering? He caught her gaze with kind brown eyes, smiled at her and tipped his hat. Harriet smiled back and watched him stride past her and up the staircase. He had a purpose. She wondered what it was.

Well, she could not rest here all day. Just a moment longer.

Mr Boothby entered the building. Harriet smiled wryly to herself. Was he here to check up on her, as her self-appointed guardian, or to conduct business of his own? It was a shame that now she must tell him her work was done. She straightened her cape and put on her bonnet. Perhaps, if she requested it, he would find another occupation for her. He had secured this job for her, after all. She was reminded of the poor man she had interviewed that morning. She would relate his tale on the walk home. Mr Boothby always offered a sympathetic ear when she told him of the poor souls who were seeking compensation from the waterworks company, and would quiz her on the size and nature of the day's claims as though he was testing her capacity for recollection. She was pleased to impress him, especially if it led to further employment. Harriet raised her hand in greeting.

He hadn't seen her. Instead, he was making a beeline for a man standing near the fireplace who was concentrating on pushing tobacco into the bowl of his pipe. They had their backs to her, and Harriet paused as she reached them, unsure whether she should interrupt what appeared to be an intimate conversation.

'The issue I have is that the share price has dropped through the floor,' Boothby was saying. 'I'm offloading mine, for tuppence if that's what it takes. I want no share in the responsibility for this whole debacle.'

'Oh, I understand you,' said the other gentleman, nodding sagely.

'We have to ask ourselves,' Mr Boothby hissed, 'will the company be able to meet its liability or does it face ruin and ignominy?'

He leaned closer to the other man, but his words were painfully clear to Harriet. 'I know something of the claims being made and I can tell you this. It'll end up close to half a million pounds. The poor of the town towards whom we are meant to show such sympathy? Well, they are scroungers, the whole bloody lot of them.'

Harriet's hand flew to her mouth. She backed away from Mr Boothby and his companion, still unseen, and without thinking ran up the staircase she had never before ascended and through an open doorway with a wooden pediment dominated by the insignia of the Crown. She found herself in a large wood-panelled room that was packed with people, all buzzing like bees. It was standing room only, and she took up position next to a woman, a wizened old thing, the lace on her white cap grey with age. Her mind was windmilling around the truth she did not want to face, that Mr Boothby had used her to unearth the size of the claims being made, and, worse, did not care about the plight of the destitute, and never had. The old woman beside her must have noticed her burning face. She nudged Harriet.

'Anyone can watch, tha knows. It's summat to do, gets thee out o' the cold, an' its free entertainment.'

There were very few female spectators in the room. Harriet looked up at the men leaning over the public gallery and then glanced down, self-consciously, at the red wool carpet she stood on. What was she doing here? The knocking of a hammer on wood silenced the room and a voice announced the resumption of the inquest. Harriet followed the progress of a handsome man in a brilliant blue waistcoat as he made his way to the witness box. Nobody had challenged her presence. She would remain here for a little while, to give Mr Boothby time to finish his conversation, to try, and fail, to locate her – it would never occur to him to look in the courtroom – and go about his business.

Raised voices caught her attention. The handsome man was asserting that the embankment was flawed, settled unequally, that pressure on the pipe joints had resulted in a blowout. Another man with a shock of white hair was remonstrating with him. At the end of the room, on a raised plinth, the judge, at least she assumed he was the judge, held up his hand to silence them. When he spoke, he held the room in the palm of his hand. Even Harriet, now.

'According to Mr Gunson yesterday,' this man said, 'the work was more than humanly perfect.'

A murmur rippled across the room and the old woman next to Harriet shook her head in apparent disgust.

The man with the wild hair was on his feet. 'The government inspectors who are now carrying out their inquiry will determine the cause of the collapse, not this inquest.'

Someone shouted, 'It's manslaughter!' and Harriet gasped along with the crowd. She could see why the old lady found these goings-on so entertaining.

There were calls for quiet and now another man approached the witness box. It was the gentleman from before, the one with the kindly eyes, except now he looked as though all the worries of the world were on his shoulders. Her heart went out to him.

'That's 'im,' the old woman nudged Harriet with her elbow. 'That's the chief engineer what caused all o' this.'

Chapter 28

Silas stood on the slick cobbles outside the King's Arms, shoulders hunched against the downpour. April's predictable showers had halted work on the barracks building site and seemed in no hurry to let up.

He was waiting.

Voices that had been loudly raised inside the inn were muffled now. A couple of the regulars had been to the inquest and reported back on the various theories for the dam's collapse. Silas had enjoyed listening to the old men who believed themselves experts in everything, but were most adroit at propping up the bar and sinking ale. It's the fault of the greedy waterworks company. No, it's nature getting her revenge on those who would gouge holes in her flanks. The real culprits are the politicians who run the town. Why? Just for being useless nincompoops, of course.

Silas had heard countless tales of those who had been in the torrent's path and survived, and he'd told his own story often enough for the sharp horror of it to begin to lose its glare. He'd thought his near-death was somehow deserved – he'd been priding himself on his good luck the day he arrived in the town and pride came before a fall, his mother always told him. Now he could see that sort of thinking was all wrong-headed. Here he was, hemmed in on all sides by grey brick and stone, the sky clouded with soot, water trickling from the spout on the wall and carrying the stink of industry along the gutter in the road. Now, it was the thought of home, where hedges were his street map, and sheep cropped in fields under a clear sky, that caused his throat to restrict in a sudden panic about being surrounded, of having the life squeezed out of him.

Yet Harriet was here.

'What are you smiling about?'

The reason for his waiting in the rain had appeared before him while he was deep in thought. He had not spotted her sheltered under a man's umbrella.

'Harriet.' He liked to say her name, but then did not know what to say next.

'Silas, you're getting soaked! Come under the umbrella. I took the omnibus here and a smelly old fellow fell fast asleep beside me. I had to keep nudging him away. Like this.'

She elbowed him, laughing, and then offered the umbrella. He took hold of the smooth curved handle that reminded him of a shepherd's crook. The crow-black shade enveloped them.

Harriet continued to chatter, but Silas was aware only of the electric pressure of her fingers curled in the crook of his elbow, all his other senses overcome. Her pale cheeks were flushed with colour, and he wondered if he was having the same effect on her that she had on him. He hoped so.

'... and I'm not sure my uncle would approve of me meeting you, and at the King's Arms of all places...'

'Aye, well, that's why I waited outside for thee.'

'... but I have told him that I occasionally visit with Louisa in her cottage off Penistone Road and if I happen to stumble into a friend en route, well I could argue that's better than being abroad alone, couldn't I?'

'He dun't like me, does he?'

'It's not that.' Now it was her turn to frown. She spoke the next words carefully. 'He's embarrassed that you caught him in a lie… and he thinks it wrong for a… for someone of your… for you to develop a friendship with me.'

'A friendship? Is that all?'

'He thinks you have designs on me.' She was blushing.

'He's right about that. I do have designs,' said Silas. 'I am smitten.' He laughed to lessen the import of his words and struck his chest. 'Smitten right 'ere.'

'Are you really?'

'Smitten?' He smiled. 'Yep.'

'I like that.'

It took a few more steps along the road before he could screw up his courage to ask, 'What about me? D'you like me, an' all?'

'You're very forward, aren't you?'

He basked in the glow of her smile. 'Do you, though?'

'A lady never tells.'

But she cut her eyes at him and his heart soared.

'So this friend we're visitin', tell us about her.'

'Well, she was our maid, but she got caught in the flood and is still recuperating. She lives with her mother, who's called Millicent, and is a housekeeper for a gentleman in town, but has moved out to look after Lou. Is that enough information?'

'Aye, I suppose. Is she a looker like thee, this Lou?'

'Silas!'

She steered him off the main road where a water pump sat at the top of a long, sloping lane between two rows of terraced cottages.

'They're about halfway down,' said Harriet. 'Oh!' She tightened her grip on his arm. 'These cobbles. I wish the rain would stop.'

'Hope Lou's got the kettle on.'

When they reached the low doorframe of the cottage, Harriet didn't knock, but simply lifted the latch and walked in. Silas folded the umbrella, squared his shoulders and ducked inside, knowing he'd be in for some scrutiny from this friend of Harriet's. He had a moment to register the warmth of the room and the sour smell of coalsmoke, and then, in a blur of movement, a black and white bundle of fur and teeth leapt at him.

Silas caught Shandy in his arms.

'Christ Almighty!' He staggered and went down with the dog, pulling at her thick ruff and holding her head back so he could examine her bright amber eyes, the pink tongue lolling over sharp white canines, her doggy breath in his nose. It was Shandy. It was. He released her so she could lick his face. 'Shandy, Shandy, it's thee all right.'

He looked at Harriet, his eyes shining. She had flattened herself against the wall and beside her an older woman was shouting something about dogs showing their true, vicious nature. Silas laughed and walloped Shandy on her haunch, marvelling at her solidity.

'No, she's his!' said another voice. 'She's his dog.' A girl fell to her knees next to him. So this was the Lou that Harriet spoke of.

'Louisa,' he said and the two of them embraced, there on their knees, Shandy dancing around them, barking wildly. He looked over Louisa's shoulder at Harriet's dumbfounded face, wanting to explain, but not trusting himself to speak.

Later, they sat around the fire with mugs of tea and bread and dripping doled out by Millicent Leigh. Shandy left his side to push her nose against Louisa's apron pocket. The girl took out of a piece of cheese and Silas watched his dog nibble it gently from her fingers. When Louisa began to tell them about her escape from the flood, her mother collected her darning needle and retreated to the lean-to kitchen. 'I can't bear to hear this tale again,' she said.

'Anyhow, the weather were wild, so I got up to fetch Shandy from the yard,' Louisa said, and smiled at Silas. 'Poor bugger were glad to get back inside. I snuck her upstairs wi' me.'

'If I'd been there, I would've—' said Silas.

Louisa touched his arm. 'I know, Silas. I'm not saying owt against thee. Nobody knew what were comin'. So I lay her a blanket on the floor and I goes back to bed. I can hear Hilda through the wall, settling the baby.' She paused. 'It woke me up, the noise of it.'

Silas said, 'I'll never forget that noise. I thought the world were ending.'

'It did, for some.' Louisa gave him a watery smile. 'But right then, I had no idea what it were. I thought the house was falling down on me. Well, it were. Nowt left o' it.'

'I saw. How did tha get out?'

'Shandy warned me.' Louisa scratched the top of the dog's head absently. 'She jumps up and starts barking and growling. At me! An' I'm sitting up in bed wonderin' if she's about to attack me. What sort o' bleedin' dog has he brought to my house that I'd then took inside?'

Silas grinned. Shandy continued to gaze up at Louisa, eyebrows twitching.

'Next minute, this roar, no, more like a hissin' sound, like a gas lamp makes, but deafening, tha knows? And a groan like the ground – the ground *under* the ground – is tearing itself apart. All o' a sudden, I'm breathing water and the house is gone. I mean, no walls, nothing, just the wave, and me in it.'

'It were the same for me,' said Silas. He shuddered. 'I won't say no more about it.'

Louisa said, 'Reight enough. Well, there were no sign o' Shandy, but I weren't exactly lookin' out for the dog.' She bent to kiss the top of Shandy's head. 'Sorry, love, but I had all on not to be pulled under or bang into summat. It were so dark, just blackness all round, and me lungs choked. I knew I were drowning, knew it. Knew there were other people in the water. There were some screaming, but I couldn't see anybody. That were bad, hearin' 'em, but not seein'. Then a tree went by and I threw mesen over it, just clingin' on. I shut me eyes. Then I got hit. Something smashed the back of me head. The next thing, I wake up, thinkin' I'd find meself in bed again, but I knew. I knew straightaway it weren't the bad dream I wished it were, tha knows?'

Silas nodded. He hadn't been aware of Harriet taking his hand in hers, but he was glad of it.

'Anyway, I'm starin' up at the blue sky above me, birds flying about. It's the mornin' and I'm on the riverbank, clarted in mud, but still wearing me nightie, thank the lord. Me head's pounding, I'm dyin' of thirst, and this animal...' she laughed shakily, '...this good dog I'd not long known were layin' next to me, right as rain. I'd lost everythin'. I had some savings, tha knows, I kept in a drawer. All gone. But I were alive and many weren't.' She gulped back tears. 'Hilda, an' baby Betty. An' your Alice, too.'

Harriet let go of Silas and went to Louisa and hugged her. Silas felt like the outsider he was. Both women had lost people close to them. Not him. He'd even got his dog back.

'Louisa,' he said. 'I don't know if I can take Shandy wi' me. They might not be keen on a dog in the lodgings I've got. I'm at the King's Arms.'

He looked at Shandy. She cocked her head, one way then the other. 'What I'm askin' is, Shandy feels at home here wi' you, I can tell. D'you think you can hold onto her a while longer?'

Chapter 29

'That was kind.'

'What were?'

'Allowing Louisa to keep Shandy.'

'I've not.'

Harriet hummed gently as they strolled on, a few notes of a song she could barely recall her mother singing to her. It was a shame the rain had stopped because she had no reason now to nestle her gloved hand in the crook of his elbow. Silas was carrying the furled umbrella in his fist, like a weapon, whereas Uncle Walter would have used it for a walking cane, swinging it along the pavement.

'I still can't comprehend it,' she said. 'You, and Louisa, and Shandy.'

Silas stopped and faced her. 'Listen, I have a secret to tell thee.'

'I don't think I can cope with any more revelations.'

He made a show of looking up and down the street. The broad leaves of oak and sycamore spread overhead, a green canopy. Harriet had noticed nature regaining her hold on the banks of the Loxley, grasses and wildflowers laying a carpet over the scarred ground.

Silas moved closer. 'This secret. I need to whisper it.'

'Oh Silas,' she said, laughing, 'what are you up to?' But when his lip brushed her earlobe, a butterfly's touch, it sent shock waves through her body. She let out an involuntary gasp.

He hissed in her ear, '*Pss pss pss,*' and stepped back, laughing.

Harriet pulled a face. 'You're such a child.'

Silas reached up to snap off a twig.

'An olive branch,' he said, passing it to her.

'That's not a branch and that's not an olive tree.' But she could not keep the smile from her face.

'Why do you have that stick?'

The question caught her off guard, but she decided to answer in the same blunt fashion.

'I have a clubfoot.'

'Oh aye, I remember it. I saw it on the night of the flood, when tha were in thee nightie.' He laughed and grabbed for her hand, but Harriet snatched it away.

'Silas! Somebody might see.'

'What care I?' He skipped ahead so that he was facing her, walking backwards. He tossed his cap in the air and caught it deftly. 'Does it pain thee much, tha foot?'

'It's tolerable.' She smiled. 'Turn around, Silas, or you shall fall over.'

He fell into step beside her and they walked on in silence for a few seconds, smiling at passers-by, in and out of the dappled light between the trees.

Silas crooked his elbow and she took his arm. He patted her hand. 'This is how we perambulate, my dear, arm in arm. Are you quite warm enough, my dear?'

'My, you are quite the young gentleman.'

He dropped the act as quickly as he'd adopted it. 'I love to walk beside thee, Harriet. Even if tha does hobble a bit.'

'The cheek!' Harriet laughed. 'Do you ride, Silas? When I'm on a horse I can forget about my foot.'

'I've never learned, never had need to.'

'I'll teach you.'

This reminded her that she had promised Alice a ride on a pony, and now she was thinking about Walter, about how he had taken to sleeping in Alice's room so his coughing would not disturb Polly. How that cough was worsening to the point where he was becoming bed-bound, and how she had overheard the doctor telling Walter that his lungs were filling up with poison.

As spring gave way to summer, Harriet explored the town with Silas, happy to act as guide to such an enthusiastic companion. She knew she ought to examine her own feelings about Silas, but his company was so enjoyable it was possible to forget the half a decade difference in age, the disparity in status, and to simply bask in the time she spent with him. She recognised it as an escape from the growing oppressiveness of her home life. She was skimming the surface of things, gadding about like a mayfly.

She took him to Norfolk market hall that sat in a wide space at the crest of a hill in the town, away from the factories and chimneys. 'It's all bleedin' 'ills, this place,' said Silas, sitting on the lip of an ornamental water fountain and scooping up water to splash on his face. He had brought her a posy of daisies and they scattered them in the fountain. They smiled at other people blooming like flowers in the sunshine. They found a bench to sit on and watched a boy drive sheep along the top of the road, holding up the traffic. Silas told her about his life on the farm and about his brother.

'He were a bad 'un. Fisticuffs all day long.'

Harriet listened and when he fell silent she squeezed his arm. 'You're here now, away from all that. We'll look after you.'

'All o' you? Or just thee?'

She blushed.

They went into the grand market hall where tall windows threw light onto the shops and stalls that filled the interior from end to end. He teased her about her enthusiasm for the ribbons and silks at a milliner's shop after she exclaimed 'Look at all the colours!' He insisted on buying her a wide velvet ribbon she admired.

'It's a lovely colour,' he said. 'A bit like tha face when I say summat tha likes.'

And she had affected insult, but her heart was gladdened.

It was a Sunday and Harriet had turned up at Louisa's with a pie she had baked. Her Sunday afternoon visits were a regular occurrence and any guilt she felt about leaving Polly to spend another day without company was alleviated by the sight of Silas playing tug with Shandy or drinking tea with Louisa and Millicent, and she knew he had been waiting for her arrival. Harriet's cheeks always grew warm when he greeted her and she caught the looks exchanged between mother and daughter, but pretended not to.

Today would be different. Harriet arrived early, hoping to speak with Louisa before Silas turned up. She handed over the pie and dropped into an armchair.

'You look sour enough to turn butter,' said Louisa.

Harriet took a breath to calm herself. She couldn't meet Louisa's eye.

'I have something to tell you.' She fell silent.

'Go on then. Am all ears.'

Harriet pleated her lips and waited for the urge to burst into tears to pass.

'All right. Walter has told me I should marry Mr Boothby. It seems the two of them have reached an *understanding*.'

A brief conversation had decided her fate. Her uncle had sat her down in the parlour the previous day and told her what her future held. 'This is your best prospect,' he'd said. She had looked down, her eyes catching on the blood-stained handkerchief in his fist.

'Do I have a say?' she'd whispered.

'No,' Walter had replied bluntly. 'This is a decision I have come to on your behalf.'

She related this to Louisa, who laughed. 'Why, that's…' then stopped short. 'What agreement?'

'They have ambitions for their business. One of them is to keep it in the family.'

'What d'you mean?'

'Boothby, Simpson and Sons. I am to provide the Simpson share of the latter.' She laughed, a bitter sound. 'I knew where all this was leading, of course. I thought if I ignored the situation it would – he would – go away.'

'He has two faces, that man. At least according to Silas, what tha sees is what tha gets.'

Harriet's heart lurched. 'Don't tell Silas about this. It's… I'm embarrassed. Please don't say anything. I think he would be disappointed.'

'That's puttin' it mildly.'

'Louisa, I can't rely on Silas, he's a boy. I have to be practical.'

'Hmm. What does Polly say?'

'That it is not up to her. My uncle is ill, you know, gravely ill. His lungs...' Harriet shook her head. 'My options are limited.'

'Tha's already said that. Walter knows what he's like, this man. He must do.'

'Yes. But he's dying, Lou! He's just trying to ensure his family is looked after.'

'An' you'll do it, then? D' you 'av any feelin' for Boothby, at all?'

'That doesn't really come into it. I can learn to live with him.' She heard the grimness in her voice. 'It is not as bad as I paint it.'

Shandy jumped up from her usual space by the fireside and ran to the door with a volley of barks.

'Oh! Silas is coming,' she said. 'Louisa, I beg you, please, don't say a word.'

Harriet was restless throughout the afternoon, avoiding Silas's eye, shrinking away when he went to take her hand. Silas joked about asking for a job at her uncle's firm and she knew he caught her frown before she could hide it. When they left Louisa's cottage, she felt the grey sky press down on her.

After a few moments of walking in silence, Silas said, 'I'd like to walk thee to the door and meet wi' Walter.'

Now she noticed his new wine-coloured waistcoat over a crisp white shirt and how clean his hands were, even the nails. He'd had a haircut and, she saw with dismay, his green eyes were narrowed with purpose. Polly would find him handsome. Walter had no use for a handsome young man in Harriet's life, especially now. She ached for Silas, knowing that Walter would not tolerate him, that Silas's kindness and gentleness and his obvious devotion towards her counted for nothing next to Albert Boothby's wealth and connections.

They had reached the river and were now minutes from her aunt and uncle's home. Harriet trailed her fingers over the darkened stone of the low wall leading to the bridge, slowing her pace as they crossed to look down at the water. It was flowing quickly today, invigorated by an early summer squall. The sandstone on the new section of bridge was still pale, fresh as a wound.

Later, Harriet cursed herself for not demanding that Silas leave her there as usual, on the bridge.

Silas reached forward to grab Harriet's hand when they entered the house, which was quiet as the grave. She shook him off, imagining what her uncle would have to say about that, and walked down the corridor and into the kitchen where he joined her at the window. They gazed, unseen, into the back garden. All three boys were running up and down between the tilted bamboo cages that supported the thick tangle of peas on one side and asparagus on the other. Walter was standing by the gate that overlooked the common, deep in conversation with Mr Boothby.

'Oh no. Silas, I think we should…'

Her eyes widened in surprise when he took her face between the warm palms of his hands and kissed her on the mouth. His lips were soft, but insistent, and the taste of his kiss sour and sweet at the same time. There was space between their bodies, a few inches, and Harriet yearned to press herself against him, overwhelmed by an instinctive need to feel more than the squeeze of his hand, the touch of his lips. Then the contact broke and she opened her eyes – she hadn't realised until that moment that they had been closed – and Silas's gaze filled her vision.

He was smiling. 'I should say sorry, but I've been wantin' to kiss thee for—'

She didn't let him finish. She felt the curve of his smile as she put her lips back to his.

The slam of the door was a gunshot that made her leap back in shock. Walter was in the kitchen, his fists clenched and his face a mask of fury.

'Uncle.' Harriet moved away, putting distance between her and Silas. 'Uncle.' She had no idea how to continue. Walter glared at Silas, then at her. He didn't speak.

Silas did. 'Sir, I am...', but Walter leapt forward to grab Harriet by the arm and she went limp with shock. She heard Silas call her name as her uncle dragged her through the house and into the parlour. He slammed the door behind them before releasing his grip. Harriet retreated before him.

'I won't demean myself by trying to reason with you in front of that boy. You risk all our futures!' He made a visible effort to calm himself. 'Harriet, my beloved niece. You cannot intend to throw your lot in with him, one of the great unwashed? You know I won't allow it. You debase yourself with this behaviour.'

The door was flung open and Silas was there. She was suddenly afraid for him.

Without warning, Walter lashed out, catching Silas with a backhanded slap across the face. There was an instant where nobody moved and the only sound was Walter's rattling and ragged breath. Silas's face was white and there was blood on his chin. Her uncle had split his lip. Another figure appeared in the doorway and Harriet was dismayed to see who it was.

Mr Boothby broke the spell.

'What's going on here? Walter?'

Her uncle held up his hand and pressed a handkerchief to his mouth, his Adam's apple bouncing up and down as though it would tear itself from his throat. He staggered past Silas, who adroitly stepped out of his path, and reached out to support himself against the mantlepiece, a deep and dragging cough finally wrenching its way from his lungs. Harriet watched in horror as her uncle fell, coughing, to his hands and knees, then slipped forwards, his head hitting the grate with a dull thud of flesh and bone against iron.

Silas crouched beside him, his hands hovering over Walter's shoulders.

'Get off him!' Mr Boothby bellowed the words and Silas jumped to his feet.

'Fetch the doctor,' Harriet whispered. 'He needs the doctor.'

Mr Boothby stood in front of her, blocking her view of Walter and Silas, and waited for Harriet to look up at him. 'The police, too, Harriet.' He looked scornfully at Silas. 'I knew you'd be trouble.'

Walter lay face down, head and shoulders on the tiles of the fireplace, and his legs stretched out on the carpet. Rust-coloured blood spotted the crumpled handkerchief in his fist and black liquid bloomed on the lacquered tile.

Chapter 30

'So, will you be going to your club tonight?'

There was a sharp edge to his wife's voice. Charlotte was hardly ever querulous, and Gunson realised she was as overwrought as he. The inquest was consuming him – had consumed him. She needed reassurance and so there was really only one answer he could give. He laid his knife and fork down carefully, flinching at the gentle clink of silver on china. 'No. I think not.'

They had dined on lamb and new potatoes, sprouts and peas and mint gravy. The meal sat in his stomach like a rock. Rather than meet Charlotte's eye, he examined the familiar pattern on his dinnerplate; dominating the white glaze was a black tree trunk with stubby roots, thin black branches reaching to the edges on which were blooming oversized flowers of no variety he'd ever seen, almost Oriental in design, and beautiful. The plate was part of a dinner service that had been in his wife's family for many years and came with her when they married. Plate from Derby, utensils from Sheffield. Assuredly, a quality combination. He should placate Charlotte, tell her that he would rather spend the evening in her company, sipping his brandy by the fire while she played the piano for him, but he couldn't summon the energy to utter the words and stared instead at this design on his plate.

'There's no point dwelling on it,' she said. 'Let's look ahead to the weekend we'll be spending with James and Anne and little Freddie. Your grandson dotes on you.'

He finally met her gaze. 'I may have to send you alone. If I am to be sacrificed to satisfy the town tomorrow, I don't think I'd have the stomach to face James.'

He had survived the inquest, despite Webster's best efforts to ruin him. The jury had rejected any suggestion of criminality in the collapse of the dam, and concluded that Thomas Fairest, a furnaceman selected from among the victims to represent them all, came to his death by drowning in the inundation caused by the tragic bursting of the Bradfield dam. There would be no charge of manslaughter laid at the door of the Sheffield Waterworks Company.

But two days after the verdict, Gunson had retrieved the newspaper before the maid could finish twisting the pages into balls to layer the coal fire. He read and re-read the inquest report until he could recite by heart the jury's declaration that, '*in our opinion there has not been that engineering skill and attention to the construction of the works, which their magnitude and importance demanded.*' There has not been that engineering skill. *There has not.*

There it was, in black and white. Committed to print. A permanent stain on his reputation.

Then came another deeper blow.

At the end of May, the Rawlinson Report, the government inspector's findings on the catastrophe were presented to Parliament. It was damning. The design was flawed, the construction method faulty. David Craven had flown into Gunson's office in a fury. 'This is my good name being dragged into the gutter!' The report came with the Chief Constable's updated list of the dead, a list that twisted Gunson's heart. He had tasted sour dirt again, a recollection of sprawling in the mud after the miller had told him about the tailor's search for his newborn son's body. He realised he didn't know where – or whether – the infant had been found and it had felt important, suddenly, that he should have this information. He had wondered who he could ask.

Gunson had wrenched his attention back to Craven.

'And now we are to have a public meeting about the company's decision to increase the water rates by twenty-five per cent.' Craven had paced the room. 'Can't you see that this adds insult to injury, John?' He didn't wait for a reply. 'Oh, I know, I know, money must be found for the compensation claims.' Craven flapped his hands. It was like being trapped in the room with an angry crow.

And now, after the passage of several weeks in which he dared hope the dust had settled, Gunson's superiors had asked him to report to them first thing tomorrow. He was to be sacrificed on the altar of popular opinion, he was certain of it. Parliament had approved the increase in water rates and voices were growing louder in support of wrenching the company from private hands. A scapegoat might appease the mob, and the rifle sight had settled on his head.

Charlotte laid her hand on his arm. 'You are a million miles away. Self-pity doesn't suit you, John.'

'I'm not...'

'I say they would be foolish to let you go, but consider this. We are comfortably off, are we not? Retirement might suit you. It might suit us both.'

He threw up his hands in despair. 'I've done all the work on Agden, and a decision is going to have to be made soon about Bradfield. The millers still need their supply to keep the new wheels turning.' He paused, thinking about the new specifications he had begun working on. 'You know, I think Dale Dyke could be rebuilt not far from the original location. If we are able to find—'

His wife cut him off. 'John, it doesn't have to be built by you.'

'I know that.'

'You are not indispensable. That company doesn't care a fig about you. I do.' She took his hands. 'You're indispensable to me.'

'I know.' He tried to smile.

'See what tomorrow brings, then. You survived the flood, John. Think on that.'

'I do. Every day, I do.'

The next morning dawned bright, and after break-fasting with Charlotte – he could manage just a cup of coffee – Gunson walked to the imposing Palazzo-style building that had been designed and built for the company, as if he was on his way to the gallows. He nodded to the early morning passers-by, certain that the fright that twisted his gut must show on his face. Even at his slowest pace, he arrived within a few minutes at the short flight of steps that led up to the entrance. The stone heads of mythical water gods stared out from above the apex of the arched ground floor windows. Today, he acknowledged them with a grimace. Would Achelous, Greek god of rivers, fall upon his head or did he have the sympathy of these deities? He had worshipped at their altar for long enough.

Although he was hardly ever in it, the chairman had his own wood-panelled office on the second floor, plushly furnished with thick velvet drapes in the window and red flock on the walls. He was sunk in a leather chair behind a gleaming walnut desk that held nothing but a lamp, pen, ink and blotter. Gunson thought fleetingly about his own desk, the surface of which was invisible, buried as it was under stacks of books and paperwork. Who would pore over his drawings once he was gone, and make their careless marks upon his life's work?

The chairman smiled at him genially. 'Please sit down, John.'

'Good morning, Mr Smith. I trust you are well.'

'Well, these are trying times.' William Smith looked enquiringly at Gunson, clearly requiring some sort of response to this most obvious of statements.

'They are, indeed.'

'The shareholders are most unhappy, and who could blame them? We are in a precarious position in terms of both our profits and our future. I certainly do not wish to see us fall into public hands, do you?'

'No.'

'You don't sound too sure.'

Gunson shifted in his seat. 'Can I be frank? I don't have a political bone in my body. All I want to do is build reservoirs. I have built eight,' he paused, recalling the reaction at the inquest to this same phrase, *eight mistakes*, 'and Agden is progressing well. I also have an idea for—'

'John, I do not mean to interrupt, but I'm not questioning your ability. Unfortunately, the situation we find ourselves in is political, and there's no way around that. I would go so far as to say we are fighting for survival. We spent sixty thousand pounds on that embankment, only to see it washed away.'

'One cannot put a monetary value on the human cost,' said Gunson quietly.

'No, indeed one cannot. However, this Rawlinson report has handed the town all the ammunition it requires to—', he broke off and leaned forward in his seat, '—do you know, the town is gaining support for a compulsory purchase, claiming that because the embankment was poorly built that means that this company is unfit for purpose? That we should be monitored like infants?'

Gunson could imagine it all too well. 'If you are alluding to Mr Webster, I would say that man produces more hot air than the furnaces at Atlas Works.'

'You are a friend of his, or you were, before the inquest.'

'He is an acquaintance of long standing, no more.'

'Well, there is to be this public meeting over our bill to Parliament and Webster and his ilk will take advantage of this opportunity to call for the waterworks to be taken into public ownership. I wonder if we can influence Mr Webster's mind? Perhaps sit down with him, away from the public arena, and press upon him how seriously we take the terrible responsibility of holding in our hands the sole supply of an indispensable necessity of life?' He wiped a handkerchief across his brow. 'I am sorry, as you can see, I feel quite passionately about our little endeavour.'

Gunson waited for the chairman's breathing to calm.

'Mr Smith, am I still the chief engineer of this company?'

'Why, yes, of course. We can't allow the townspeople to believe shoddy workmanship caused this catastrophe, and sacking you would only reinforce that... mistaken impression.'

'The dam was sound,' said Gunson. 'The fault lay with an underground—'

'Yes, yes. As I have already said, you possess great natural abilities and your extreme conscientiousness is not in doubt. I have not called you in today for an appraisal.'

Gunson felt the tremor in his hand again, the intermittent palsy that had afflicted him ever since the flood, but he kept his voice steady. 'My chief pleasure has always been in my work, in building dams.'

'Oh, I did not ask you to attend my office to remove you!' The chairman laughed.

Gunson wiped his face. 'Then why?'

'It is nothing really, a trifle. As I was saying, I'd simply like you to renew your friendship with Mr Webster, to see whether the man can be brought around to our way of thinking. He's a man of the people, a judge, a councillor, a champion of the poor. You can help him to recognise that we act only in the best interests of the town. Clean water for everyone is our priority, not profits. Somebody like you, John, who doesn't have a political bone in his body, is just the man for the job.'

Chapter 31

It was almost midnight, closing time, and the sky had darkened into full night. Plumes of white smoke from a nearby works obscured the stars that would be visible at home. They were there, just the same. Silas gathered skittles and balls from the pub's garden and stacked them in the snug. He picked up six tankards with a practised ease and deposited them on the bar.

Job done.

He sighed, desperate for the night to pass so he could return to Harriet's side, to apologise, to make it right with her uncle. He clung to the idea there was still hope as fiercely as he'd clung to the lamp-post in the torrent. She had saved him then. She would not desert him now.

He'd engineered this disaster, there was no doubt. He should not have kissed her. It had been a wonderful kiss. He was stupid, impulsive, acting like he was back at the farm, trying to catch hold of one of the country girls. No better than an animal. Silas chewed his lower lip, and flinched. The skin was torn where Walter's ring had caught it and now he'd set it bleeding again. He blotted the blood on the sleeve of his shirt.

'Come on then, auld Syd,' he said to the white-haired man who was sitting on a stool in the corner, hiding in the shadows. 'Don't be thinking Elsie won't spot thee. Get thee cap on. Home time.'

He heard Elsie Broomhead's tread on the wooden stairs that led up from the cellar. 'She's comin', Syd. Up tha gets.'

The old man muttered under his breath but managed to find his feet, swaying a little on the spot before shuffling towards the door.

'Your 'at!' Silas put the man's cap in his hands. 'It's parky out tonight.'

He reached past Syd to unlatch the door and watched him weave down the street before closing the door and bolting it. When he turned, the landlady of the King's Arms was wiping the counter down. She eyed him knowingly. He knew she'd clocked his swollen lip earlier, but she had said nothing about it. He wondered whether he ought to tell her.

'You've had a mardy face on you all night, Silas. Have you been in a fight? Over this girl you're sweet on? Has she told you to sling yer hook?'

'What girl's that then?' But he couldn't keep the pretence up. 'It's not her,' he admitted, leaning on the bar. 'It's her uncle. I'm not good enough.' He sighed. 'An' it's as simple as that. I went to see him, tha knows, to show him. I wanted to do it proper, make sure he knows I'm not after his money or owt. I went in there and made it ten times worse for meself. I'm a daft sod.'

'No, Silas, you're not daft. Here.' She poured two glasses of whisky and handed one over. 'What happened?'

'Well...' He felt the blush rising and bent his head to sip the whisky. It stung the wound on his lip, but it was not the blow from Walter he thought of. 'I did give her a kiss.'

'Silas Hinchcliffe!' She laughed. 'I bet she kissed you back an' all.'

'Who could resist, eh?' Then Silas swallowed, serious again. 'Her uncle, he's her guardian, he saw us. He had some sort o' coughin' fit…'

'A coughing fit?'

'Yep. He's poorly, Harriet says from the flood water. So he falls into the fireplace and knocks himself out.' Elsie's eyes widened. 'An' she asks me to fetch the doctor, who's a neighbour of theirs. He comes straight out. There's another man there – I've met him before, Boothby he's called – an' he won't let me back in! Says Walter's woke up an' he's sittin' in a chair and he's talkin'. The fella sends me packin'.'

'I'd say that's probably for the best. Let them sleep on it.'

'I don't know who this fella thinks he is…'

A furious hammering on the door startled them both. Was this Syd back again? He'd been known to circle round on himself and would then have to be set back on the path home. But that little old man couldn't put this much force into it. Another volley of thumps echoed round the room.

'Keep your hair on,' muttered Elsie, bustling over to draw back the bolt.

'Wait,' said Silas. 'Let me…' He was suddenly afraid for his landlady, but she was already opening the door. She cried out in protest when two burly figures in black capes and tall hats pushed past her. Police constables.

'Oy!' shouted Silas. 'There's no need for that. What's goin' on?'

Elsie clutched the back of a chair. Then she pulled herself up to her full height and anger flashed in her eyes. 'What can I do for you gentlemen at this hour? You can see we're closed.'

One of the men stepped into the middle of the room, towards Silas, while the other remained by the door.

'We're looking for Silas Hinchcliffe,' said the constable closest to him.

'What for?' said Elsie, at the same time as Silas said, 'Tha's found him then.'

The constable closest to him took Silas's arm roughly. 'You're under arrest. Come with us.'

Now the second man came forward and seized his other arm, digging his fingers painfully into Silas's bicep. He decided it would be foolish to struggle and allowed them to march him towards the door.

'What 'ave I done?' He spoke quietly, not really wanting an answer. He knew why they were there. He could see in Elsie Broomhead's eyes that she knew, too.

'What's the lad done?'

'Mrs Broomhead, he's not the innocent boy he looks.' The constable pointed to Silas's swollen lip and the blood on his sleeve. 'Look at the state of him. You can see he's been up to no good.'

'What is he charged with?'

'Come on.' The constable was breathing heavily in Silas's ear. He stank of onions. 'No messin' now.' Silas's hands were cuffed behind his back and he was shoved onto the pavement. The nearby houses were silent and dark. He looked back at his landlady who stood on the doorstep, light spilling out from behind her.

'He's not done owt wrong,' she hissed quietly, mindful of the hour.

One of the constables laughed. 'Oh, he has. This one'll be charged with grievous bodily harm, might even be manslaughter if the gentleman doesn't recover.'

Silas gasped. 'I 'aven't…'

'Shut your gob.' His arm was squeezed again, painfully. 'Don't struggle, lad, or you'll be getting more than a split lip.'

Silas dropped his head.

'That's better.'

'Sorry, Mrs Broomhead.' The other constable gestured to the door. 'Lock up tight, now. You never know who's abroad. At least we've got this vagabond off the streets for thee, eh?'

Chapter 32

Harriet leaned against the bannister, gripping the bowl of soapy water tightly with both hands as she descended. She was halfway down when the front door opened and Mr Boothby strode into the porch, dropping his umbrella in the stand as if he was the master of the house.

'My dear!' He bounded up and took the bowl from her.

'Thank you.' Harriet shook her wrists in relief. 'I'm sure I would have dropped it. Would you mind carrying it through to the scullery?'

'You should not be doing a maid's work,' he called over his shoulder as she followed him to the back of the house. He was practically skipping with glee.

'I was helping Uncle to wash,' she said warily. 'You seem to have all the joys of spring in your step, Mr Boothby.'

He tipped the contents of the bowl into the scullery sink. 'Is Walter up to a visit today?' He didn't wait for her reply. 'I have news. That ruffian has been arrested and locked up.'

A chill ran through her. 'What ruffian?'

'Come, come. You know exactly who I mean.'

He shepherded her back down the hallway and into the front parlour.

'Please, sit.'

She did.

'That boy who attacked your uncle. He's reflecting on his sins in the cellar of the constable's house where they stow the drunks and the harlots – excuse my language – which is where he belongs. He'll be taken to the town hall cells and then he'll be charged.'

Harriet folded her hands in her lap. She would show a calm demeanour and not give him the satisfaction of witnessing her fear, or rising anger. 'Mr Boothby, I hope you did not give a mistaken impression of events? Silas did not attack my uncle. He's just a boy...'

'He's eighteen. Old enough to swing.'

'Swing?'

'A grievous assault. An attempted murder.'

Harriet laughed. 'You are not serious? This misunderstanding must be rectified. My uncle...'

'Is gravely ill.'

'From floodwater on his lungs. Not from his injuries.'

'Injuries inflicted by the boy...'

'Injuries he sustained in a fall from coughing.'

'Why are you defending someone so far beneath you?'

'Silas is a friend.'

'Then you should choose your friends more wisely.' He looked around the room. 'The new maid could do a better job. Where is she?'

'Sadie is with my aunt.'

'And your cousins?'

'They are on the common.'

'Then we are alone, at last, and I hope I may speak freely.'

As freely as you enter my uncle's house, Harriet thought. She bit her lip and studied her clasped hands.

Silas was a prisoner because of her. She would not persuade this man of his innocence by antagonising him.

Mr Boothby was waiting. '*May* I speak freely?'

She looked up and nodded brightly, feigning an interest while her mind was fully occupied with Silas's predicament. Serious crimes were dealt with at the York or Leeds assizes, but Silas would appear first at the local court where any charges would be levied, and then transferred to jail. She needed to find a way of halting the process before the charges were laid.

'Walter asked me to protect you, all of you, and that is what I shall do. I shall do it for my friend and business partner.'

Harriet inwardly flinched, but kept her expression neutral when he reached forward to cup her chin, lifting her face so that she was forced to meet his eye. 'I know you must feel ashamed. I'm sure we can find a way of helping our little temptress to behave herself, eh?' She couldn't prevent her eyes from widening. 'Do not be so hard on yourself. You are not a woman of the world, Harriet. At your age you should be married with a family of your own. Of course, you have your disability – forgive me for making mention of it – and Walter has been content to have you look after his family.'

He relinquished her – she could still feel the imprint of his fingers, but resisted the urge to rub her chin – and sat back. 'Why, look at all the roles you have played. Governess, housekeeper, hostess... a fine set of attributes...'

Her thoughts returned to Silas, casting about to find a solution. There was something she might do. She straightened, gazing at Mr Boothby's mouth, paying no heed to the words coming out of it. She would go to the town hall. Yes, this is what she would do. It would have been unthinkable once. Now, stepping inside the municipal headquarters of the town was no longer a daunting prospect. She would seek out the clerk who had thanked her for helping to record the claims, and ask a favour in return.

She realised Mr Boothby had stopped speaking and was regarding her, a self-satisfied smile on his face. 'I rattle about the place since my wife passed on. We were not blessed with children.'

Harriet went back to staring at her hands. It was the seemly thing to do. Meanwhile, her thoughts raced. If she could make a case for Silas, explain what had really transpired, surely he would be freed? Would any attention be paid to her, a mere woman? All she knew was that she had to try.

'A pretty young woman such as yourself should not be considering aught except how to become a devoted wife and mother.' He coughed. 'Harriet.'

She looked up. 'Yes?'

'Walter has spoken to you about joining our two families. I hate to flatter myself, but I'd like to think you will be agreeable to my proposal.'

'Um, sorry, I am confused.' She had become so distracted by Silas's plight she had not seen the danger directly before her. She cursed herself for allowing Mr Boothby to steer the conversation in a direction she might have been able to change, had she been paying attention. It was too late now. He was making the proposal of marriage her uncle had told her would be forthcoming.

'You will not get a better offer!' He laughed, his smug certainty echoing around the room. 'And I am gentlemanly enough to forgive one kiss stolen by a ne'er do well.' He put his hands over hers. His touch was clammy and she suppressed a shudder. 'It is time for you to act according to your status. I know you enjoyed the work I secured for you, helping the poor of the town. Up until the time we start our family, you may continue to assist those less fortunate. Your kindness does you — it does us both — much credit.'

He had insulted Silas again. He had insulted her, perhaps without even being aware of it, but perhaps not. It occurred to her this proposal might be Silas's only hope. Mr Boothby would be sure to grant his fiancée her dearest wish. She swallowed, and tried to smile. 'Perhaps,' she said, 'we could begin by showing mercy to Silas.'

'So you are agreeable? Walter said you would see the sense of it.' He took her hands and kissed them. She gazed in dismay at the bald spot on the top of his greying head.

'And… the boy?'

'Put him out of your mind, my dear.'

'I will, of course. I only wish you would explain the truth of my uncle's fall.'

He squeezed her hands. 'You are too good, Harriet. That rogue should never have taken advantage of you. He'll get his just desserts!'

She understood then that only she could save him.

Chapter 33

She managed to send Mr Boothby on his merry way by telling him they ought to check on her cousins, who had gone out to play.

'It gets very muddy on the common. I shall need my Wellingtons,' she said, casting a critical glance at his polished shoes.

'Ah, in that case I shall leave you to it.'

At the door, he stroked her arm; he seemed to need to be always touching her in some way. She moved imperceptibly away and he dropped his hand. 'You do mollycoddle those children. In my day, we'd be left to our own devices from morning to night. Never did me any harm.'

Harriet smiled politely. 'It's my aunt's wish that I keep a careful watch over the boys. You understand why.'

'Of course, of course.' He nodded soberly. 'Well, I'll bid you adieu, my dear.'

She found the boys kicking a football about in a noisy group of about a dozen children. She watched them for a few moments, but couldn't see a method to their play. They all chased the ball in a solid clump, like a shoal of fish, towards one small and solitary boy standing on the line where the common met the road. He seemed braced to catch the ball and all the boys behind it. Harriet walked carefully across the wet grass so she would not have to shout like a common barker to gain the attention of her cousins. She beckoned Adam over. He cast a wistful glance at the ball, but came to her. She told him she had an errand to run and wouldn't it be fun for the boys to visit Louisa so they could play with the dog? Luckily, he agreed and coaxed his brothers away from the game.

They ran back to the house ahead of her and were fighting over who would be first to pet the dog when she caught up with them. She shooed them upstairs to tell their mother that cousin Harriet was taking them on a jaunt and eased her Wellingtons off, massaging her foot to ease a painful cramp. She closeted herself in her bedroom, sitting on the edge of her bed to think carefully about what she was about to attempt. Her stomach contracted whenever she thought about what she was going to do, and then she reminded herself where Silas was, and where he might end up if she did not act. She would need to consider what outfit would best serve her needs.

She picked out a day dress in fawn-coloured satin, the high neckline trimmed with a thin collar of black braid that matched the seaming on the bodice and full skirt. The matching bonnet was wide-brimmed in the old style, the better to shield her face from prying eyes. At the mirror in the hallway, shouting to the boys to hurry, hurry, she threaded the red velvet ribbon Silas had bought for her into the bonnet and surveyed herself critically. Her outfit was simple, understated, serious, the treasured ribbon the only splash of colour. She was ready.

'I'll be back by teatime,' she told Sadie, who had appeared at the end of the corridor that led to the kitchen. 'Tell my aunt I'll bring her back some of those sugar mice she loves.'

The boys were waiting for her in the porch, tumbling and yapping like puppies. The walk would do them good. Harriet stopped, tears springing to her eyes. Alice should be running to join her brothers, her pink calfskin boots thumping on the polished floorboards, Adam should be reaching for his little sister's hand and bending to kiss the top of her head. Harriet felt her lips moved soundlessly, 'Be careful not to slip, my love.' She blinked her tears away and Alice's apparition with them.

They walked to Penistone Road. From there, Harriet would take the horse-drawn omnibus into town.

Louisa nodded tersely at Harriet when she opened the door.

'To what do I owe the honour?' She cocked her head and raised a knowing eyebrow. So she knew about Silas.

Harriet smiled desperately. 'News travels fast in this town. Please, Louisa, I had to bring the boys for an excuse to get out, but I can't take them where I'm going. I'm not sure how long I'll be. I'm going to try to help Silas.'

'Tha'd better get theesen off then.' The coolness in Louisa's voice was wounding.

'Louisa…'

'He shouldn't involve himsen wi' people like thee. He's likely to get trampled on.'

'Louisa, none of this was my doing.' She didn't believe her own words. She could have prevented Silas from entering the house, if she had really wanted to. 'I'll do my best.'

Louisa softened. 'That's all tha can do, I suppose.'

Once inside the town hall, Harriet stopped and took off her bonnet, smoothing her hair away from her face with gloved hands. She knew there were cells beneath the polished wood under her feet and that Silas was already, or soon would be, locked in one of them. The court rooms were upstairs. Perhaps he might appear in the very same room Harriet had observed the goings-on of the inquest at the end of March. It felt an age ago. How her life had changed in a few short months. But it wasn't Silas she had come to find.

'Hello, Miss Wragg!'

She was gratified to see the same clerk who had thanked her for her help with the claims walking towards her.

She put on her most charming smile. 'How lovely to see you again.' She had forgotten his name. 'And how fortuitous! I believe you are the very person who can help me today.'

The clerk led her into the chamber in which the inquest had been held, past the empty benches and to the back wall of the room. He rapped his knuckles on the wood panelling and turned to wink at Harriet. She raised her eyebrows, playing along; she had already spotted the vertical crack that indicated a hidden door. There was a muttered 'Yes, yes, enter' from behind the wall which, when the clerk pushed on it, swung open to reveal a cell-like room dominated by a mahogany table and a floor-to-ceiling bookcase. A small window framed a view of the grandly appointed Royal Hotel on the opposite corner of the boulevard, the first port of call for many of those who disembarked at Victoria Station. Her brother had stayed there on his most recent visit from London and she and Walter had taken tea with him in the ground floor cafe.

Partly obscuring this view was a man sitting on the windowsill, using a magnifying glass to examine the small print in a book he was holding. When he looked up

Harriet recognised him as the judge who had presided over the inquest.

'I see Frank has shown you my hidey-hole,' he said to her, smiling.

'This is Miss Harriet Wragg. She's begged a few minutes of your time, sir.' The clerk nodded encouragingly to her and left the room.

'A few minutes is all I have, Miss Wragg.'

How should she begin? 'I wonder if you can help me, sir...' She stopped, frustrated with herself. She was here now. She must not waste the few minutes granted her.

'If Frank brought you to my den then I am sure you must be deserving of help.' He shut the book with a snap. 'You might think this room is a sign of the overcrowding that results when you try to pour a quart of civic business into a pint-pot of a town hall, but it is my very favourite space in the whole building. John Webster, at your service.'

Chapter 34

A bucket was suspended by a rope from a gantry. Gunson watched it swing, empty, in the breeze. Beneath it stretched the temporary railway laid to carry supplies to the site, depressingly deserted. No navvies leaned on shovels, complaining about the mud in the tunnels, the ache in their back, the imperviousness of the ground in the basin that would become Agden reservoir if only work could be resumed.

A raven shook the branch of a nearby tree and croaked loudly. In a distant field a cow mooed. Then silence reigned. Gunson sighed and turned back to Webster, who was standing at the foot of a slope of rubble three times his height.

'Will this form part of the embankment, John?'

'Yes. You see the rails here,' he pointed, 'that run along the base of it. They'll be used for infill when they've served their purpose. It's ugly sight now, during construction…'

'Of course.'

'… but Agden will blend into the valleyscape, and in years to come, visitors will not question why or how, they will simply enjoy the tranquil beauty of it, on the very doorstep of the town.'

He'd driven Webster out to the site hoping that the man would be as dismayed as he to see it laying idle. Agden was a mile from the gorge that had been Dale Dyke reservoir and the journey here had taken them through some of the altered landscape. They had skirted a wrecked mill, its crumbled walls jutting into the sky as useless as rotting teeth in an old crone's mouth, and passed near the home of George Swinden, the site foreman who had pulled Gunson from the path of the deluge. Were it not for George, he would have been crushed to death in the valve house, another victim to add to the chief constable's tally.

He shuddered. He'd escaped the deluge only to be swept up in political machinations that had him swirling out of his depth.

Webster was picking his way carefully over the rails. 'A feat of engineering, indeed.'

One of his peers had even gone so far as to describe his dam as lamentably defective. *Lamentably defective.* A wave of loneliness engulfed Gunson.

'… never thought I should become so knowledgeable about the efficacy, or otherwise, of puddle walls. John?'

Gunson grunted.

'You were in a world of your own there.'

'It merely disconcerts me to see the place deserted,' he said. 'The inquiry is now complete and we are eager to resume work here.'

'I have enjoyed learning about your business. Recently, I've been reading about Toxteth, the new Liverpool reservoir that has been built underground. I have seen illustrations. It is most impressive.'

'Yes.' Gunson smiled. 'I am cognisant with Toxteth.'

'At least that type of reservoir does not hang dangerously over one's town.'

Gunson hid his impatience. 'The one cannot be compared against the other.'

Webster nodded. 'There is beauty and power combined in our reservoirs, I can appreciate that. I suppose we would lose the majesty if they were buried away, though it is a shame when that majesty turns savage.' He cleared his throat. 'I am not trying to rile you, John. I do enjoy the architecture as much as the lake, the turrets and balustrading, the careful thought that goes into the design to make it more than workmanlike. Perhaps that is where an underground reservoir fails to please.'

'I was thinking more of the cubic capacity,' said Gunson. 'Toxteth holds only two million gallons of water to serve a small area. Our reservoirs aim to satisfy the demands of the town now and in the future.'

'Well.' Webster turned to look down the valley. 'It is always a pleasure to escape from the soot and smoke of the town and breathe in the fresh country air. You want to resume Agden works and I am sympathetic to that, despite the very many and wonderfully contradictory opinions in your profession about the cause of your last dam's collapse.'

Gunson kept his tone mild. 'We contend a landslip was a contributing factor. In any event, we're mindful of the points that have been made. Agden here,' he gestured to the scene below, 'we can't delay for much longer. The mill owners, the factories and the inhabitants of the town need clean water and it will be on our heads if supplies dry up again this summer and we are forced to apply curfews.'

'I agree with you on that.' Webster laughed. 'I fully agree. So instead of preaching to the converted, tell me why you really asked me to accompany you today.'

'Why, getting construction underway again was certainly one of the reasons,' said Gunson. 'I must admit I had not expected you to be so sympathetic, especially after

Rawlinson's report, which may have leaned towards your jurymen's assertion that the engineering was at fault...'

'It did more than lean, John. It positively genuflected.' Webster tucked his thumbs into his waistcoat. 'But let us get to the point.'

Gunson rubbed his beard. 'I am a mere employee...'

'The chief engineer, no less, and architect of our water supply. Sometimes your diffidence does you no credit, John.'

'Let me speak, then. I see how diligent the company is and how committed to supplying this town, and has been for the past thirty years. I doubt the town could run water services more cost effectively.'

'Ah, we are back to that.'

'Of course. We're setting the rate increase not for the benefit of shareholders but so that we can meet our obligations to the town, and that is in the provision of a constant supply of water, as well as meeting the costs of compensation to those who suffered losses in the misadventure.'

'Misadventure, you say.' Webster sighed. 'An interesting choice of word. I saw the bodies laid out in the workhouse, young and old together. I saw the people come in to identify their dead. You were there, too, John. And yet you speak of "misadventure".'

'I have heard the flood described otherwise, for example, as a disgrace to science. I prefer not to use such inflammatory language. All I want to do is build reservoirs.'

'You could build them as an employee of the Corporation.'

Gunson sighed. 'Shall we return to town?'

Webster said, 'I am sorry, I do not wish to toy with you. You must know I admire you, John. I know you are a man dedicated to his work. It's a simple matter. The council is proposing to purchase the waterworks company, but it is contingent on whether you put up the rate by twenty-five per cent. Some twelve thousand people of the town have signed a petition against it.'

'It is difficult to follow the correct path when it is befogged by the stirring up of enmity between men.'

Webster nodded slowly. 'You are correct. I admit I may have been less than impartial at the inquest and spoke more strongly than certain people might have liked.'

Gunson couldn't hide his exasperation this time. 'You went too far. The courtroom is not the place for the realm of imagination.'

Webster spread his hands and chuckled. 'John, John. I am agreeing with you. I can see that work must resume as soon as possible on this reservoir and on a replacement for Dale Dyke. But your company has such stringent power over the inhabitants of this town. Legal warfare is sometimes the only recourse. But I would not wish to hinder the supply of water in anyway, and can lend my voice in support of that. I will promise to keep an open mind when the resolution to purchase is put to the vote in council.' Webster found a patch of scrub and shuffled his feet through the green stems. 'My goodness, mud sticks, doesn't it?'

He waited for Gunson to follow.

'Do you know,' he said, 'Her Royal Highness sent a personal cheque for two hundred pounds to help those destituted by the flood?'

'She can afford it,' said Gunson, gruffly.

'Ah, but what about the working man who needs every penny he earns? All of Sheffield's workers gave a day's wage.'

'That is commendable.'

'They did their bit. Perhaps you can do yours, John.' He inspected the soles of his shoes. 'That's better. Still need a good polish though. I have a small favour to ask of you.'

'What is it?' Gunson regarded the man beside him warily.

'Oh, nothing onerous, John. An impetuous youth, in need of employment and some help in being steered back onto a righteous path. I wonder will you take him on, guide him? It would save him from jail, or worse.'

'My goodness, what has he done?'

'He entered the home of a gentleman and attacked him, allegedly. The man sustained grievous injuries and might have died.'

'You think this boy is innocent, though.'

'Yes, I do. A most persuasive case was made by a young lady of the town whom the lad is most fortunate to count as a friend. Take him on as your protégé and show me that your company has a heart.'

'I believe you are enlisting me in one of your causes.'

'Yes,' Webster chuckled. 'I believe I am.'

Chapter 35

Silas heard the bolt drawn in the cellar door above him and scrambled up, stiff and clumsy. He'd spent the night on a wooden pallet with a horse blanket for a cover, finally making a nest of the scratchy material and huddling in a sitting position against the damp wall.

But his lack of sleep had just as much to do with his companion as the cold. A filthy creature had been curled up in the corner of the cellar, stinking of alcohol and piss and snoring heartily. At one point during the long night, this cellmate had got up from the floor and climbed on the pallet. Silas felt hot breath in his ear and slim fingers ferreting under the blanket, searching for his crotch. He'd cried out and felt the terror of knowing that nobody would come. His wrist had been seized and his hand placed on a heavy, bare breast before he could snatch it away. Silas gave the woman a hard shove and she retreated to her corner, muttering under her breath.

Now, a square of light from the top of the cellar stairs brought scant illumination into the room. Silas could see a head of wild grey hair poking out from the bundle of rags in the corner.

'Come on then, Meg. Let's get thee up and out.' A man trod heavily down the wooden stairs and prodded the bundle of rags. Silas recognised him as one of the two constables who had taken him from the King's Arms, the man who had gripped his arm so hard he'd thought the muscle would pop. He shrank back.

'A five-shilling fine this'll cost thee, so better get earnin' again, eh?' The constable looked across at Silas. 'Tha's got a visitor.'

Silas's heart leapt, but then he remembered where he was. Harriet must not see him in this state, sharing the cellar with a drunken prostitute. He must stink to high heaven, too. How had he been brought so low, so quickly? The constable was pulling the woman to her feet.

'Come on, let's have thee.'

The pair of them disappeared up the stairs, but the door remained open. Was he expected to go up or would that be viewed as an attempt to escape, and added to his list of transgressions? It might well be a trap. Silas stood in the centre of the room, uncertain. He needed to urinate and eyed the bucket. A visitor. Perhaps it was Mr Boothby, come to gloat. The door remained open and there was nothing but silence beyond it. An age passed. What should he do?

Then the light from the doorway was eclipsed.

'Silas. I've brought thee summat to eat.'

It was Louisa. She edged down the narrow stairs, carrying a wicker basket. Silas turned his back but there was nowhere to go, nowhere to hide his shame, and so he sat down on his makeshift bed and put his head in his hands.

'Don't fret, love. Here, 'ave some o' this.' She shoved a still warm wedge of bread into his hand. 'I brought thee this an' all.' He took the bottle of ale from her. Now his hands were full and he had to look at her.

'Thank you.'

'I got a bottle for 'im upstairs an' all, a bottle o' whisky. Loosened 'is lips nicely.'

She sat beside him.

'What's goin' on?' he said. 'I've done nowt wrong.'

'I know that, o' course. But it looks like they're charging thee wi' grievous bodily harm.'

'But I never…'

'Shush up.' She patted his knee. 'Eat your bread and sup your ale an' listen. Do as tha told for once.'

Silas's mouth was dry. He squeezed the bread in his hands and listened. Louisa told him he'd been brought to the station in Hillfoot after his arrest. The station was the constable's cottage and miscreants were locked in the cellar until they could be taken to the police headquarters at the town hall. There he would be formally charged and transferred to jail – a proper jail, probably Wakefield – until his trial.

'How did you know?'

'Your landlady. Elsie, is it? She asked yer pal Jim if you 'ad any people, any family, and he pointed her to me.'

A lump rose in Silas's throat.

'I can't eat this,' he said.

She took the bread off him. 'Here.' She rummaged in the basket. ''Av a go at this.'

He bit into the apple she handed him. It was juicy and sour. He'd had a bag of apples when he ran away from home. He recalled they had a sweeter taste. Shandy had one, and he gave his last apple to the horse that was hitched to a gig near the reservoir. It could have been a hundred years ago, and only yesterday.

'I'm told they won't charge thee with attempted murder, although they reckon tha could 'ave killed 'im.

Tha'd definitely 'ang for that, so it's a mercy the uncle's still breathin'.'

Silas gulped to dislodge the piece of apple that was stuck in his throat like a piece of glass. 'No mercy at all! Not if I'm to spend the rest of me life in jail. I might as well 'ave drowned in that flood.' He dropped his head. 'What about Harriet? She were there. He were fallin' and I tried to steady 'im, an' she were there. Has tha seen her?'

'Harriet? No. She'll not be allowed anywhere near thee. An' it'd be her word against two so-called gentlemen. And tha's a foreigner here, don't forget that. That friend of her uncle reckons tha's been gunning for Walter Simpson for a while.'

'What's that mean?'

'Stalkin' him. Chasin' after his riches, pretendin' a friendship wi' his innocent little niece.'

He jumped to his feet and threw the apple she had given him against the wall, where it exploded satisfyingly against the flaking whitewash. He clenched his fists. 'No!'

'Calm theesen down, tha worse than a bairn. Tha'll be stamping tha foot next!'

'But it's lies, the lot o' it.' A terrible thought occurred to him. 'Harriet doesn't think I were 'aving her on, does she?'

'No.' Louisa frowned.

'What?'

'They reckon you 'ad a go at Walter in the King's Arms. Drove him out, he were terrified. So what were that all about?'

Silas frowned and spoke slowly, recalling the time he'd seen Walter and his friend drinking whisky and had wanted only to thank the man. 'Aye. I did go over to 'im. I were polite.'

'So tha weren't demanding to see Harriet?'

'No! Well, I weren't demandin'. I asked, that were all. I'll tell the judge that, an' all.'

Now he was filled with the desire to tell his side of the story. His name was being blackened while he remained down here, as helpless as a rat in a trap.

'I have to ask thee summat else, Silas. Did tha follow Walter and his friend home, so tha could find out where he lived?'

His stomach dropped.

'Oh Silas, I can tell from tha face that tha did.'

After Louisa had gone, the constable returned, waving a set of handcuffs in Silas's face. 'Come on, lad.'

To his horror, the journey to the town hall was to be made on a public bus. He was led to the back, his neck prickling from the curious stares of the other passengers. Pushed down onto the bench, he dropped his head and studied the straw around his boots. The constable sat tight against him, as if afraid he'd make a run for it. His humiliation was complete. It couldn't get worse than this. He'd never bear it.

At the town hall, he was walked down to the bowels of the building and wished that he had paid more attention to the outdoors, even just a glimpse of the sky or a tree or a chimney stack might have lessened the dread of another windowless room. His new prison wasn't much bigger than a coffin. A shelf bed took up most of the space. He had a blanket and a bucket. There was no pretending this was a cellar in an ordinary house. He was in a proper cell now, but at least he had it to himself. The thought of sharing a cell filled him with terror.

He had been confined for three or four nights when he received a new visitor.

It had frightened him how quickly the monotony of the days caused him to lose track of time. Louisa had been to see him twice more, bringing bread and fruit and ham. Otherwise he'd be sustaining himself on the milk porridge, meat hash and weak coffee that was delivered daily by the young lad who also had the job of removing Silas's waste bucket. Silas had attempted to communicate with him, had said hello, told him he knew another boy about his age who was called Adam and what was his name? 'Joseph,' the youngster whispered, clearly terrified of him. He wanted to tell the boy his side of the story, but how could he expect to be believed, a foreigner locked up in a cell with a bucket of piss for company?

Now, he could hear the key in the lock and Joseph appeared with a chair which he placed just inside the door. He sidled away, ignoring Silas's inquiring look.

A woman about his mother's age came into the cell and looked around nervously before settling her eyes on Silas. She wore a spotted green silk dress with a white lace collar and cuffs and her pale hair was netted. A simple, but expensive rig-out, even Silas could see that. His mother had never owned such a dress.

'Good morning, I'm Mrs John Gunson,' she said in a voice so soft he could barely make out the words. She sat on the chair.

Silas brushed his fringe away from his eyes and waited. He didn't want to say anything that might incriminate him further.

'Do you have parents, Silas, that we might contact?'

'No!' He'd startled her. 'Sorry, but no. They're not bothered about me.' This sounded self-pitying and was not what he meant. 'I mean, I got my landlady to write to 'em, after the flood, just so as to say I was alive, but I never 'eard back.' He was impatient now. Was this why she was here? 'It doesn't make no odds. They don't need to know. I don't need 'em.'

'I understand. My husband asked me to come and see you – to see what I thought of you – before he makes his decision.'

'What d'you mean?'

'Mr Gunson has been asked to mentor you. Do you know what that means?'

Silas shook his head. 'Is it better'n jail?'

She laughed a little, in a nice way, and he found himself warming to her. 'Much better, yes. At least, I hope you would find it so. Your friend made a persuasive case for your release.'

His heart thudded. 'My release? What friend? Louisa?'

'Be still and I'll explain. A young lady called Harriet Wragg.'

'Harriet!'

'Yes. She visited one of the town judges to explain the events that transpired at her uncle's residence. It's been suggested you should come to stay with us and be set to work. You have been treated unfairly, it seems. I wouldn't presume to take the place of your mother, but I have raised three boys, so I do have some experience in that regard.' She held up her hand, as if to forestall any argument, when Silas jumped to his feet and began pacing the cell. 'I understand you are not a child, but you are not a man yet, and hot-headed youth might benefit from some advice intended most kindly.'

'Harriet? She's helpin' me, then? Has tha seen her? Will I…'

'Calm down, Silas. You are like a caged lion at the zoo.'

He stopped in his tracks. 'What's this judge like? Is he really takin' her word for it, o'er Walter and that other one, tellin' their lies? That Boothby fella has it in for me. I've never done owt to 'im.'

An amused voice startled them both.

'I hear the judge is a fair man, and perhaps a bane in the lives of some.'

A man stepped into the cell, the starched high collar of his shirt only emphasising his short stature. His beady eyes were penetrating, but he smiled genially enough at Silas.

'How do you do, I'm the presiding judge in your case. You must be Silas.' He bowed to Mrs Gunson. 'Good afternoon.'

'Good afternoon, Mr Webster.'

'I see you have already met our troubled young man.'

Silas opened his mouth to protest, thought better of it and closed it again.

'I am sorry for your plight,' the judge said. 'I think I may have a solution for you that might avoid the Assizes court entirely. The young woman who came to visit me on your behalf presented your case very forcefully. I think she may have saved you.'

'Again,' said Silas.

'Again, Silas?' said Mrs Gunson.

'Harriet already saved me once, from the flood.' He found his legs could no longer support him, and Silas sat on the bed, and wrapped his arms around himself.

'I was the coroner for the inquest into the flood. You've probably read all about that farrago in the newspaper.'

'No. I 'eard enough about it in the King's Arms, though.'

'Well, it seems your young lady saviour has come to the rescue again.' He took out his pocket watch. 'To be brief, I believe what she told me about the circumstances that have brought you here, but you can recognise the difficulty. We have two upstanding gentlemen of the town accusing you, a seeming vagabond with nobody to stand for you.'

'Harriet stands for me.' Saying the words made it real. Silas shook his head, wonderingly. 'Harriet stands for me.'

'She does, she does. But a woman's word won't be taken against that of her uncle or the Grandmaster of the Masons. I have spoken to Mr Boothby...'

'Why not her uncle?'

'He is indisposed. The least said about that, for your sake, the better.' He raised his voice to pre-empt Silas's protests. 'Walter Simpson is dying because of exposure to flood water, not of the injuries he sustained in your presence. Unfortunately, that dreadful calamity continues to claim lives. Calm yourself, Silas. I've spoken to the parties concerned and I now intend to lay out the terms of your release, which all are agreed upon. You should consider yourself a very lucky young man.'

Mrs Gunson nodded her agreement.

Silas felt at once grateful and guilty. Harriet had not visited him and although he suspected it was because she had been forbidden, he had nevertheless felt abandoned by her. Now he was learning that she had fought his corner. The judge was still talking, but Silas wasn't listening. He was overwhelmed by the urge to find Harriet, to kiss her again and again and again and damn the consequences.

'And so you come full circle, Silas, to find gainful employment in helping to rebuild the very thing that nearly killed you.'

He had no idea what the man was talking about, but he looked very satisfied with himself.

'Now, Silas. There has also to be a reckoning in these things, a punishment that must be endured.'

'A punishment? But I've done nowt wrong!'

'Please, just listen, Silas,' said Mrs Gunson.

'Mr Boothby is not satisfied. He wanted to see you hanged or locked up for life where you'd spend your days picking oakum. I'm afraid it pains me greatly, but there has to be a public atonement, a warning to those who would prevent the inhabitants of the town from feeling safe in their own homes. Additionally, it will be viewed as a further crime—'

'I've not committed a crime at all.'

'—if you attempt to re-establish your friendship with Harriet Wragg. It would not be appropriate. The young lady is betrothed to be wed. These are the terms. I strongly recommend them to you.'

Silas interlaced his fingers behind his skull and lowered his head to his knees. He stared at a crack in the flagstone, followed it to the thin thread between the next flagstone and the next. A beetle lumbered out from under the bed and wandered towards the toe of the judge's polished shoe. Silas stared at his own dusty boots. Betrothed. It was impossible. And who to? That Boothby fella? Harriet never would marry that man. The judge was lying, a ruse to discourage him from seeing Harriet. He would see her again. Let them try to stop him.

'What punishment?' he mumbled.

'Silas. Sit up. You are making me impatient. Remember I am trying to help you.'

They could run away together. He had done it before and now he had money stashed in a bureau in his room at the King's Arms and believed himself wiser to the world. The town he'd had such high hopes of had betrayed him, twice. He was done with it. They would go far away, to Chesterfield or Nottingham, or even to the coast to live out their days by the sea. Betrothed. The word was a boulder pressing on his neck.

'Aye, I know thou art.' He lifted his head. 'What's this punishment then, that'll get me out of 'ere?'

Chapter 36

Harriet Wragg would disappear. She would be transformed, turned to a new purpose. Mrs Albert Boothby.
Turning meant curdling, too. Milk gone sour.

'Ow!' She inspected the bead of blood on her finger
and sucked it, laying aside the offending needle. How
many times had she consoled Alice over a punctured
fingertip? If she had a daughter she would name her
for her cousin and teach her the art of embroidery. She
would be an obedient wife by then. She had always been
obedient before, accepted her lot. But since the flood,
rebellious thoughts had stirred the silt of her mind. The
old Harriet Wragg would never have taken matters into
her own hands in an attempt to save Silas from the noose.
And she could see clearly now that Mrs Albert Boothby
would not be allowed to ink her delicate fingers in a
clerical job.

What sort of future might await a woman named
Harriet Hinchcliffe?

She looked up from the tapestry, momentarily blinded
by the shaft of sunlight she was sitting in. Ludicrous
thought. She would not secure a future on one kiss, albeit
a thrilling kiss, a kiss she had returned, wanting the feel
of Silas's full lips against hers. Albert Boothby had a thin
mouth. How would it feel to kiss those lips? She could
not imagine. She would soon find out.

Harriet took a slow deep breath, in and out. Her bedroom still gave off the woolly aroma of new carpeting and the cloying scent of freshly varnished furniture. It was not her furniture. It belonged to Walter and would pass to her brother James to hold in trust for her cousins when Walter died. Her uncle had told her he would live to see her married, but the doctor thought otherwise. 'Let him believe it,' the man had told her. 'It does no harm.'

Her finger had stopped bleeding. Harriet picked up the needle again. She had redrawn the outline of the princess on the precious embroidery her mother had started but never got the opportunity to finish, of a gowned and crowned girl with red hair. After the flood, she had found the fabric on the ruined carpet. The red thread of the girl's hair was intact and Harriet had carefully washed the cotton. It came out miraculously unmarked. She had re-stretched it over a new wooden frame, determined to finally finish the piece her mother had started. She kept the tiara because the stitching around that was already complete and she could not bear to undo any of her mother's work. But she altered the gown to reflect the latest fashion, sharpening the waist to a point, supplying a bustle and a high-necked collar. The princess was no longer a fluffed up, feathered thing on her way to a ball to meet her prince. She was dressed for an outing, wearing a tiara. An eccentric. She had added a delicate umbrella with lace trim. The face she kept blank.

A series of thuds and shouts from upstairs interrupted her reverie. Harriet sighed. She ought to have known the boys would not keep to their spelling and numbers for long, despite the promise of a magic lantern show if they applied themselves. She would set them straight and visit Polly.

Her aunt was sewing, too, stitching into shape a series of knitted garments for the children of the poor. Polly had started on this after the flood, when Harriet told her she had donated all the clothing they could spare for the poor souls who had lost everything. Polly enjoyed knitting and sewing tiny jackets and bonnets and boots for babies, to be delivered to the workhouse for distribution. The plain work was taken on by Sadie, who complained mightily about the boys' ability to wear holes in the seat and knees of their trousers on what she reckoned was a daily basis.

Sadie was sitting on the chair by the bed when Harriet entered.

'Hello, Aunt. I'm restoring Mother's embroidery and lost track of time. Shall I make some tea?'

Sadie swung her head from side to side, an affectation of world-weariness that set Harriet's teeth on edge. 'A young lady and her fancy work. I wish I had the hours in the day. It's not me that's getting wed to a rich gentleman though, is it? No need for me to get familiar with the finer accomplishments.'

Polly smiled, a thin-lipped smile that Harriet couldn't interpret.

'Yes please, I would like tea,' she said. 'Is Mr Boothby joining us tonight?'

It made no difference to Polly, who would have her dinner brought up to her on a tray, as usual. Walter ate very little and never left Alice's room now. Harriet wondered how long it had been since her aunt and uncle saw each other. Polly never complained about his absence.

Harriet either ate with Mr Boothby in the dining room or had an early meal with the boys in the kitchen. On his most recent visit, Mr Boothby and Harriet had repaired to the parlour after supper and he had watched her read by the fire until she became uncomfortable and the words made no sense. He had waited for her to look at him and had laid his pipe aside.

'I wish you to call me by my Christian name, as my late wife did,' he said. 'I think it would be appropriate.'

She had nodded.

'I should like to hear you say it.'

'Of course. Albert.'

It felt alien on her tongue.

'And you will end your association with that girl.'

Harriet cast about, trying to think who he might mean. 'Louisa?'

'Yes. We shall find you new friends who are not of the servant class. Do you know, Walter does not approve of your friendship either. It doesn't do. They begin to take advantage when it comes to discussion of wages and suchlike.'

Harriet had been stung, but was determined not to show it. 'As you wish, Mr... Albert. I have to say that Louisa has been a good friend to me.'

He had looked pained. 'I can inform you through certain sources I have that the girl keeps unsavoury company. A pretty face can be a curse for a poor young woman.' He had paused, his mouth slightly open, his lips moist-looking in the firelight. 'She's been seen lifting her skirts in Spital Hill.'

Harriet had no idea what he was talking about. 'What does...'

He had licked his lips and interrupted her. 'I'm glad it's beyond your understanding. Suffice to say, I shouldn't be surprised if that girl ends up in a reformatory. Don't frown, you'll ruin your lovely face, Hetty.'

Hetty. Silas had occasionally shortened her name, in jest because he knew she disliked it. His teasing had given her the opportunity to tickle him, to play her fingers over his vest and feel the hard muscles of his stomach. When Mr Boothby called her Hetty, all she felt was revulsion.

'No,' she said now, to Polly. 'Mr Boothby isn't joining us tonight. In fact, I have been invited to a supper party he is hosting.' Albert Boothby had told her to look her prettiest. 'I want to show you off,' he'd said.

Later that evening, Harriet re-entered Polly's room, bashful in the dove-grey taffeta and custom-made satin boots she had purchased with money sent from her brother in London. In his accompanying letter, James had instructed her to buy an evening outfit suitable for the wife of a prominent townsman, and had even given the name of the tailor she should use. The boots had been made by the shoemaker on Fargate she had always gone to; the man had a knack for sculpting a shoe that cradled her bad foot so that she hardly limped. They were as comfortable as a pair of slippers.

Harriet could feel Polly's eyes drinking in every detail of her outfit and she fussed self-consciously with the folds of the skirt. The belt that emphasised her slim waist was rose-coloured, the same shade as the fringes on the short, puffed sleeves and on the neckline that skimmed her collarbone, exposing the tops of her shoulders. She had, for the first time and with Sadie's assistance, used tongs on her hair to create curls and Sadie had twined a black velvet ribbon through them.

'I haven't had the opportunity to wear this yet,' she said. 'Will it do?'

'I should say so.' Polly smiled. 'It's an interesting choice of colour.'

'You don't like it.'

'Harriet, on anybody else it would look dull, but on you it's perfect. It brings out your red hair beautifully.' Her aunt's eyes filled with tears. 'You look lovely, you really do.'

Mr Boothby sent a cab to collect her and she waved gaily to her cousins as she stepped into it, allowing the smile to slip from her face as she settled back for the journey, her stomach clenched in anticipation of the ordeal that lay ahead.

Albert Boothby greeted her at the door to his house, elegant in his white cravat. She was introduced to his friends, immediately forgetting every name as soon as she was given it. Mr Boothby assured her this was an informal gathering, a simple three-course supper for sixteen people, prepared by his cook and served up by hired waiting staff. Of course, he told her, once they were wed she would be in charge of all such arrangements, and he hoped she would indulge any mistakes he made as a mere man trying to do his best on the domestic front.

Harriet was seated beside a woman close to her own age who whispered a joke about the limp and yellowing pineapple that was the table centrepiece, and she found herself relaxing, and thought she might enjoy the evening after all. It was certainly gratifying having her food served to her, instead of making and serving it for others, and exhilarating being in the company of adults. The soup and the main course of roasted pheasant, glazed carrots and peas, were delicious. She declined a second glass of wine when the cheese and croutons were served, although Mr Boothby pressed her to take one; the first had flushed her skin and she knew a second would make her drunk.

After supper, the guests retired to the parlour to admire the new grand piano Albert had bought, an early wedding gift for Harriet. One of the ladies agreed to play and Albert sank into a settee and indicated Harriet should sit by his side by patting the cushion. He talked over her head to the gentleman seated on her other side, remarking that the guest list for the annual Cutler's Feast did not feature any of the directors of the Sheffield Waterworks Company.

'I think you could say the knives are out.' This remark from retired town alderman Mr Gatesby-Taylor generated snorts of laughter from the men and titters from the ladies.

Harriet spoke quietly. 'It is a shame to make jest when so many lost their lives.' Heat rose into her cheeks, but it soon became apparent her remark was being ignored, if it had been listened to in the first place.

'Cutler's Hall is to be expanded, I hear,' Albert said.

One of the men pointed at him. 'A fine project for Boothby, Simpson and Sons?'

'I wouldn't presume. We're up to the job, that's for certain.' Albert drained his glass. 'I'll tell the Master Cutler as much.'

Harriet said, 'Cutler's Hall seems like a grand enough edifice. What more could be added to it? There is much greater need in the town.'

'Such as?' asked the man on her other side.

Harriet said, 'We should build housing for the poor. They suffered more from the flood because they have no reserves to draw on. Oh!'

Albert had nipped her, twisting the soft flesh of her underarm between his fingers. He spoke under his breath, without looking at her. 'Harriet, my dear, you are stepping outside your sphere.' He released her and continued, more loudly. Harriet resisted the urge to rub her arm. 'The Company of Cutlers owns one of the finest Georgian buildings in the town, but their banqueting hall cannot accommodate more than two hundred men. Now,' he gestured to a man standing nearby, 'since four years past, steelmakers are included in this august body. Sheffield steel deserves premises that reflect its standing around the world!'

'Cheers to that!'

Albert held up his glass and a servant came forward to replenish it. 'Now, Harriet.' He offered her his hand and when they were both standing, squeezed her fingers and said, 'I shall leave you to enjoy the company of the ladies.'

Her potential new friend was taking a turn at the piano. Harriet watched the woman's slim fingers, half gloved in a fine black net, move delicately over the keys.

'I cannot play half so well as you,' she said.

'I'm sure that's not true. Let's duet!'

'Not in front of an audience. Perhaps you'll visit me and we can play.'

'Come! Don't be shy. Sit by me.'

Harriet laughed and moved away. 'No, no. I'll only embarrass myself. Perhaps the next time we meet.'

'I shall look forward to it.'

Warmed by this encounter, she approached an older woman, an elegant lady who wore her hair piled high in the old style, a sparkling emerald at her throat, thinking to engage her in conversation, but the woman turned eyes like glass on her, a cold, unyielding gaze that somehow found and pierced the treachery in Harriet's heart. *Why are you here? Don't insult us with this pretence. I see through you.* She spun away, fussing with a doily on the sideboard and fighting down a wave of grief. She was afraid she would faint, and all from a look she had no doubt misinterpreted. She leaned against the wall, partly hidden by the heavy velvet drapes in the window, and tried to compose herself. She had entangled herself with a man she didn't love in order to achieve her uncle's ends, and her own. It was guilt she was feeling; not the heavy burden of guilt she carried over Alice's death, but a nagging feeling of wrongdoing.

She glanced around the room. Nobody was paying her any attention, a relief. Her fingers brushed the wallpaper's soft nap and she closed her eyes, and Silas's face swam before her, his narrow green eyes mocking her, his long fingers delicately lifting her braid so he could put his mouth against her ear. 'She's right, tha knows. What tha doin' wi' this lot when tha should be wi' me?' Harriet smiled, then dropped her eyes, overcome by sadness.

Chapter 37

Rolling waves of terror threatened to overcome him at the thought of the punishment that lay ahead. But he could rant and rave all he liked, locked in this cell in the pitch dark. No one would come.

Mrs Gunson had delivered what she termed 'good news'. The serious charges laid against him had been dropped. There would be no appearance at the York Assizes and Silas would not end up with a criminal record. He had protested his innocence – again – but was coming to the realisation that guilt or innocence had little to do with anything. There were those who meted out punishment, and those who took it, and he was in the latter category.

Mrs Gunson had taken his hand. 'Silas, what is happening to you is wrong, there is no way around it. But listen to me, it will be over by this time tomorrow and you will be able to put it behind you. And we will help you, Mr Gunson and I. We'll keep you to a straight path.'

He had nodded wearily.

After Mrs Gunson had gone, a youth with a patchy beard and a pox-scarred complexion brought in an extra blanket that Silas took from him wordlessly.

'The lady asked me to fetch this. Don't they teach thee any manners where tha from?'

'I thank thee for the blanket.'

'Sarky bastard.' He made fists and jumped lightly from foot to foot, his shadow leaping up the wall behind him. Silas flinched away and the youth laughed and picked up the lamp. 'Farm boy, stinking o' cow shit. Tha knows nowt. This cellar's haunted by a low life like thee that hanged himself in 'ere and good riddance an' all. Watch tha don't bump tha head on his swingin' feet.'

He took the light with him.

Silas cocooned himself in the blanket and lay curled on his side. The pitch dark was a suffocating, almost tangible presence so he closed his eyes against it and tried pretending he was in his own bed at the King's Arms. His ears were as attuned as a bat's, pricking at every sound from outside his cell – a murmur, a rattle of keys, muffled footsteps on the street outside – and then there were no more sounds and he guessed it must be the dead of night. He imagined he felt a breeze across his face, a motion in the air as if it was being disturbed by a swinging body, and he began to sob quietly.

A constable he had not seen before came for him the next morning.

'Put out your hands,' the man said, not unkindly.

Silas did. Humiliatingly, they were shaking hard, his own body betraying him. Similar wrought iron bracelets had been used to circle his wrists when he was taken from the King's Arms, his shoulder blades forced painfully together as his arms were pulled behind his back. This time, his hands were bound in front, almost as if he was in prayer, and he was grateful for this smallest of concessions, recalling his animal terror on the night of his arrest of being unable to save himself should he stumble and fall.

Silas's hair fell in his eyes and he automatically lifted a hand to sweep it back, and bit back a cry of distress when the other followed.

He was led up a narrow flight of stairs. At the top, two burly men stepped forward, dressed in rough wool and wearing heavy boots, and took up position on either side of him. Guards, the constable told him, as he handed over to one of the men the screw key for the handcuffs, come from the prison to carry out your punishment.

Outside, Silas squinted up at the white overcast that was too bright for his eyes, a light drizzle falling on his face.

'Tha's a lucky bugger not to be comin' back wi' us to Wakefield.' The guard who had spoken peered into his face and said to the other man, 'Lad's white as a sheet.'

'Swooner?'

'Prob'ly.'

He was put in the back of a cart where three or four men, all handcuffed, were already sitting, heads bowed. Silas kept his eyes on the sawdust-covered planks. It was a five-minute journey to the marketplace where people swarmed like wasps around the stalls and the air was rich with the smell of fruit and vegetables and fish. As he was pulled from the cart, he saw a boy dart among the gigs and carriages, pushing a barrow full of potatoes before him, and wished he was that boy. A group of half a dozen men in toppers crowded around a nearby tobacco stall and glanced curiously at the new arrivals.

Silas flinched from the yells of costermongers touting for trade and was jostled by those on the fringes of the crowds around the carts. A few of these strangers glanced at him and his captors, then away, and he understood that in their eyes he was just another ruffian, a poor sort, under arrest for stealing or affray. On his way to pay for his sins in the public arena. Worth a look, maybe, if they had time for the spectacle, but otherwise not deserving of a second thought.

Fresh pain twisted his guts. Harriet would be there, he was sure of it. She would be made to witness the degradation orchestrated by Walter Simpson and Albert Boothby. Silas stumbled and was caught by the arm. 'Steady, lad,' said one of the guards. 'We're 'ere. There's a few of thee today. Tha's first, though. Gettin' the most licks. What did tha do to deserve that, eh?'

'I did nowt,' he mumbled.

'Aye, I might've 'eard that one before.'

The other man tugged him to a halt. 'Soon be over and done wi'. Might make thee think twice about gettin' theesen in trouble.'

Silas had kept his eyes lowered during the short walk across the cobbles, but raised his head now and saw he was at the top of the town square where the market was held. A black-hatted woman about his mother's age, wearing a long apron over her skirts and wielding a wicker basket, glared at him and muttered words he was glad he couldn't catch. In front of him was a wooden frame. He felt his gorge rise and swallowed painfully. Silas flicked his eyes away from it, breathing heavily through his mouth. A small barefooted boy was staring at him, the thumb of his dirty hand wedged in his mouth and snot coating his upper lip. A girl darted forward and pulled the small boy away. He watched her disappear into the crowd with smarting eyes.

Then the guard blocked his view.

'Yer shirt. Here, I'll do it.'

248

Silas gulped as the man unfastened his shirt and pulled it down from his shoulders and away from his body in one fluid movement. Silas crossed his arms around his torso. There was a jeer from the crowd. The lash could not be worse than the shame of this. He dropped his chin to his chest and squeezed his eyes shut.

A sudden shout – 'Don't thee go fallin' asleep now!' – and more laughter.

Naked from the waist up, he was turned to face the frame and his hands placed through metal rings and secured tightly. He thought his legs were going to be parted and tied to the lower struts of the cross – he had not had anything explained to him, and he scrabbled for purchase with his fingers, panicking – but his feet were left on the ground. Something hit his lower back and he yelped and there was more laughter. A cabbage rolled between his feet.

He turned his head so his cheek rested against the rough wood. He lowered his eyes to the ground, focusing on the wilted and veined leaves of the cabbage and then on the wheels of the empty cart parked behind the frame, the wooden spokes poking from dirt-crusted rims. A high whine in his ears competed with the roaring waterfall of market sounds at his back. Time stood still.

Nothing happened. The rain fell more heavily now, plastering his hair to his face and trickling down his back. Perhaps they'd call it off, this public spectacle, because of the inclement weather. Hysterical laughter bubbled in his throat. He clamped his teeth together.

A pair of feet encased in scuffed boots appeared on the ground alongside him. Silas swivelled his eyes, straining, and saw a man's hand gripping a thick wooden handle from which dangled nine thin cords, each with a knot in the end. The cords almost reached the top of the man's boots.

He'd been whipped before by his father who'd used a leather belt and told Silas he was lucky not to be getting the buckle end. *Next time tha'll get it and tha'll know about it then.*

The feet and the hand holding the whip disappeared from view and Silas was staring at cobbles again. They gleamed blackly in the rain.

There was a soft voice in his ear – 'Turn your 'ead the other way' – and a handful of his hair was grabbed and now he was staring at the pavement on the other side. This was it.

He saw movement nearby, a black bird swooping to the ground, pecking at spilled grain. A foot in a polished black shoe kicked at it and the bird took off.

'No respect for the occasion,' a voice said, and Silas looked up into the mocking eyes of Albert Boothby. The man nodded, satisfied Silas had seen him, and walked away.

The fury that rose through his body numbed the first strike of the whip, but the second was a lion's claw raking the skin between his shoulder blades. Silas gasped and quivered in anticipation of the next blow. It came, white-hot agony against his lower back. He had been determined not to scream. On the fourth blow, which followed the same path as the first and ripped open skin that was already on fire, he did. The fifth blow flicked his ribs, less forcefully. There were boos from the spectators. Then the sixth struck him below the nape of the neck. Silas jerked in surprise and bit down on his tongue, flooding his mouth with the metallic taste of blood.

A pause. He pressed his forehead against the wet and unyielding iron, swallowing blood. They had told him there would be twenty-five lashes. Were they showing some mercy, at last?

Two sets of boots stamped past in opposite directions.

'That were weak, Georgie. My turn. Gi' thee weedy arm a rest.'

Chapter 38

Harriet woke early to a silence so deep she knew immediately that Walter was dead.

She swung her feet out of bed and stood on the rug, suddenly at a loss. What should she do? Alert the doctor. Then tell Polly and her cousins. No, no, that wouldn't do. Tell Polly and the children first, then send Sadie for the doctor when she arrived for work. Harriet looked at the clock. It was five in the morning, still dark. What had woken her? The absence of sound. She had fallen asleep listening to Walter's weak coughs and groans through the ceiling, his drowning lungs effortfully dredging up the frothy phlegm that made the sheets stink. It had been a week since the doctor said he could do nothing for Walter other than increase his medication. Her uncle had already been drinking enough laudanum to make into gibberish the few words he was capable of saying. Harriet threw a shawl over her nightgown. She could not risk one of the boys discovering their father dead and she could not trust that they would remain sleeping until it got light.

That meant she must go immediately into her uncle's room, to confirm what she already knew.

Harriet lit a lamp and climbed the stairs quietly. She could hear Polly snoring in the master bedroom. There was no sound from the boys' rooms. She hesitated, clutching the cool porcelain of the doorknob to

Alice's room, trying to picture the scene, to ready herself. He would be lying on the sickbed that had replaced his daughter's smaller cot. Would he be safe under the covers, or half out of bed, his head hanging limply over the bucket, the white nape of his neck exposed? She closed her eyes, relinquished the doorknob and instead knocked gently on the door, clinging onto the hope that she might be wrong. No sound from within. She could not delay any longer. Harriet eased the door open, leading with the lamp. In the dim light, Walter was a hunched shape on the bed, his face turned mercifully away.

'Uncle?'

The room stank of sweat and vomit and something rotten. Breathing shallowly, Harriet screwed up all her courage and reached out to touch his shoulder. The thin material of his nightgown was damp and chill.

'Uncle Walter?'

A choking sob broke the deathly silence. Harriet realised the sound had come from her and clasped her hand over her mouth. She backed away quietly, keeping her eyes on the shape in the bed, her heart hammering, waiting for him to rise up and point an accusing finger. She was to blame. He had saved her and lost Alice and was finally a victim of the flood, condemned to the slowest of deaths by drowning.

Albert Boothby arrived two days later to pay his respects and Harriet showed him into the room where her uncle lay. He approached the coffin sideways, like a crab, and she was afraid she would laugh and then become hysterical. She pressed her fingers against her lips. Now she was overwhelmed by sadness and allowed tears to slip down her face. Mr Boothby wouldn't notice her distress in the gloom. The curtains were drawn, as they were throughout the house, and all the mirrors had been covered at Polly's insistence. And when Walter was taken out of the house to be buried, her aunt had instructed that the body must go feet first so that Walter could not beckon the living to follow him into death. Silly superstitions, but Polly must be indulged. As for Harriet, she would be relieved when Walter's corpse was gone. There was nothing of him in the cold body laid out for all to come and see.

She had been doing some half-hearted gardening when Mr Boothby arrived. Now, she slipped out of the mourning room to wash her hands in the scullery. She was scrubbing her fingers with a nailbrush when he tracked her down.

'I shall arrange for Walter to have an obituary in the *Telegraph*,' he said.

He paused then, and she wondered if he was waiting for her to thank him for honouring her uncle with a notice in the paper. She rubbed her cheek, which was damp.

'You have dirt on your face,' he said. 'Harriet, I thought you might be happier to see me. You must allow yourself to look to me for comfort now. I'm to be your husband and protector.'

'I have been looking forward to your visit.' She wondered whether she should broach the subject of delaying their impending nuptials, whether he would understand that she was suffocated by grief and needed space to breathe. She swallowed. 'Albert, I...'

'Look at this.' He touched her face and showed her his dirt-streaked fingertips.

She let out a sigh. 'It must be soot. I had some kept back for me when the chimney was last swept, to spread on the soil. I've been planting out, Albert.' It still felt unnatural, saying his name. 'Onions, asparagus, beets.' She smiled gamely. 'It cheers me, to grow things.'

'Soot? I would have thought there's more than enough of that in this town.'

Without warning, he took her chin in his hand, wet his finger and rubbed her cheekbone with it. 'There's a perfectly serviceable greengrocers not half a mile away. You're doing the poor fellow and his family out of trade. Did you think of that?' He kissed her firmly on the lips and stepped back. Harriet was stunned. She used the back of her hand to wipe away the spit he'd left on her cheek.

'Come, Harriet,' he laughed, clearly delighted with himself. 'We are to be wed soon, in accordance with your dear uncle's last wishes, joining our two families in blood as well as business. I think a kiss is permissible.'

She forced herself to meet his gaze. 'I've been thinking...'

'Always a dangerous occupation for a woman.'

'Haha. You are droll.' She untied the strings of her gardening smock and pulled it over her head quickly. 'I'd like to suggest that after the funeral we observe a suitable period of mourning before we have our celebration.' He looked at her, his face unreadable. 'I think it's appropriate to delay the wedding, just for a short while. I'm worried for my aunt, now she is alone. Adam is soon leaving for boarding school...'

'Quite. Funded by me. And the younger two shall follow him if I have a say in it. Polly has Sadie to look after her and can continue to lig around, growing fatter and more stupid with each passing day.'

Harriet was aghast. He would never have dared to speak so when Walter was alive.

'And your duty will be to your husband.' He cocked his head, reminding her of the parrots in the botanical gardens, and now she was thinking about Silas and was certain it must show on her face. She watched the water swirling in the sink. 'Really, Harriet. You should be grateful that I am prepared to take responsibility for you. Come to me.'

He held out his arms and she could think of no reason not to step forward. She had made her bed and now she must lie in it. She managed to suppress a shudder at the thought of laying in a bed beside this man; she could not imagine it and it was better not to think of it. Not yet. She did not love him; she did not even respect him. She could go to London, to live with James and his fiancée. James would take her in. But then what would happen, with Walter gone, to Polly and Adam and the younger boys? Her marriage to Albert Boothby would secure the future of her cousins and keep Polly safe, and Silas, too. Boothby had won, and he would be satisfied with that and let Silas be. She could engineer no alternative fate for herself. She could hear Polly's voice inside her head. *Men hold all the cards in this world and are permitted to cheat, while women must make the best of the hand they're given.*

Albert Boothby enfolded her in a tight embrace. He smelled of sweat and cigars. She returned the embrace, resting her head lightly on his shoulder. Walter would still be alive if she had managed to keep hold of Alice, if Harriet hadn't lost her in the swirling torrent, if Walter had not dived into the filthy water time and time again, filling his lungs with the poison that had eventually killed him. Dear Alice. She would name her first girl Alice. That thought brought some comfort. She would keep herself busy, running the household, raising her children, and perhaps eventually she would come to love, or at least respect, the man whose arms caged her now, and forevermore.

Eventually, he released her and examined her tear-stained face.

'Grief can addle the mind. You must trust me, Harriet. You threw a spanner in the works when you consorted with that boy, I have to say it. But reason prevailed and three weeks from now you shall be my wife.' He patted her back. 'He's had his licks. If I were him, if I could conceive of putting myself in his grubby shoes, I should return from whence I came.'

Harriet stiffened and he stepped back to scrutinise her face, holding her by the shoulders. She wanted to affect disinterest, but her reddening cheeks betrayed her. Her eyes filled with tears again and she flinched away from his huff of disgust.

'What is the appeal of that low life?'

'What do you mean,' she whispered, 'by licks?'

'Cat licks.'

The kitchen door slammed and they heard Adam call out a greeting. Boothby's fingers squeezed her shoulders before he let go of her.

'No fewer than twenty-five cat licks,' he said, a smirk of satisfaction on his face. 'I was there, to witness it. I heard you had intervened on his behalf. It's to your credit, my dear, that he finally had some sense beat into him.'

Chapter 39

The red and white bricked facade of the Royal Voluntary Hospital on West Street was spitting distance from Gunson's office and he decided it would do him good to stretch his legs before returning home, even if that involved entering a cesspit of death and disease.

A viewing of the young man was required before Gunson brought the youth into his home. He could remain dispassionate, establish whether he was dealing with a nefarious individual, or a victim of mistreatment, as John Webster asserted. Charlotte had also spoken up for the boy, but his wife's womanly qualities of compassion and pity, while admirable, might well have clouded her judgement.

He followed his nose to the main ward, trying not to breathe in too deeply the stomach-churning stench that seemed to be made up of a combination of cabbage, blood and dirty bodies. Every bed was occupied by patients in varying degrees of distress and nurses and visitors milled around. He recognised his doctor, Doctor Jepson, who volunteered at the Royal as he claimed, 'for the experience of treating the variety of disease', honing his skills at the infirmary, while making a private income from people such as Gunson who could afford to be treated at home. Jepson was surrounded by relatives at the foot of one of the beds, but waved his arm to direct Gunson to the bed at the end of the noisy room.

The patient he was here to see had no visitors in attendance.

His first sight of the boy drew a gasp he hoped went unheard. He lay curled up, facing the wall, the flayed skin of his back exposed for all to see, as vulnerable as an unguarded infant. Gunson was aghast. He moved closer to examine the wounds, shaking his head in disbelief. The boy would be deeply scarred for life. Whatever crime was alleged to have been committed could not have warranted such barbaric treatment. He moved his gaze to the head of dark curls that rested on the pillow; they reminded Gunson of his oldest son and he wondered where this boy's people were. Obeying an urge to show some tenderness, he began to pull up the sheet that was puddled around the youth's waist, but a young nurse hurried over and laid her hand on his wrist.

'Better to let the air get to it,' she said.

He nodded mute agreement. The deep, livid gouges covered the boy's back, with only a few patches of uninjured skin pinkly shining in the mess. The poor fellow looked like a pummelled piece of meat on a butcher's slab.

Gunson walked around the bed, half-hoping he would find the boy sleeping, but he lay awake, staring at the wall. He turned his gaze on Gunson as he arranged his coat-tails to sit self-consciously on a chair hurriedly carried over by the same nurse who had prevented him from covering the boy's wounds.

He coughed, unsure how to start.

The boy spoke first. 'When d'you reckon I'll be out of 'ere?'

His voice was faint and came from lips that were still cracked from the fever he'd endured.

'Tomorrow, I'm told,' Gunson said, and smiled as encouragingly as he could. It wasn't returned. 'You'll be coming to stay at my home and…'

'Tha's not the doctor?'

'Ah, I'm John Gunson. Mr Webster has arranged for you to…'

'Aye, I know. I'm to work under thee.' He coughed and his voice was stronger when he spoke again. 'A *remarkable opportunity* for the likes o' me, eh?'

Gunson smiled again, recognising Webster's patronising tones.

'You have met Mrs Gunson. My wife thinks that we can help you to, er, find a better path, one that won't cross with those that may still wish you harm.' He hurried on when Silas's eyes widened in fear. 'Not that I believe anybody does, now that you have had your… well, it's best to keep a low profile. That's all I shall say about that.'

'All right.' The boy shrugged his shoulder and winced. 'I were set on a steelworks, but I've been labourin' since the flood. I were in a forge when it…' He stopped and gulped. Gunson fought back the urge to stroke his hair. This boy wasn't his son; he was a stranger being offered an opportunity to turn over a new leaf. 'I came to town the same day as that dam burst. Bad luck to me, eh?'

'Bad luck for us all,' said Gunson. It would be best to adopt a brisk tone, to encourage the boy out of his funk. 'But there is work to be done. The thirst of the town is no less.' He paused, but it seemed there were to be no more interruptions. The boy was looking at him, neutrally, but a nerve jumped rhythmically in his cheek. 'Perhaps you'll help me sate that thirst. We've collected your possessions from the King's Arms and you shall take our housekeeper's room. She has moved in with her daughter since the flood. It will please my wife to have an extra pair of hands to help. We have a cook, and a maid of all work, and a stable boy who I think is about your age. How old are you?'

'Nearly nineteen.'

'Ah, good, good. I could use a driver to run errands for my wife. If I need to be anywhere I prefer to drive myself. It's been agreed you'll learn engineering, a fine profession.'

'Engineerin'?'

'Yes, I'm sure you're very grateful for the opportunity?'

'I know nowt about engineerin'.' He seemed to perk up suddenly. 'I've 'eard of Brunel. Railways, bridges. Built half the country, I were told. Aye, I've 'eard o' him.'

Gunson chuckled. 'Have you indeed? Well, you must not run before you can walk. I'll start you with the navvies on the Agden site. You'll get along with them. Um. I mean to say, they are more your people, aren't they?'

'I don't know owt about navvies neither.'

'Never mind. They'll teach you the basics. Evenings you will study reading and writing and mathematics under the expert tutelage of Mrs Gunson. You'll come to my office at the end of each day after working on the site and I'll show you the theory of it.'

He was on comfortable territory now, and warmed to his theme. 'Reservoir building is an essential industry, perhaps the most essential. You know, without a clean and reliable supply of water this town – any town – would wither and die, the wheels of industry stop turning. Stagnation set in. It's our job to prevent that from happening.'

'I saw that dam, Dale Dyke. It were some size.'

'One of the biggest we'd built.' Gunson sighed. 'God knows, I'm taken for granted until there's a catastrophe, and then I'm blamed for it.'

He'd gone further than intended.

The boy lifted his hand a few inches off the mattress. 'I'm Silas Hinchcliffe.'

Gunson shook his hand gently. 'Pleased to meet you, Silas. Can you walk? Millicent will come tomorrow to take you to our place.'

'Millicent?'

'My housekeeper. Millicent Leigh.'

He was surprised to see the boy attempt to lift himself up, his eyes searching Gunson's face eagerly. It crossed his mind the boy wasn't all there in the head.

'Please don't exert yourself. That's it. Lie down, Silas.' He looked around but the nurse was nowhere in sight. 'You must rest.'

The skin around the boy's mouth was white with strain.

'I know Milly,' Silas said. 'I know her daughter, Louisa. She's lookin' after Shandy for me.'

'Shandy?'

'My collie. An' Louisa's friendly with Harriet. Harriet Wragg, Walter Simpson's niece. D'you know her?'

The boy's cheeks were flushed. Gunson was at a loss. He didn't recognise the names Harriet Wragg nor Walter Simpson. 'It's a small world indeed,' he said politely.

'Tha doesn't know of her, nor Walter Simpson?' He closed his eyes. 'That man's the reason I'm in 'ere.'

'Ah, well. You must put all that behind you now.'

'Aye, that's what the judge told me.'

'The gentleman is correct.'

'I've had my fill of gentlemen.'

'I dare say you have.'

Silas opened his eyes and looked at Gunson, a resigned smile on his face. 'Least said, soonest mended in this town, eh?'

Gunson smiled wryly. 'It's a workable philosophy.'

'You built the dam that burst.'

'I did.' Gunson hesitated. He shouldn't have to justify himself to this humble creature, a member of the working class with no vote to cast and no interest in politics, although the urge to defend himself was strong.

'I'm sorry for it,' said Silas. He lifted himself onto one elbow, grunting with the effort.

'So am I, young man, so am I.' He looked at his hands then back at Silas. Perhaps Webster had glimpsed some potential in this boy and was not simply punishing Gunson for his own amusement. Charlotte had told him her first impression of the boy had been that he had a good soul, that he had indeed been mistreated and deserved a second chance.

'Let me tell you about the progress we are making on the Agden dam. Lay down. Rest, and listen. Do you know the basic principles behind dam building? No? You're entering a truly exceptional field of work. There's much to be done even before we break the first sod...'

Chapter 40

He'd been nicknamed 'Silas the Shadow' by the sneery clerk who sat in the outer chamber, and it was fair to say he stuck close to Gunson whenever he was required to enter the building that housed the waterworks company. He found the place and its stiff-collared inhabitants intimidating and was more at home on the Agden site, where he'd soon overcome the initial suspicion from the navvies who travelled together from site to site and were as thick as thieves.

'Related to the boss, are tha? Come to keep tha beady eye on us?'

This question had come from a short and burly man who thrust out a spade for Silas to take and pointed to a row of men who were scratching out a foundation trench. Silas had taken the tool from the man wordlessly and tramped away. He hardly knew what he was doing there himself – on the Agden site or in the Gunson's home. Later, when the sun was at its highest point, he stripped to the waist.

The man nearest him whistled low and long through his teeth.

'Looks nasty,' he said.

'Yep,' said Silas.

'Tha shunt expose theesen to the sun wi' that mess on thee back.' He'd patted Silas's arm, a friendly gesture, and the other men had turned back to the job at hand.

Charlotte Gunson had told Silas the angry red weals on his back would fade to pink then silver, in time. He hated the feel of the ridged and puckered skin when he tentatively reached around with his fingertips. 'Already, your young skin is healing,' Mrs Gunson had reassured him. He liked Mrs Gunson and had confided in her his fear of re-entering a steel forge, and told her about his recurring dream of Fred smeared across the boiler, his mouth frozen open in a scream of horror. She hadn't laughed at him. 'Just remember that you will succeed in life,' she had said, 'if the thing you are doing is the thing that you most want to do. You're learning engineering and I'm sure it will come in useful if you want to go into steel-working. You've already shown you can apply yourself.'

He didn't tell her he had strolled past Walter Simpson's house late one night, keeping to the shadows, hoping for a sight of Harriet. He had not yet repeated the journey, having no reason to be in that part of town and being wary of falling foul of the night watchman, but he yearned to see her, a need that Louisa mocked – 'Hasn't that family caused thee enough grief? Steer clear, Silas. That's what I say.'

He followed Mr Gunson into his office in the Division Street building, nodding to the clerk and rolling his shoulders. A thousand insects swarmed up and down his back. Mrs Gunson had warned him about this peculiar sensation. She had told him the intolerable itching was part of the healing process.

His boss set about unfolding a sheet of paper covered in straight and right-angled lines and shaded curves. He clipped it to the drawing board that dominated the room and gestured to Silas to take a closer look.

'The front elevation of the embankment at Agden. I'm going to increase the size of the by-wash, here, on the right, do you see?'

Silas nodded. He was struggling to relate the clean, sharp lines of the drawing to the muddy site he was working on.

'And it's stepped, not sloped.' Mr Gunson ran his finger over the elevation. 'The outlet pipes, here and here... and the puddle wall...'

Silas had been taught how to manipulate wet clay to form a watertight seal between the embankment and the reservoir, and learned the method was an old one, adopted from canal building, but vastly scaled up. He knew now that the puddle wall had been a bone of contention in the investigation into the collapse of Dale Dyke. The outlet pipes, too.

Gunson's voice washed over him. '...the basin will hold five hundred and fifty-nine gallons of water and covers twenty-five hectares. The material we excavate goes here, into the embankment, nothing is wasted... one hundred feet high and eleven hundred feet wide... aesthetics are important. The slope is sewn with grass and becomes part of the natural landscape...'

Silas's eyes slid to the daguerreotype that was pinned to the wall next to the easel. It was a blurry black and white image of part of the valley, photographed in the immediate aftermath of the flood. The Loxley was a muddy swamp, its meandering banks a jumble of rubble and uprooted trees. A group of people posed in the foreground, tiny grainy figures on the edge of the scene. An old woman in a bonnet and apron over her long skirts, a younger woman standing slightly apart and clutching the hand of a small boy in a cap and four older bare-headed children holding each other's hands like paper cut-out dolls. When Silas had first examined the daguerreotype, Mr Gunson confirmed it had been made the morning after the flood. He didn't explain why he had it on the wall and Silas didn't ask.

Gunson clapped his hands together.

'We're moving forward at a fair lick, eh, Silas? There'll be a new Dale Dyke to follow Agden.' He glanced up from his drawings and Silas saw that the skin around the older man's deep-set eyes was smudged by fatigue. 'I've been preoccupied and I'm afraid Mrs Gunson will be displeased with me this evening.' He was holding a brass compass, absently pressing one of its two miniature spears against the soft pad of his thumb. 'The nights are drawing in again. Have you noticed? And I shall have to work late once more.'

'So there will be a new dam at Bradfield?'

'Yes, of course.' Mr Gunson laid the compass down, a tremor in his hand making it clack against the desk. 'The millowners expect it and so does the town for all it likes to criticise. Well, we go on. What was destroyed is rebuilt.' He smiled at Silas. 'It's seven o'clock and Charlotte will be waiting to give you your lessons.'

It was three days later when Silas opened the door to the Gunsons' residence to be met by silence. Usually, he would hear the sound of piano notes from the front parlour or the chatter and laughter of the ladies who called to take tea with Mrs Gunson. Occasionally, he would hear her voice among others coming from the back parlour, where she hosted meetings of the local relief committee. In the wake of the flood, clothing and feeding the poor, not to mention the workers struggling to get back on their feet, was a full-time job, she had told Silas. This had given him the opportunity he'd been seeking to say Harriet's name aloud.

'I know somebody like thee,' he had said.

'Like me?'

'Aye, a girl called Harriet. The pair o' thee'd get on. She's as kind as thee, and likes to 'elp people.'

'Why, thank you! Tell me about her.'

He had told her everything and, at the end, she had said that he should be patient, and focus on his rehabilitation. Silas had agreed, to be polite. Inwardly, he chafed to be free to visit Harriet, to hold her hand again, to kiss her. In the meantime, he could talk about her to Mrs Gunson. It was better than nothing.

Now, he shrugged off his jacket and walked through the house and down the short flight of stairs that led to the kitchen, similarly deserted, the scullery beyond and the stable-yard. The second maid, a robust girl taken on after Silas's arrival to do the heavy-duty housework, was standing at the scullery sink twisting the tap.

'Ey up, Ethel.'

'Silas!' She spun around. 'Tha freetened me to death. Come and get this bleedin' thing going, it's stuck again.'

'I'd do owt for thee, Ethel.'

'Gerrout on it.' But her eyes crinkled with pleasure and a pink blush rose on her cheeks. 'The missus is in the dining room.'

'Already?'

'No, daft sod. It'll be another hour before tha gets tha hoity-toity supper.' She put her hand in the sink, swirling the water. 'I need to heat some watta. Freezin' cold, this is. Have a feel.'

'No, thanks.'

'Mrs Gunson says tha to go an' see her. Best get theesen in there.'

'Si thee later, Ethel, me lovely.'

'Gerrout on it.'

Mrs Gunson was sitting in her husband's chair at the head of the dining table when Silas entered. A large vase in the centre of the table was filled with yellow and red blooms from the climbing roses she cultivated on a small iron fence behind the house.

'They look pretty as owt,' said Silas.

'Good enough to grow in the limited space I have for gardening,' she said, plucking at the tablecloth nervously with one hand. The other hand held a letter.

'What's the matter?' He closed the door behind him and leaned on it. 'Am I in bother?'

'No, Silas. You are wanted, though. Will you sit down, please? You're making me nervous looming over me like that.'

He pulled out a chair and sat down. 'Go on then, Missus Gunson.'

She reached forward to touch his sleeve. 'Well, there are two matters. I have some bad news for you, Silas.'

His stomach contracted. 'Is it Harriet?'

'No. No, it's nothing to do with that family.' She put the letter on the table in front of him. Silas picked it up. He could read quite well now, thanks to Charlotte Gunson. It had been opened. He looked up at her and raised his eyebrow. 'I'm sorry, Silas. It is addressed to you, but I was worried it was from the court or the police and I thought I might be able to deal with it, without causing any more upset to you. You've been through so much.'

'But it is bad news.' He couldn't bring himself to look at the page he held. It was covered in a spidery half-remembered hand.

'Yes. Silas, it's from your father. Do you want to read it yourself, or shall I tell you what it contains?'

'Here.'

He held out the sheet and she took it from him and laid it flat on the table, and looked into his eyes.

'Silas, I'm very sorry to tell you that your brother has died. Peter had an accident on the farm and a Reverend James has written on behalf of your father to tell you that you must return home as soon as you possibly can.'

Silas looked away from her sympathetic gaze. Outside, a horse and rider clopped slowly by. A fly bumped and buzzed against the windowpane, trapped behind the net curtain. He should let it out, or kill it. 'Does Father give a date for… for the funeral?'

'No. They've had the funeral already. I'm sorry. You should read the letter from your father, Silas. Whatever you decide to do, you will have the support of myself and Mr Gunson.'

'Aye, thank you.' He was surprised to find his throat was thick with tears. He took the letter back and folded it and put it in his jacket pocket.

'I'm so sorry, Silas.'

'It's not tha fault.' He spoke more roughly than he'd intended.

'Your father says there's a widow…'

'Aye. Ginny.'

'… and a baby boy to consider. Your father wants you back to run the farm. Forgive me for asking, but did you leave on bad terms? He's most insistent that you obey him.'

Chapter 41

A meeting was taking place in the master bedroom. Polly had been persuaded into a bed jacket and thence into Walter's armchair. Albert Boothby and the family solicitor stood before her and Harriet took up position beside her chair. It was explained that Walter's share of the construction business would pass to Harriet's brother, in trust, along with the house and its contents, until Adam came of age. Albert told Polly that he would pay a nurse to provide round-the-clock care for her, to free Harriet from the burden. Harriet shuddered as the gilded cage of her future life closed around her. In any event, he remarked to the solicitor, Walter's young niece would be embarking shortly on her new life as Mrs Albert Boothby.

Polly had remained mute, and moved only to pat the hand Harriet had laid on her shoulder.

'Is this a new symptom, this refusal to speak?' Albert asked Harriet, in front of Polly, after the solicitor had given his condolences and bade them a good afternoon. The two of them had got Polly back into bed.

'Thank you for your help. Excuse me,' Harriet replied, and lifted the lid of the commode. She was grimly satisfied when he muttered an excuse and soon after left the house. Polly didn't speak or look at Harriet when she returned with a clean bucket, but lay with her chin on her chest, seemingly half asleep.

Harriet found Sadie cleaning the dining-room furniture, her sleeves rolled up.

'Shall I fetch the polish, Sadie?'

'No, thank you. Nowt wrong wi' using a bit of elbow grease.'

'I'm walking to the haberdashers on Infirmary Road.'

Sadie raised an eyebrow.

'I need lace to trim my new bonnet.'

Satisfied with the flicker of scorn on Sadie's face at so frivolous a pursuit, Harriet escaped. It was a dank afternoon, darkening rapidly. She took the omnibus the few stops to Louisa's cottage, recalling an earlier journey, to meet Silas, when a dozing man had slid sideways and come to rest his head on her shoulder. She had been happy then. Why was happiness only recognised in hindsight? If she was ever happy again, she would try to capture it in the moment, relish it like a precious jewel.

Harriet opened the door to Louisa's cottage without knocking, as she had been accustomed to doing during frequent visits during the summer. Shandy lay by the fireplace, chin on paws, and sprang up to greet her with a single welcoming bark. Louisa was hanging clothes on the rack above the fireplace. Her eyes at first lit up when she saw Harriet, but then a shadow fell across her face. 'Shandy! Go on.'

She spoke harshly and the dog gave her a wounded look as she slunk back to her place by the fire and lay down, replacing her chin on her paws, her eyes flicking between the two women.

'I'm sorry. I should have knocked,' said Harriet. 'It's been a while. I've surprised you.'

Louisa hoisted the rack and wound the rope around the double hook on the wall, paying close attention to an action she must have carried out hundreds of times and surely could do with her eyes closed. She rearranged some of the garments. When she finally glanced at Harriet, there were angry spots of colour on her cheeks.

'I wondered when tha'd finally show thee face.'

Harriet had braced herself for this. 'I'm sorry, Louisa. I was forbidden from seeing you. I still am. My uncle demanded it before he died and now I have Mr Boothby breathing down my neck. I'm sure he's got the new maid spying on me. Oh, Louisa. I have agreed to marry him.'

'All right for some, eh? He's rich enough.'

'Louisa, please! I'm trying to apologise. I know I'm at fault, that if it wasn't for me... I don't know what to say. Can I sit?'

Louisa's face softened. 'Well, all right. Yes, of course, sit down.'

'Have you seen Silas?'

'A few times, aye, since the flogging.'

Harriet winced.

'He's doing all right, considering.' Louisa's voice hardened again. 'Don't know how he'll get over it, meself. A whipping for all to see at the Saturday market. Folk were laughing, tha knows what these spectacles get like.'

'I've never...'

'No, course you won't ever have seen one, will you? Soft life for some, int' it?'

Harriet put her hand to her mouth and dropped into a chair. 'I went to the King's Arms...'

'So tha knows he's moved out of there, at least.'

'Won't you tell me where he is, Louisa?'

'I don't want him gettin' in trouble again. Nor should you. I've told him, no goin' near her place. That bloke wants thee dead, I said. That bloke tha says tha goin' to be wed to.'

Harriet bowed her head, crushed by the harshness in Louisa's voice. 'I wish I could see him just once, to apologise. I did what I could for him.'

'Aye, that's summat, at least.'

'He must hate me.'

'I don't know about that. I've told 'im he shun't be dwellin' on it. Look, it's no use cryin', love. I'll put the kettle on.'

'Where is he, Louisa? Has he gone from the town?'

'Who'd blame him if he did go? Way he's been treated.'

'The judge was sympathetic. He said he'd help…'

'Aye, an' he did. Pair of you kept him away from the rope. How did you persuade him?'

'He saw that what I was saying was the truth of the matter!' Harriet sighed. 'I also told him that Mr Boothby's insistence on the worst punishment was to do with me, and that we were to be married and I would never contact Silas again.'

'An' yet here you are.' Louisa's mouth twisted into a bitter smile. 'I'd leave it at that, love.'

'Maybe we could meet here, Louisa, like we used to.'

She flinched away from Louisa's candid look. 'Go back to the way it were? No, Harriet. He's got good people lookin' after him now. Leave it, like I say. I saw what they did to him, tha didn't. Go back to your comfortable life an' forget about Silas.'

Harriet laughed bitterly. 'Silas is free now. I'm the one in jail.'

'Harriet.' Louisa handed her a mug of tea. 'Don't be so bleedin' dramatic.'

They smiled at each other and Harriet swallowed a sob of relief.

'Can I come to see you again?'

'Aye. Let the dust settle for a bit first, eh?'

When Louisa waved her off from the doorstep, Shandy at her side, Harriet's vision blurred with tears. She might salvage Louisa's friendship but her friend's refusal to give her Silas's whereabouts stung. She blinked her tears away, staring into the distance at the tall brick chimneys propping up the sky over Atlas steelworks. The familiar columns were already losing their substance, no more than faint smudges on the darkening horizon. The cold air stung her nose.

She had reached the midpoint of the long straight road that sliced like a blade through the maze of streets in the smoke-choked east end, when she decided she might as well walk the rest of the way. It was quiet in the late afternoon hour, the day holding its breath in the minutes before factory workers spilled out from behind high iron gates.

A two-wheeled curricle scooted by, rattling over the cobbles, making her start. The carriage's sole occupant was urging on the horse, a white creature, ghostly in the gloom, and did not spare her a glance. Man and horse seemed to drag the last part of the day away with them.

Harriet adjusted her cloak and hurried on. The pavement was empty except for a lamp lighter who stepped into the gutter to allow her to pass, his eyes glittering under the brim of his cap. She nodded her thanks, aware of his head turning to follow her. Another half a mile and then she would be turning left to walk downhill towards the river. Across the robust stone bridge built to replace the wooden one lost in the flood and she would be home.

She crossed a junction onto the long stretch of road where high ivy-covered sandstone walls hid a handful of gentlemen's residences from view. Mr Boothby had built some of these grand edifices with their turrets and octagonal bays, and lived in one. His villa sat in the middle of a wooded garden, a large plot, well screened for privacy. The floors in Mr Boothby's home were of darkly polished wood, the staircase teak and the walls covered in dark plaster, mahogany panelling or burgundy flock, making it oppressive, despite its size.

Albert had told her they would fill the bedrooms with children and she would have charge of a full staff, including a lady's maid of her own. She saw how easily she might sail into a life that was not hers, steered by other's hands.

As she passed the iron gate in the wall that led to his residence, Harriet averted her gaze.

A shout in the distance only served to highlight the desertion of this part of the street. Harriet glanced behind her, again. The pavement was empty, except for the drifts of leaves. She reassured herself that the factory whistles would soon blow a hole in the silence. She would be just one more body in a crowd of them, not alone and easily singled out, a rabbit scuttling along a hedge, easy prey to a beady-eyed hawk.

A scuttling from behind found its echo in her chest. Harriet increased her pace. A leaf or some other street detritus blowing along, no reason to look back. But now her mind was flooded by the memory of the crunch of leaves under little Alice's boots, her cousin's delighted giggle. And now the sound was the rasp of Walter's drowning lungs, finally suffocated by the same flood that had carried his daughter away, and she could not help herself. She spun around.

The empty street faded into blackness beyond the pool of light cast by a gas lamp. She was not being followed, except by the dead that her fevered imagination was raising. The lamp lighter had gone, leaving flickering yellow stars in his wake.

A shadowed figure emerged from an alcove in the wall right beside her. She froze, a scream trapped in her throat, as his bare fingers grazed her gloved hand.

His low and steady voice made her heart leap in her chest.

'Harriet.'

Chapter 42

'Silas!'

Her eyes widened and he thought she must be afraid of him, but then she took both his hands in hers, clasping them tightly, peering up into his face. 'I thought I'd find you at Louisa's. She wouldn't tell me where you'd gone. I'm so sorry, Silas. I didn't know, I didn't know that you'd be punished like that.' The words were tumbling out of her, almost too quickly for him to follow. 'I told them you were innocent. I tried. I went to see the judge to plead on your behalf. Walter was just trying to protect me.'

He laughed gently. 'Tha does witter on.' Harriet's face fell. 'No, I like it. I missed it. I missed thee, the sound o' tha voice.'

'I've missed you, too, Silas.'

'I had a speech planned, for when I next saw thee.' He examined the pale oval of her face. 'All I can think about is kissin' thee again.'

She laughed, nervously. 'Look where that got us.'

'It were worth it, though.'

'Oh, Silas. It's lovely to see you.'

He bent his head to kiss her, but she jerked away.

'Tha like a scalded cat.'

'I'm sorry but we can't, Silas. I can't.' She looked back, at the empty street. 'And what were you doing, creeping up on me like that?'

'Aye, well, I can hardly pitch up on tha doorstep, can I?' He cocked his ear to the rising sound of a factory whistle and a church bell ringing out the hour. 'I've got Mr Gunson's gig and can take thee 'ome in it, most o' the way at least. Will tha let me kiss thee first though, before they all turn out?'

As she opened her mouth to protest, he pressed his lips against hers. She stepped back, biting her lip, although their hands were still joined. 'We shouldn't do this, Silas. And I am almost home. It would be a very short journey.' She looked over his shoulder. 'Where is it?'

'Tied up at the Horse and Plough. Come wi' me. Go on.' He saw that she was wavering. 'Come an' sit wi' me.'

He would have said more, but was drowned out by whistles and bells. Workers spilled out from factories in the surrounding streets, noisy cross waves pushing her body against his. He stood firm, ducking his head to inhale her scent. Fresh, like lemons and oranges.

'Are tha gunna stand in't road all day?' The gruff voice that came from behind reminded Silas of his captors and he flinched and hunched his shoulders, raising both hands into fists. The damaged skin on his back prickled as he twisted his torso to confront the man, who was already gone. His heart was pounding now and he took a deep breath to calm himself.

He forced a smile to reassure her – 'Somebody's got an ale waitin' for him' – and steered her in the same direction. They turned onto a narrower street, where men were hailing each other as they arrived at the inn on the corner. He saw one or two of them look Harriet's way, sizing her up.

'This way.'

'Silas. What if we are seen?'

'We're more likely to be seen 'ere on the street, aren't we? Here we are.'

He waited for her to gather up her skirts then offered his arm to help her up the step and into the cushioned seat. He sprang up after her and they sat back together, shielded from view by the fabric covered hood of the gig. Silas took her hand. His heart had been empty, a parched crock, and just looking at Harriet, the sight of her, filled him up to the brim again.

'What are you smiling about?' she said.

He was seized with an impulse to drive them both away, now, to escape with her and not look back.

'Could tha stand to be a farmer's wife?' He whispered the words and Harriet leaned closer.

'I beg your pardon?'

Silas kissed her and this time she returned his kiss. He broke the lingering connection to look at her face again, and laughed – 'I feel drunk' – and twined the ribbon of her bonnet between his fingers. 'Remember when I bought thee a ribbon?'

She touched his fingers, still entwined in the ribbon. 'I thread this into my bonnet whenever I hope to see you.'

'That's the ribbon I gave you?'

'I'd expected you to recognise it.'

'It's too dark to see t'colour. I remember, though. A red ribbon.'

He recalled he had made her laugh by telling her his wages were burning a hole in his pocket. Who else would he want to spend them on?

But now she looked sad.

Silas put his hand into his jacket pocket, closing his fingers around the small box he'd stowed there along with the letter from his father. His gut knotted in fear at his own audacity, but he knew this was the only moment. The pounding of his heart told him so. Now or never.

'Harriet, listen. There's summat I want to ask thee…' He began to withdraw the box from his pocket. The thin paper of the letter rustled.

The Gunson horse whinnied gently as another gig drew up alongside theirs. Harriet shrank back. 'This is no good,' she said. 'Why don't we arrange to meet at Louisa's house, like we used to? It's safer there. I can find an excuse to come. I'll make sure I'm not followed.'

Silas froze. 'What's the point o' that? Why should we skulk around? I've a job now, tha knows. Only a temporary thing, really, summat forced on me out o' pity. I'll get back to steel. It's my ambition to run me own factory. I'll have a steelworks wi' me name o'er the gate.'

'I'm sure you will. I believe you will. My situation is complicated. Oh!' She put her hands over her face. 'I do miss you, Silas. I miss our afternoon walks and our talks. Why can't we go back to the way it was, before the, before you…' she trailed off.

He relinquished his grip on the box containing the plain gold band he'd finally scraped enough cash together to buy second-hand. It fell back to the bottom of his pocket.

'Does tha miss this?' He gently took her hands and tried to kiss her again, wanting only to drown the voice in his head that told him he'd been a fool to think this woman might ever consider marrying him.

Harriet pushed him away. 'You can't solve this with kisses, Silas. You're a child. I have to go. I'll be missed at home.' Her mouth was set and he was not allowed to soften it with a kiss. 'You think we can do whatever we like. We can't.'

'Why not?'

'You see? That response only shows your immaturity.'

'I know what I want, Harriet. Does tha? I know what I don't want an' all. I won't visit thee at Louisa's, hidin' like I'm some sort o' criminal. I did nowt wrong. It's not right. It's not enough.' He tried to get her to meet his eye. 'Harriet, I thought I were set on a path wi' thee. I thought that felt the same way I did. Louisa's told me about 'im…'

'About who?'

'Tha knows. I can't believe tha's thick wi' him.'

She stared at the floor of the gig. 'It's foolish to get on the wrong side of influential men. You've already learned that, I think.'

Silas took her hand. 'Look at me,' and she did, at last, but her gaze was unfocused. He knew he'd lost her.

'Haven't you learned that, Silas, even now? Help me down, please.'

'It were 'is idea, gettin' me flogged.' His lip curled, he couldn't help it. 'Harriet, I thought tha were better than that. I'll provide for thee. Don't go off wi' that bastard.'

'Stop it!'

'We need to have this out.'

'There's nothing to have out!'

There were tears on her cheeks and he went to brush them away, but she batted his hand down and there was determination in her eyes. 'This is no good, for either of us. I am to marry. Please don't say anything. Just help me down. I *have* to go. Silas. Do I have to beg?'

He climbed out of the gig and stood on the pavement, and offered his hand. When Harriet was safely down, he tried to keep her hand in his.

'Tha's makin' a mistake,' he said, and he could hear the desperation in his voice.

'Let go of me, Silas. Let go.'

Later, he ate his supper listlessly, separating the bones from the flesh of the fish on his plate with a silver fork while the Gunsons conversed over his head. He could tell they were being careful around him, believing he was grieving his dead brother, knowing he had a decision to make, and they left him in peace to slowly chew and swallow food he could not taste and for which he had no appetite.

For she had gone off without another word and had not looked back.

Chapter 43

Charlotte dusted breadcrumbs from her fingers and rose from the table to pour his coffee. He knew her so well he could tell simply from the way she looped her hair behind her ear that she was out of sorts.

'What's wrong?'

'I know this does not interest you, John, but Christmas is three weeks off and I am not prepared. I forgot to order the bird.'

Gunson patted her arm. 'Silly goose.'

Charlotte didn't return his smile. She set the coffee pot down with a sigh. 'I'm afraid you can't have sugar in your coffee this morning. I have ordered a packet to be delivered with today's groceries.'

'I don't mind. I can take it without sugar.' He waited until she sat. 'What's really the matter?'

'I should think it obvious,' she said tartly. 'Silas has made his choice. I wish it were a different one.'

'You've enjoyed having a boy in the house again.'

'I have. He's a sweet boy.'

'He steals all the sugar, I'm not surprised.'

This won him a faint smile.

'I'm driving him to the station. Would you like to come along? We're collecting his dog from Millicent's place.'

'Yes, I will come. Oh John, I hope he'll keep in touch. He promised to write to us.'

'Then I'm sure he will. He's a boy of his word.'

'I've enjoyed teaching him so much more than I expected I would. He's a fast learner. Won't you will be sorry to see him go?'

'Yes, of course,' said Gunson. 'I thought he might make a fine engineer. But, as you say, he's made his choice. I like the boy, he reminds me of our Thomas at the same age. He's a hard worker, and he has a knack for numbers.'

Numbers. His fevered mind printed them on the bedroom ceiling during the dark sleepless hours. The cost of rebuilding Dale Dyke; it would by financial necessity be a smaller dam. The number of the claims made against the company; six thousand. The number of lives lost, and the age in days of the youngest, a number that haunted him.

'He has had his heart broken, I think. Poor boy.'

'Hmm.'

His dam had not been defective. He could keep telling himself he was not at fault, but his nightmares told him otherwise. 'Well, time for me to leave for work, dear. I'll return later this morning to collect you both. Where is he?'

'Upstairs. Packing.'

She tilted her head for a kiss on the cheek as Gunson rose from his chair.

'Millicent tells me he might have stayed if he thought he had a chance with that Harriet Wragg,' said Charlotte.

'What does Silas say to you about it?' Gunson was suddenly curious.

'We talk of other things, of his old life and his mother and father and what he might expect when he returns.'

'He doesn't talk of her?'

'He doesn't mention her at all.'

The animal–skin valise squatted on the bed like a toad, mouth gaping.

Silas skirted around it and opened the window. Over the roof tops, the November sky was a pale canvas painted over with widening columns of smoke from the stacks of the steelworks. A cold breeze tattered the smoke and carried the scent of sulphur and soot, hops from the brewery, and manure from the stables which his room overlooked.

He would miss the sharp stench of the town, the smog that on still days snaked through the back lanes, making them appear insubstantial. Silas turned from the window to gaze at the candlewick bedspread. He had not slept long in this room provided by the Gunsons. He could not call it his. He remembered the thrill of being led into the attic space in the Hilda Armitage's house, the prospect of renting a room, an adult now, not a runaway. He had not even spent a single night there and it was gone now, along with all the occupants except for Louisa, who had saved his dog. He'd stayed long enough in the King's Arms to believe he was establishing roots, only to be ripped up and thrown into another maelstrom. He'd had enough. His mother would be happy to see him, his father would set him to work. His reason for leaving home no longer existed. Peter was dead. The thought made a curious numbness invade his body. Would Silas be expected to marry his brother's widow? To bring up their child as his own? He pictured Reverend James sitting at the kitchen table, warming to another theme, which this time would be the pairing of Silas with a dead man's wife, all the wonders of the steel age forgotten.

Mr Gunson was waiting downstairs for him. If he left it any longer he would miss the Wicker Station train.

The valise was lined inside with canvas and had strong leather handles, an expensive bag. He hadn't wanted to take it, but Mrs Gunson had insisted, telling him, 'You can return it when you return yourself.'

'I won't be coming back,' Silas had replied.

'Then keep it,' Mrs Gunson had said kindly, and Silas's guts had twisted in doubt.

It was time to feed the blasted toad.

First, his work boots and his shoes stowed in the bottom. None of the clothes he had arrived in had survived the flood, some left in the satchel in Mrs Armitage's kitchen, the rest ripped from his body as he had rode the wave. He'd followed Fred Sharrow to the forge wearing a smock, his trousers tucked in at the knee. Country-boy clothes. Now he wore short boots inside more finely cut trousers and was cultivating a patchy beard. Bum fluff, Louisa affectionately called the hairs sprouting from his chin. If he'd had a full beard, if he was closer to her age, perhaps Harriet might have taken him more seriously.

He wrapped the relics he'd purchased from the girl on the pavement in the wake of the flood – the teacup and saucer, the porcelain cat – in the new waistcoat he'd worn in a futile effort to impress Walter Simpson. He wondered whether he'd ever have the opportunity to wear it again.

Next, three pairs of britches, his undershirts and vests.

He could not stay in the same town that contained Harriet, knowing she had agreed to marry the man who was responsible for the scars that covered his back. He couldn't face her betrayal.

A purse, bulging with coins, many more than would be required to refill the housekeeping jar he'd raided all that time ago when he stole away as the sun rose behind him. He tossed this into the top of the valise for easy access. He had a train fare to pay, would need coins for the coach ride at the other end, and didn't want to be fishing around inside the bag. Silas then closed the valise, picked it up, and left the room without a backward glance.

He was travelling light, if he didn't count his heart.

Chapter 44

Mr Boothby arrived with a trunk for Harriet to pack her clothes into. He produced, with a flourish, a purse of coins for Adam who was leaving within the hour for boarding school and packets of sweets for the younger boys, who were to pass into Sadie's care when she was promoted to housekeeper and moved into Harriet's room, at Mr Boothby's expense, an offer he had qualified with 'for now'. He consoled Harriet as she wept on the doorstep, waving an equally tearful Adam off, promising they would all be together again at Christmas. He patted her waist and said he hoped she would be growing him a son by then. Harriet hoped for this, too, and said so. She told herself it was a boon that they both wanted children. This shared goal was enough of a basis for a marriage, for her transition from one secure life to another. She would honour and obey, and perhaps love would grow over time. Her feelings for Silas were girlish, romantic nonsense. She had recently celebrated her twenty-fourth birthday and should act like the grown woman she was. This is what she told herself.

'That went off very well,' he said, rubbing his hands. 'I shall not see you for supper tonight, Harriet.' He handed her the newspaper that had just been delivered. 'However, I do have a little job for you.'

'A job?' She felt her spirits lift. 'I thoroughly enjoyed my time at the town hall. I believe I have an aptitude for...'

'Hmm? I'd like you to peruse the entertainments column of this publication.'

'Entertainments?'

'Select an event I might take a prospective new business partner.'

'New business partner?'

'Must you echo everything I say?'

She followed him into the kitchen where Sadie was building the fire.

'Sadie, a pot of tea and a round of sandwiches if you please,' he said.

Sadie bobbed. 'Yes, sir.'

Harriet stared at her. Had Sadie really just curtsied? She spread the newspaper on the kitchen table, wondering what a new business partner meant for the future of Boothby, Simpson and Sons, and whether her brother, who held Walter's interest, knew about this. James had recently written to Polly to inform her he was now in a strong enough financial position to support a family of his own and had found a fiancée. He had assured Polly he would honour his obligations to Walter's widow and dependents. Unspoken was the assumption that Harriet would soon be another man's responsibility. Should she tell him about Albert's plan to bring someone else into the business? She was sure she would be scolded for interfering in the business affairs of men.

Harriet sighed and scanned the page. The Sheffield Choral Union was putting on a concert in a few days' time. Or Albert might take this potential business partner to the Alhambra where there was music five nights a week.

'The Theatre Royal has booked a troupe of comedians for three days hence. That sounds jolly,' she said.

She looked up at the ceiling when a floorboard creaked above her head. Some heavy object was dropped and bounced across the room above in a series of diminishing thuds before coming to rest. A football, probably. She returned her attention to the newspaper.

'Oh dear,' she said. 'Dreadful news from the courts. A gang of robbers left a seventy-year-old man for dead. The poor old soul was walking from Chesterfield. All he had on him was two half-crowns, a knife and a tobacco box. How awful. They even took his shoes.'

'I don't know what the world is coming to,' said Albert. 'It's not safe to be abroad, eh, Sadie?'

'No, sir.'

Here was an advertisement for Hartley's teething powder, which reminded her of Louisa telling her about baby Betty's rash. Betty had been cutting her teeth when the flood took her and her mother. That had been on the eve of the disaster, the very day that Silas arrived in town and found his way to Hilda Armitage's house. He was thus already, though neither of them knew it at the time, connected to Harriet in a distant way. As if fate decreed it even before he was thrown into her orbit by the great wave. Harriet pursed her lips and turned the page, looking for a distraction. It always seemed to her that any thread she allowed her mind to follow had Silas at the end of it.

'We should attend church this Sunday,' said Albert, taking a bite of the sandwich Sadie laid before him. 'Our marriage banns are being announced.'

Tradition dictated that the banns were to be read at three consecutive Sunday morning services. The attendance of the Simpson family at church had always been sporadic, to say the least, but Mr Boothby rented a pew and liked to appear in it with his young fiancée by his side.

'Will our names be read out?'

'Of course. Do not be shy, Harriet. In three weeks, all the eyes of the town will be on you as you walk down the aisle. The banns are a formality. There will be no objections to our union.' He lifted his teacup into the air and Sadie hurried over to refill it.

Harriet wondered whether marrying outside one's class would count as reason enough to deny a wedding from going ahead. She rubbed her brow. There her mind went again, veering off course to seek out Silas. She recalled his teasing grin, the way he narrowed his eyes at her as if he could read her innermost thoughts. Had he already found another girl to test his charm on, to kiss and send dizzy?

The kitchen door swung open, and Harriet blinked in astonishment at the woman who stood there, smiling at her.

Chapter 45

Polly crossed over the threshold, wearing a black silk day dress, flanked by two triumphant-looking little boys holding their mouths to stifle their giggles. Harriet could not recall the last time she had seen Polly in any garment other than a nightgown. She had even put on stockings and shoes, and a jewelled barrette sparkled in a bird's nest of grey hair.

The boys were ecstatic: 'Harriet! Look!' and 'We helped mother get downstairs!'

Polly took in the scene. 'How... inviting,' she said, her chest heaving.

Sadie was the first to react. 'Mrs Simpson!' she cried. 'What on God's good Earth...?' She bustled over and took Polly's arm, shooing the boys away. 'Harriet, a seat, and be quick about it.'

Harriet pulled out a chair and Sadie guided her aunt into it. Polly's colour was hectic and her breathing came in ragged gasps, reminding Harriet of Walter in his final days.

She had never seen Albert Boothby look so unsure of himself. He coughed and began to speak, but Polly held up her hand for quiet and he obeyed. Sadie put a glass of water on the table, and they all watched her take a sip.

She should have known he would not remain still for long. He slammed his hand on the table, startling all three women. 'What are you playing at? We have just buried Walter! Are you intending to follow him so soon?'

Polly smiled thinly and pointed her finger at him. '*You* may leave. I wish to have a private conversation with my niece. Sadie, take George and William outside, please. They need to be aired.'

'It's lookin' like snow,' said Sadie dubiously.

'Boots and hats then. Five minutes only.'

Polly sipped from her water glass while Sadie fussed with hats and coats and shooed the boys outside, throwing an aggrieved look at Harriet before following them.

'You just missed your oldest son's departure, unfortunately,' said Albert.

'Mr Boothby, do not presume to sneer. Adam and I shared breakfast together. We had a conversation about his future.' She took a deep breath. 'All is well.'

'Well? Let me tell you, Mrs Simpson, that when I am head of this family...'

'Why are you so aggrieved to see me out of bed, I wonder, Mr Boothby?' Polly smiled tenderly at Harriet. 'I'm sorry for the shock of it.'

Harriet crouched by her side. Beads of sweat gleamed on Polly's face. The wedding band and ruby signet she wore on her left hand were sunk deep into pale and puffy flesh. 'But, aunt, has the doctor allowed it?'

'I should say not! If Walter were here he would not allow it either.'

'Mr Boothby, please,' said Polly. 'I'm sure you have important matters to which you should attend.'

'I shall remain to hear...'

'Albert,' said Harriet. 'I would have you stay, but we must obey my aunt who has just risen from her bed and will be feeling weak from it. Let us not distress her.'

He looked from Harriet to Polly and back. Harriet smiled at him and touched his arm. 'I shall see you tomorrow, Albert, and every day after that.'

He nodded stiffly. 'Good day to you both.'

Polly held Harriet's gaze as they listened to his footsteps recede and the front door open and slam. Harriet waited, wondering what was to come. A log snapped like a gunshot in the grate.

'Dear Alice,' said Polly. 'You were a good mother to her.'

Tears welled up in Harriet's eyes.

'I'd longed for a girl after three boys, but I could not find any love in my heart for her. I had just lost my sister, your dear mother. I am not making excuses, only trying to explain. Walter brought you and your brother here, and I was overwhelmed. I was afraid for Alice, for you and James, for the boys. There was danger everywhere. Then Walter told me that the danger came from me. I was the cause of my fears and would be their effect. He told me I was unstable and brought the doctor who gave me pills. I took to bed.'

Harriet followed Polly's gaze to the window. A blur of fat white snowflakes blew against the pane, swirling and softening onto the posts of the gate at the end of the garden path. The boys were running up and down the path and Sadie watched them, stamping her feet and rubbing her hands together.

'I wanted to keep my family safe,' said Polly. 'But look at us, Harriet. We are so reduced.'

Harriet wiped her eyes with the handkerchief Polly handed her. Her aunt's eyes were dry and full of pain.

'I gave you too heavy a burden to carry alone and I am sorry for it. Now,' she tapped the table with one finger, 'tell me about your wedding preparations.'

'The wedding?'

'Yes, the wedding. You have heard of it?'

Harriet laughed, relieved to hear humour in her aunt's voice. She blew her nose.

'You will be getting nervous, I imagine. The anticipation of it all. I remember my wedding day.'

'Do you?'

'Well, yes, Harriet. It was my wedding day. What of your dress?'

'Albert's sister has shown me the dress she was married in, an ivory silk. I think something like that would do. Albert likes it.'

'You don't seem enthusiastic. Harriet, I hope you understand that you are permitted to have second thoughts.'

'I'm content to take Albert's advice on it.'

'I'm not talking about the dress, child. You think to continue to see this boy, don't you? I may have been in bed for six years, but I see the light in your face when you've been to visit Louisa. Sadie is a gossip and sharper than you give her credit for.'

'Aunt!' Harriet laughed, but she was rattled. Polly was bringing out of the shadows things she did not want to think too closely about, and emotions she had thought she'd been successfully holding in check.

'Don't deny it. You'll contrive to meet him, won't you, even once wed?'

'No, of course not. I wanted to remain friends. He would not agree to it.' Harriet felt colour creep up her neck and into her cheeks. It was devastating to think of her last meeting with Silas. She almost wished Polly back in her bed.

'Your own face betrays you. I would like to say something. You should give what I say due consideration.' Polly paused. 'It is not too late to avert the course you are on.'

The fire hissed in the silence that followed. Harriet's mouth was dry.

'It was Uncle Walter's wish that I marry Albert Boothby.'

Polly's hand shook as she lifted the water glass and gulped the remaining contents down. 'You know, it suited Walter to keep me confined so he could go about his business unhindered, with you as his unpaid and uncomplaining servant. I am ashamed that I had not the strength to fight him, but now he is gone. He is dead and gone.' Polly looked around the room as if to confirm Walter's absence. 'And you are my niece, my beloved sister's child. I would have you happy. Your life is a precious currency, not to be spent unwisely. I know I am the last person who should say this, but,' she reached across the table to shake Harriet's arm, 'Harriet, wake up. Women's choices are limited, but they do exist.'

'What would you have me do?' Harriet said numbly.

'Answer me this. Answer quickly, without pause.' Polly narrowed her eyes and Harriet quailed. 'Who resides in your heart? Quick now.'

'Silas.' His name rode up from her throat on a sob that opened the floodgates. 'I love Silas. I loved him from the moment I saw him on Lady's Bridge. I can't forget him. I have sent him away.'

'Why?'

'What do you mean? He is too young and the wrong class and a foreigner in the town. I'm thinking of our

297

family. What will become of us without the security Albert Boothby can offer?'

'Let me shoulder that burden now. I owe you a great debt, Harriet.'

Harriet put her head in her hands. 'The wedding arrangements...'

'Can be undone.'

She looked up, wonderingly. 'Am I really contemplating calling off the wedding? What will he do?'

'He'll find another young woman with a womb for rent.'

Harriet gasped. 'Aunt!' Then they were both laughing, slightly hysterically, and Harriet clutched the edge of the table. 'My head feels light.' She took a breath. It was as if she had been submerged in silt beneath deep and still waters and was finally realising it was in her power to rise, to test her limbs, and swim for the surface. A bubbling laugh escaped her. She knew what she wanted, and she would summon all the courage she had in the getting of it.

Chapter 46

John Gunson followed his wife and Silas into the cottage, removing his topper as he ducked over the threshold. His hands jerked involuntarily, his nerves getting the better of him, and he peered around the smoke-hazed room, rather than meet the eye of Louisa Leigh. She would view him as the engineer of all her losses.

'Goodness me, it's warm in here.' He coughed. 'You have a snug little place.'

'"Little" being the word. It does the job,' said Louisa drily, getting up from her seat by the fireplace. A dog leapt up, a sharp-eyed collie who bounded over, ignoring him, thankfully, to run in tight circles around Silas's legs. Silas dropped his valise and crouched on his haunches. 'Hello, girl. Time for me to round you up, eh?'

Gunson was crestfallen to have offended Louisa. 'Young lady, I don't mean to patronise.'

Charlotte gave him a look and turned to Louisa, smiling. 'Your home is very convivial.'

This was the truth. Rocking chairs covered in plump cushions and colourful crocheted blankets were placed either side of the fireplace, with a three-seat settee that sagged in the middle facing the glowing coals. The room was a trove for knick-knacks – the dresser, the table and wall shelves all covered with ornaments, picture frames, candlesticks and lamps. Samplers and platework hung on

299

the tacking paper that covered the walls. The room was very small. He could cross it in two strides to reach the closed door on the far wall.

To his relief, this door now opened and Millicent Leigh emerged, carrying a tray of breadcakes.

'Good morning, Mrs Gunson, Mr Gunson. Or is it afternoon?'

'Well, let's see, Mrs Leigh.' He consulted his pocket watch, glad for a task, however small. 'It's half past the hour of one.'

'Will you have something to eat? There's rabbit stew.' Millicent put the tray on the hearth and turned to the dog, now sitting to attention, nose twitching. 'Don't you dare touch those, Shandy. Louisa, take Mr Gunson's hat and cloak.'

'We won't stay long, Milly. We've got a train to catch,' said Silas. 'Me an' Shandy.'

Gunson handed his hat and cloak to Louisa and finally raised his eyes to look at her. She had her mother's startlingly blue eyes. Louisa smiled at him and turned away, throwing his cloak onto the back of the settee and casting about for somewhere to place his hat. She finally balanced it, cockeyed, on an unlit lamp and sat by Silas on the settee. 'Mrs Gunson, will you sit with us?'

'I'd be glad to,' said Charlotte, and sat herself down on the other side of Silas.

'My favourite ladies,' he said.

'I wish you wouldn't go,' Louisa said, tucking her arm into his.

Silas didn't speak.

'Mr Gunson,' said Millicent. 'Come and sit down here.'

He lowered himself into a rocking chair. 'Thank you.'

It was discombobulating, being ordered about by his housekeeper. He wondered, now that Millicent lived out, how long it might be before Charlotte was forced to find a replacement. His wife had told him she was minded to increase Millicent's wage, now she had rent and fuel to find, even though her hours at the Gunson residence were drastically reduced.

'Have one!' She gestured to the breadcakes. 'Mrs Gunson?'

'No, thank you. I had a late breakfast.'

Gunson bent down and took a breadcake. He bit into it, for politeness' sake. It was filled with butter and cheese, and might be the most delicious sandwich he'd ever tasted if he had any appetite. He chewed and swallowed painfully and allowed the hand holding the breadcake to drop over the side of the chair. The dog eyed this movement, but remained in place, panting gently. He wondered whether the animal would dart forward if he dropped the bread and relieve him of the burden of continuing to eat.

'How remarkably well trained he is,' he said.

'She's a lovely animal,' said Louisa. 'Soft as a brush. Do you like dogs, Mr Gunson?'

'Not especially, no. I encountered a mongrel on the street once that tried to make his teeth meet through the calf of my leg.'

'Oh dear,' said Millicent. 'They can be a nuisance, can't they, when they're not looked after proper? Shandy is like part of the family now.'

'I'm sorry to take her away, but she must come back wi' me,' said Silas.

'Will you keep in touch?' said Louisa.

'Aye, o'course. I'll come back one day, an' see you all.'

'And bring Shandy.'

'Aye.' Silas shook his head when Millicent offered him a breadcake. 'Nay. Thanks.'

A draught from the window laid cold air against the back of Gunson's neck. The dog flopped down, chin on paws, and observed each of them in turn, eyebrows twitching. It was unbearable. Gunson was going to have to eat the damned sandwich.

'Mr Gunson was a great support to me when I was searching for you, Louisa,' said Millicent.

'I know, Mother.' Louisa shook her head and said to Charlotte, 'She's told me the tale often enough.'

'I am glad you are well,' said Gunson, and fell silent. He rubbed his beard. 'I know you lost people dear to you and I am sorry. It was a terrible tragedy.' He stopped again, at a loss for words.

Charlotte tutted. 'What my husband doesn't say is that he has worked day and night ever since to make amends.'

He smiled at her gratefully.

'Well, Louisa is safe under my roof and I'm glad of it,' said Millicent.

He nodded gravely.

'Mrs Gunson, I met you, once, before, when I were a girl,' said Louisa. 'Mr Gunson were interviewin' mother and you took me in the kitchen and gave me a spiced bun. Tha prob'ly don't remember it.'

'Oh, I do!' said Charlotte. 'Yes, I do remember.'

'Tha wanted her to live in so from that point I were required to find me own way in the world. I din't have a father to go to.'

'I was widowed young,' Millicent interjected.

'Anyway, it were fine because I got a maid's job at the Simpsons – that ruined me hands, but, look, Silas, they're a sight better now I'm not scrubbin' all day long – an' I got taken in as one of Hilda Armitage's waifs and strays.'

Gunson didn't need reminding of what had happened to Hilda Armitage and her child.

'She sounds like a kind lady,' he said, then hurriedly asked: 'How old were you, when Millicent came to us?'

'Thirteen.'

Charlotte coughed. 'John, I've been telling Millicent about Silas helping you rebuild the dam.'

'The dam? Oh, that dam. No, no. We're not starting on that just yet. Of course, there will be a new Bradfield reservoir, perhaps not on the exact same location because, you see, we have identified an issue with subsidence. An underground spring. Nature set a trap for us and in we tumbled.' He shut off the flow of words like a tap. He could feel Louisa's gaze on him and spoke to the coals in the scuttle by his side. 'Silas has been working on Agden, and learning some engineering. He has proved to be a very able young man and my wife holds him in high regard.'

'I do.'

'As do I, of course. We shall miss him.' He took another bite from the breadcake and swallowed painfully. 'We should be leaving shortly, for the train.'

'He's a good boy, there's no doubt,' said Millicent.

'You're all talkin' about me,' said Silas, 'as if I'm not 'ere.'

'Well, tha won't be soon,' said Louisa, 'and then we can gab about thee as much as we like. Fancy that, the boy that ran away from 'ome then got his heart broke and decided to run off again.'

'Louisa! Silas has suffered a bereavement,' said Millicent. 'He has to return home.'

'Home's 'ere now,' said Louisa.

'What's this runaway rubbish!' Silas said, but he was laughing, and Louisa buried her head in his shoulder. The dog padded over and laid its head on Charlotte's dress. She patted it absently. Gunson smiled at the scene before him. Why could it not have been Louisa that Silas wanted, why had it to be this Simpson woman? The boy could have saved himself a flogging.

'I should like to see your part of the world,' said Charlotte. 'If I can ever drag my husband from his office we should love to pay you a visit.' She gave Gunson a cool look. 'Perhaps when you retire, John? Should such a day ever come?'

She was punishing him for speaking harshly to her before they left the house. She had caught him off guard, springing on him the news that one of her lady friends had found the perfect retreat for them, a house with generous grounds overlooking Walkley's green and rolling hills, four miles or more above the basin in which the town sat, and featuring a dedicated music room. He had been forced to warn her that he must delay their retirement to the countryside by many years if he was to meet his obligations to the company. 'You are not obligated, John,' she had replied, with more scorn than he was anticipating, 'When will you admit that you are now obsessed by this desire to rebuild the dam?' He had replied forcefully, hissing into her startled face when Silas turned his back to stow his valise in the carriage. She was a typically hysterical woman who knew nothing of his motivations, and must anyway comply with his wishes. It was her wifely duty.

Thinking of it now, he briefly closed his eyes. He had never spoken to Charlotte so harshly before.

Louisa got up to shovel more coal into the fire. The greasy smell filled his nostrils and Gunson rose to his feet quickly, setting the rocker in motion.

'I'm afraid we have run out of time, Mrs Leigh, but thank you very much for your hospitality.' He nodded to Louisa. 'I am very happy to meet you. Shall we, my dear? Silas?'

'Aye, Mr Gunson,' said Silas. 'I'll be just a minute.'

'Then we shall let you say your goodbyes. Come, Charlotte.'

In the lane, his breath clouding around his face, Gunson replaced his hat and fastened his cloak.

'The weather is vile,' said Charlotte.

He turned to her and rearranged her scarf, so it covered the lower half of her face. Her eyes were large and gentle above the blue wool.

'I'm sorry, my dear.'

She cupped his cheek with one gloved hand. 'I know.'

Satisfied, Gunson shuffled his feet impatiently. 'Silas will be moments only,' he assured her. He was eager to get back to Division Street, to the pile of work that awaited him. The previous day, he had bumped into Samuel Webster on the pavement and, reluctantly, stopped to exchange a few words. He had winced when Webster spoke of a stay of execution. 'The council has given you five years' grace, all the time you'll need to meet your pledge to provide a constant and uninterrupted flow of water to the town,' Webster had said, 'I should think you would be pleased with that, John.' Gunson had told the man he had a headache. 'Ah,' said Webster, 'At least you are able to continue about your day. I am plagued by those terrible headaches that force me to take me to my bed, sometimes for days at a time.' Gunson had smiled grimly. 'Perhaps you are dehydrated,' he had said, earning a surprised guffaw.

'What are you smiling about?' said Charlotte.

'Nothing, my dear.'

The ground sloped up steeply at the far end of the lane and Gunson saw a lone figure appear from around the corner and begin a careful descent over cobbles that were now snow-covered. He couldn't make out from this distance whether the shuffling form was male or female, not that it mattered. He looked in the other direction, towards the main road where his gig was waiting. It was like looking through a telescope in reverse. Townspeople on horseback and in carriages hurried across the junction and pedestrians moved quickly among them, bent against the cold, indistinguishable from one another, purposeful or not, but all cells in the body of the town. Water was its life blood, carried along five arteries to feed the ever-thirsty heart, and he, the careless surgeon, had burst one of those arteries and must forever make amends.

Chapter 47

Harriet pounded downstairs and found the boys in the front parlour, unusually placid, setting out ivory roundels on the games table and throwing glances at their mother that were curious one second, delighted the next.

'Don't run, Harriet, it isn't ladylike. We're playing draughts,' said Polly, who was ensconced in Walter's favourite armchair by the fire. Her hair was loose about her shoulders. The grate was piled high, coals squeaking under a layer of logs. Harriet was relieved to have avoided Sadie who must have been in the room to build the fire moments before. Excitement bubbled through her. Now she had made her decision she must enact it immediately.

Polly surveyed her critically. 'You may become stuck if this snow decides to settle.'

'It won't,' said Harriet. 'It's just a passing flurry.'

She hooked her reticule over her arm so that she could pull on long gloves. She was already wearing a quilted hood and heavy black velvet cape that almost reached the hem of the voluminous and heavily layered skirt that hid her sturdy ankle boots. She was starting to sweat.

'You shouldn't go out in this weather. You're not safe on that foot,' said Polly. 'And what are you intending to say to Mr Boothby? Have you considered that? You should beware a man's wounded pride.'

'Oh.' She was tucking her netted hair more firmly under her hood and paused to look at Polly's reflection through the wall mirror. 'I'm not going there, Aunt. I should like to avoid a meeting altogether with Mr Boothby. I intend to write a letter. I'm going to Penistone Road.' A wave of apprehension swept through her body, her stomach clenched, and she exhaled heavily. 'Silas might refuse me yet. I wouldn't blame him, but I have to know his answer, this moment, now that I am decided. Millicent knows as well as Louisa where Silas is lodging and where he works, but neither will tell me. I hope I can convince them.'

She turned to look at Polly properly. 'There should be no shame in this.'

'But there will be, you know that. Also know that I support you, whatever is the outcome. I shall write to your brother. James might not agree with you, but I do not think he'll forbid it – he's busy enough with his own affairs – and I do believe he will protect his sister.'

The pavement was treacherous. Harriet waited impatiently for the timetabled omnibus, keeping her eyes cast down and standing a short distance from the three other gentlemen passengers. When it arrived, the men stepped back and indicated she should board first. She nodded her thanks and found a seat. The straw on the floor of the coach was soaked and the blue upholstery damp to the touch, but it didn't matter. Nothing mattered now, except finding Silas and begging his forgiveness.

The man sitting opposite smiled back at her and Harriet averted her gaze, turning to look out of the window behind her as the coach stopped to allow off the three gentlemen she had embarked with. It wasn't far to Penistone Road. She would alight at the next stop.

'Look at this!' The woman sitting beside Harriet rapped on the glass.

The coach had stopped outside a butcher's where a small boy, woefully underdressed for the weather, was crouched under the shop window next to the thrown-back grille of the coal hole, clutching a sack. Lumps of coal were being flung out by his accomplice who had worked his body into the delivery chute so that only the legs and the dirty soles of his bare feet were visible. The boy on the pavement stopped in the act of stuffing pieces of coal into a sack to stare up at the omnibus. There was a shout from across the street, and seconds later, the butcher tore out of the shop. Harriet put her hand to her mouth as the boy with the sack dropped it and leapt to his feet – which were as unshod as his companion's – and ran off up the street. She was fleetingly grateful the butcher was not carrying a meat cleaver before he grabbed the leg of the boy in the chute and yanked him out. The little fellow hung onto the lip of the coal hole then, screaming, was dragged along the pavement. The sound of jeers rang in Harriet's ears as the coach pulled away.

The woman beside her was cackling. 'Cheeky little buggers,' she said. 'The birch will warm their backsides.'

'They were little children,' said Harriet, shocked.

The woman shrugged.

'Right enough,' said the man on Harriet's other side. 'These kids today have no respect. Little children? Little thieves, the lot of them. It's fiendishly cold, isn't it?' His leg was pressed against her skirts, and he dipped his head towards her, encouraging her to engage with him as if he mistook her for a streetwalker. Harriet nodded curtly and turned away from him.

The coach was approaching the junction where she would disembark. Tatters of grey smoke from the chimneys of a terrace of houses rose to mingle with darker columns from the tall factory stacks behind. Beyond the immediate horizon was a blur of whiteness, as if the wider world had been rubbed out. Harriet's breath caught in her throat as the enormity of the choice she had made finally hit her like an ice-cold wave. It was not too late to change her mind.

'That were a sharp exit,' said Louisa.

Silas shrugged. 'He's got a lot on his mind. Anyhow, I'd best not keep them waitin' in this mucky weather.'

He gathered both women in his arms. 'I'll miss thee.'

Louisa was laughing and crying at the same time. 'I'll miss thee dog more. Go on, then. Out tha goes. Bye bye, Shandy.'

'You look after yourself, love,' said Millicent.

He took a last glance back at the two of them, nodded once and quickly opened and closed the door behind him to preserve the heat inside. Gunson straightened up when Silas appeared, still holding the half-eaten breadcake in his gloved hand. His nose was red with cold, and he sniffed mightily then cautiously offered the bread to Shandy. She gulped it down.

'Are you all right, Silas?' said Mrs Gunson.

'I am.'

'Let us hurry then.'

Heads down against the falling snow, they tramped away in the direction of the waiting carriage.

There was no time to feel anything, not now. He had a train to catch.

Harriet trod gingerly over the cobbles as she turned onto the steep descent down the lane, trailing her fingertips along the wall, although she knew this would not provide any real assistance if she slipped and fell. She could feel the unforgiving cold of the brick through her gloves. Three figures were walking ahead of her in the distance, black bulks made insubstantial by the falling snow, a dog padding alongside them, and Harriet slowed her pace, acutely aware of her vulnerability as a lone woman abroad in the town. She was relieved to see the silent shapes diminish into the distance.

A set of bells began a muffled call, an afternoon service, or perhaps even an out-of-season wedding. Harriet shivered. Albert attended church regularly whereas Walter had got out of the habit, tired of fending off enquiries about Polly's health, of pretending not to see the greed for gossip that masqueraded as concern. Silas had been a churchgoer in his own village – he had told Harriet all about the vicar who set him on the road to Sheffield, she would get down on her knees to thank that man, should they be lucky enough ever meet – but he had not, as far as she knew, joined a local parish of the town. There was plenty of time. Silas had only been in the town for less than a year, and had a hard time of it, but had not given up. Could she smooth his path now, or would she make his life more difficult still?

She reached Louisa's door. She took a deep breath and knocked on it.

The branches of the trees that lined the road they drove under were bare of leaves, as they had been when Silas arrived in town in the early spring. He realised he had not even managed a full year. He watched fat flakes of snow melt on the pavement. If snow was falling at home it would blanket the fields and low farm buildings in white and the streams would grow icicles. It could not smother the turrets and hot chimneys of the town so effectively. He had assured Mrs Gunson and Louisa and his old landlady that he would return, as a visitor rather than runaway, but he knew this was unlikely once he was back at the farm. The fact he was already accepting this weighed on his heart. It was Harriet's town, not his, and she had made it clear that she did not want him.

The wheels of the carriage sprayed slush onto the pavement and the feet of passers-by. Silas bent forward to fondle Shandy's ears. She would find herself usurped on their return, no longer top dog. Yet Silas would be promoted. A far cry from his previous status. Would his homecoming make him happier than remaining here? He wished he could convince himself of it.

Louisa opened the door instantly. 'Oh! What are you doing here? I were just on me way out.'

A heavy shawl covered her head and she wore a scarf across her face. Harriet flung her arms around Louisa. 'Is Silas here? I have to tell you, Polly is up and...'

Louisa pushed her gently away and the scarf fell, revealing a painted face. Harriet had never seen rouge on Louisa's cheeks before.

She frowned. 'Why are you...'

'Never mind me. What's up wi' thee?'

'I need you to tell me where Silas is, please. Is he here? I have to speak to him and it cannot wait.'

'Well, it might have to.' Louisa had regained her composure. She closed the door on the snow swirling outside, but replaced the scarf over her face. Millicent stood up from her seat by the fire.

'What is it, dear?' she said. 'What's happened?'

'Nothing!' Harriet began to laugh. 'Everything. Milly, where will I find Silas? You will tell me, won't you?'

'I thought Louisa might have let you know.' Millicent looked at her daughter, who merely shook her head. 'Silas has gone home, back to the farm. His older brother died and he's needed by his parents and by his brother's widow and child, to take over.'

Harriet looked from Millicent to Louisa and back again.

'He's gone back to run the farm,' Millicent repeated.

'Yes, I…' she trailed off. There was something missing. 'Where's Shandy?'

'Gone wi' him. Right.' Louisa seemed to come to a decision. 'Come wi' me. I think tha might be able to catch 'im.'

'You just missed him,' said Millicent. 'The Gunsons have taken him to the Wicker.'

'Who are the Gunsons?' She was becoming impatient.

'Kind people, both o' 'em,' said Louisa.

'How will I get there?' Harriet was afraid she would begin to wail. She shook her head and whispered, 'I've left it too late.'

Louisa pushed her towards the door. 'I'm gettin' the bus. It's due any minute. Come on, come on! It'll take thee reight there.'

Along the viaduct, over the road that ran through the Wicker district, the locomotive engines pulled their carriages through the sky. Mrs Gunson, ever the teacher, had told him the name of the man who designed the impressive structure, but Silas had immediately forgotten it, the names of famous engineers no longer being of any use to him. Instead, he repeated to himself the time of departure and the platform he should wait on, otherwise he would end up in Manchester. He'd watched the great steam engines cutting through the countryside but had never pictured himself sitting in one of the carriages being pulled along behind. It was an unhappy realisation to find he could not muster the slightest bit of anticipation at the prospect.

'Forty-one arches in total and this one the tallest at approximately forty-five feet,' said Mrs Gunson. Mr Gunson was staring ahead, his expression melancholy.

On the platform, Mr Gunson shook Silas's hand. 'Well, you must hasten on your journey. I hope we will see you again. You should come back when I have built the new dam and the town has put the last traces of the disaster behind it.'

Silas nodded. He could see that while he himself had been scarred by the events of that night, Gunson would be forever submerged, fighting a deep current of guilt that would never let him go.

Charlotte hugged him. 'You're like one of my own boys now. Stay in touch.'

'I shall. Goodbye, Mr Gunson. Goodbye, Mrs Gunson. An' thank you both.'

Harriet hoisted her skirts to aid her ungainly progress up the steep set of steps that led to the station platform. Her boots spattered grey slush onto the hems and cuffs of the people edging carefully down. The snowflakes had been replaced by a thin cold drizzle, and she spared her cousins a fleeting thought. The boys would be disappointed they could not go sledging on the common.

She was fighting the tide. All these bodies descending the steps to the street, frustrating her progress, must be passengers who had recently disembarked. This meant a train would be idling at the platform, the guard waiting with whistle in mouth for the carriage doors to finish slamming like falling dominos. Silas might be sitting in a carriage now. Harriet hastened, and pushed through to the platform, which was clearing quickly.

A great cloud of white smoke blossomed from the underside of the steam engine on the track beside her. She could see two men inside, one feeding coal into a glowing, gaping maw and the other manipulating levers and knobs. Harriet stopped, breathless. The last time she had been here she had been holding her younger brother's hand, waving off their parents on a trip to London, promising to look after James for the few days they would be away. A few days that had turned into forever. She had been kept safe ever since, by her uncle, and was now being offered a similarly secure existence by Albert. There were no such guarantees with Silas, however much he swore to look after her. It might be better if he was on this train, soon departing. She was rooted to the spot, and could not untangle her thoughts.

The station guard walked briskly towards her, along the row of carriages.

'Miss, are you all right? D'you want this train? You'll have to look sharp. Shall I find you a seat, love?'

'No, no. I mean, no, thank you.' She began to turn away, all her earlier resolve evaporating like the steam from the locomotive. She had been acting like the heroine of a penny dreadful, the eternally foolish girl who follows her heart and ends up molested or murdered. She had caught some sense of delirium from Polly. She should return...

The whistle blew, a shrill sound that pierced her heart. The engine hissed into fresh life, a plume of smoke lengthening along the top of the carriages as the train began to chug slowly away. There was another sound over the hissing and grinding. Sharper, insistent.

It was a dog, barking.

Silas pulled on the leather strap to drop the sash window of the carriage that he was sharing with five others, a couple of whom muttered about the cold he was letting in.

'Only for a minute,' he said, 'while we clear the station. I'm sayin' me farewells to the town. Whoa, girl!'

Shandy had leapt for the open space and would have been through the window if he hadn't grabbed her around the hips. Her upper body was hanging out as the train began to move and she was barking furiously.

'That dog'll lose her head shortly,' said the man sitting opposite Silas.

'Aye, I know that. Come 'ere, yer mad animal!' Silas yanked her back inside.

'P'raps you'll shut that window now,' said one of the other passengers.

Silas wedged Shandy between his legs. He'd heard of this mania known to seize hold of certain people once they were put in the confined space of a train carriage, a wild hysteria that had them kicking and screaming. He'd had no idea dogs could be infected by it. Shandy was whining now, a high keening sound that he didn't think he'd ever heard her make before.

'Quiet, girl!'

He kept her trapped as he stood to close the window. They were nearing the end of the platform now and he could see on the edge of it the figure of a woman. She was wreathed in steam. The smoke cleared for an instant.

It was Harriet.

She gasped, disbelieving. There was Silas, framed in the open carriage window, and now Shandy jumped up and Silas locked his arm about the dog's neck to prevent her leaping from the train, while his other hand waved frantically. The unbridled joy on his face found its answer in hers, and Harriet burst out laughing. He was almost level with her now, and she could see curious faces behind him. She didn't care. She was filled with a reckless elation. She knew they understood each other perfectly. They always had.

'I'm not getting married!' She was shouting wildly, surprising herself. 'I'm not!'

Now they were level and already he was moving away. He slammed his hand repeatedly on the outside of the door as the engine tugged the carriages away, gathering speed, leaving Harriet behind.

'Thou art!' He shouted back at the top of his lungs. 'Tha marryin' me!'

Chapter 48

Silas Hinchcliffe reached the top of the rise that would show him the view down the valley. Here, he paused.

Across the bare fields, patches of melting snow were dissolving in the cold drizzle that Harriet would say was the barely-there rain that soaked you through. A curtain of heavier rain moved in the far distance, obscuring the view towards the Pennine hills. Silas wiped his face and glanced down at Shandy, who had planted herself by his side. 'Good girl,' he said absently. He was thinking.

The thrilling jolt that ran through his body when he saw Harriet at the station had set his heart hammering and he could barely contain himself during the tearing, rattling journey to the next station a couple of miles away. Shandy had caught his mood, jumping from one side of the carriage to the other as they raced through a tunnel, and only settling when he dropped the window as they emerged into open countryside and allowed her to raise her nose to catch the various scents rushing by. It was all he could do not to open the carriage door and throw himself out.

The other passengers had been glad to see the back of them.

When he realised he was west of Bradfield, he had decided to walk back to town over the hills, in order to calm himself and to think.

The last time he'd stood at this vantage point there had been a vast reservoir beneath his boots, and a man on an embankment, battling the elements. The reservoir and the dam that had failed to contain it were gone. Instead, he was looking down on a ragged gorge between the valley sides, an untidy tumble of escarpments and rocky hillocks with a thin river threading through it. No sign remaining of the monster that had almost killed him. To think, he'd been afraid of re-entering a forge. He wondered what Mr Gunson would say – or Harriet, come to that – if he told them that the ambition he first held, of becoming a steelworker and operating the great Bessemer machine, was back with him, stronger than ever. He would be at the cutting edge. Or he might even start his own business, small scale at first, forging edge tools, saws, knives, then building an empire as big as Atlas. Why not? Anything was possible in a boom town and now he had good reason to make something of himself, the best reason in the world.

And he wondered how his father would react to the letter he now intended to write. *Tek on a tenant to run the place, what's that soft git on about? Does he think we're made o' money?*

Silas looked away from the scar on the landscape and turned his feet towards the landscape of chimney stacks beneath the steep valley sides. Shandy barked once, a sharp sound in the still air.

'All right then, girl. C'mon. Harriet's waitin' on us.'

Author's Note

On a stormy night in the early spring of 1864, a reservoir burst its banks above the Loxley Valley and seven hundred million gallons of water were unleashed on the unsuspecting people of the town below.

I came across an account of the disaster whilst researching my grandparents' early working lives as file cutters and was surprised to find that one of the most significant events of the Victorian era earned little more than a footnote in history. Yet almost two hundred and fifty lives were lost, engulfed by the wall of water that tore through the valley and into the industrial basin; whole families swept from their beds, night shift workers killed in mills and forges with no comprehension of what had befallen them.

Silas and Harriet and most of the characters who appear in this novel are fictional, but the chief engineer is based on the real John Gunson, who continued to build reservoirs for the waterworks company until his death in 1886.

Acknowledgements

This debut novel could not have been written without early readers and cherished writer friends Emma Clark-Lam, Sara Cox, Sarah Daniels, Asha Hicks, Carly Reagon, and my daughter Jess Cooke, or completed without my wonderful agent, Kate Nash, and amazing editor Emily Bedford. My gratitude to Rose Bray, and to Suzannah Dunn and the Curtis Brown Creative team. Loving thanks to my family and friends for putting up with me, especially my husband Alan, who never had a doubt. Finally, apologies to my Labradors, Piper and Mini, who weren't walked enough by half when deadlines loomed.